Praise for *Phoebe's Light*

"Fisher weaves together a pleasing romance that sets a high standard for future series installments."

Publishers Weekly

"Fisher's superb command of her historical setting is particularly commendable as she launches her Nantucket Legacy series, and many readers will find themselves fascinated by how the Quakers were treated when they first arrived in the New World."

Booklist

"Based on actual historical events and people, Suzanne Woods Fisher has taken her research to the next level and brings to life the forgotten beginning of Quakers on Nantucket Island."

RT Book Reviews

"A book that will sweep you up and take you away."

Interviews & Reviews

"In this brand-new series, bestselling author Suzanne Woods Fisher brings her signature twists and turns to bear on a fascinating new faith community: the Quakers of colonial-era Nantucket Island."

Fresh Fiction

STITCHES
IN TIME

Books by Suzanne Woods Fisher

Amish Peace: Simple Wisdom for a Complicated World
Amish Proverbs
*Amish Values for Your Family: What We Can Learn from
the Simple Life*
The Heart of the Amish

LANCASTER COUNTY SECRETS

The Choice
The Waiting
The Search

SEASONS OF STONEY RIDGE

The Keeper
The Haven
The Lesson

THE INN AT EAGLE HILL

The Letters
The Calling
The Revealing

THE BISHOP'S FAMILY

The Imposter
The Quieting
The Devoted

AMISH BEGINNINGS

Anna's Crossing
The Newcomer
The Return

NANTUCKET LEGACY

Phoebe's Light
Minding the Light
The Light Before Day

THE DEACON'S FAMILY

Mending Fences
Stitches in Time

THE DEACON'S FAMILY
- 2 -

STITCHES IN TIME

SUZANNE WOODS FISHER

Revell

a division of Baker Publishing Group
Grand Rapids, Michigan

© 2019 by Suzanne Woods Fisher

Published by Revell
a division of Baker Publishing Group
PO Box 6287, Grand Rapids, MI 49516-6287
www.revellbooks.com

Printed in the United States of America

Library of Congress Cataloging-in-Publication Data
Names: Fisher, Suzanne Woods, author.
Title: Stitches in time / Suzanne Woods Fisher.
Description: Grand Rapids, MI : Revell, [2019] | Series: The Deacon's family
Identifiers: LCCN 2019006994 | ISBN 9780800727529 (pbk.)
Subjects: | GSAFD: Christian fiction. | Love stories.
Classification: LCC PS3606.I78 S75 2019 | DDC 813/.6—dc23
LC record available at https://lccn.loc.gov/2019006994

ISBN 978-0-8007-3707-8 (casebound)

Scripture used in this book, whether quoted or paraphrased by the characters, is taken from the King James Version of the Bible.

Published in association with Joyce Hart of the Hartline Literary Agency, LLC.

To my daughter-in-law, Amanda.

We are so blessed that you married into our family.

A moment I'll never forget:

your delicious "heartbreak" cake.

On top of you just being you,

you've also given us the *best* gift: grandchildren.

"'LORD, WHAT DO YOU WANT ME TO DO TODAY?'"
THE OLD BISHOP TOLD THE CHURCH LEADERS.
"THAT'S A DANGEROUS PRAYER. BUT IT'S MORE
DANGEROUS NOT TO ASK."

Cast of Characters

Mollie Graber—niece to Fern Lapp. Moved from Ohio for a fresh start and is teaching school in Stoney Ridge.

Sam Schrock—younger brother to Luke Schrock. Trains young horses from the racetrack for buggy work. Originally introduced in The Inn at Eagle Hill series.

Luke Schrock—recently returned to Stoney Ridge after a stint in rehab (or two. Or three). Originally introduced in The Inn at Eagle Hill series. His story continued in The Bishop's Family series.

Isabella "Izzy" Miller Schrock—wife to Luke Schrock. Introduced in *Mending Fences*.

Amos Lapp—deacon of Stoney Ridge, husband to Fern, owner of Windmill Farm. Originally introduced in the Stoney Ridge Seasons series.

Fern Lapp—wife of deacon Amos Lapp. Originally introduced in the Stoney Ridge Seasons series.

David Stoltzfus—bishop of Stoney Ridge. Originally introduced in *The Revealing*, book 3 of The Inn at Eagle Hill series. Main character in The Bishop's Family series.

Hank Lapp—uncle of deacon Amos Lapp. Originally introduced in the Stoney Ridge Seasons series.

Edith Fisher Lapp—wife of Hank Lapp. Originally introduced in the Stoney Ridge Seasons series.

Jesse Stoltzfus—son of bishop David Stoltzfus. Introduced in *The Revealing*, book 3 of The Inn at Eagle Hill series. His story continued throughout The Bishop's Family series.

Jenny Stoltzfus—wife of Jesse Stoltzfus, half-sister to Izzy Schrock. Introduced in *The Lesson*, book 3 of the Stoney Ridge Seasons series.

Alice Smucker Zook—wife of Teddy Zook. Introduced in *The Haven* and *The Lesson*, books 2 and 3 of the Stoney Ridge Seasons series.

Teddy Zook—Amish carpenter, church Vorsinger (music leader)

Freeman Glick—former bishop of Stoney Ridge who experienced a "Quieting" and was removed from his responsibilities. Introduced in *The Imposter*, book 1 of The Bishop's Family series.

Ruthie Stoltzfus Kelly—wife of Patrick, daughter of bishop David Stoltzfus. Manages The Inn at Eagle Hill. Main character in *The Devoted*, book 3 of The Bishop's Family series.

Patrick Kelly—husband of Ruthie. Together they manage The Inn at Eagle Hill. Main character in *The Devoted*, book 3 of The Bishop's Family series.

Mattie Riehl—wife of Solomon Riehl. Main character in *The Choice* and *A Lancaster County Christmas*.

Carrie Miller—wife of Abel Miller, mother of Rudy Miller. Main character in *The Choice*.

Rudy Miller—son of Carrie and Abel Miler. Introduced in *Mending Fences* as an ardent admirer of Luke Schrock.

Foster teenagers from the Stoney Ridge Group Home

Tina and Alicia—foster teens for Mollie Graber

Cassidy—foster teen for Fern Lapp

Chloe—foster teen for Alice and Teddy Zook

Social workers from a private foster care agency in Stoney Ridge

Roberta Watts—supervisor

Mavis Connor—assistant to Roberta Watts

ONE

It took a lot to shock Luke Schrock. Generally, he was the one who did the shocking. So on the day that Bishop David Stoltzfus received whispered suggestions from each church member of Stoney Ridge to choose a deacon to replace Amos Lapp, it never once occurred to Luke that his name might be submitted. Never ever crossed his mind. Not once. Why would it? Luke was newly married, only twenty-five years old, and on his best days, he was just now starting to feel like a grown-up.

Yet someone had indeed whispered Luke's name to David as a choice to be deacon. Just *one* person. Who? Who would do such a thing, think such a thought? Surely not his wife, Izzy. When a man drew the lot to become a minister or deacon, it was a lifelong obligation. The poor wives of church ministers took the brunt of their husbands' responsibilities. Year after year, Luke had seen Amos called away from family gatherings for deacon business, and his wife Fern was left to manage alone. No, definitely not his Izzy.

Fern wouldn't have whispered his name, would she? No. No way. She, more than anyone, knew that Luke wouldn't be any good at deaconing.

What about Fern's niece, Mollie? She was new to Stoney Ridge, stepping in as a much needed schoolteacher. Mollie loved to play practical jokes. Was she playing him for a fool? Sammy might know. His brother, he had a hunch, was sweet on Mollie.

Hank Lapp! It had to be him. He was sitting right in front of Luke with his wild and wispy white hair, blocking the view.

Luke leaned forward and gave Hank a poke in the ribs. "Did you give my name to David?"

Hank jerked like a fish on the line. "WHAT'S THAT, BOY?"

Luke sighed. Hank Lapp had one volume: loud. "Hank, don't say a word. Just nod or shake your head. Do not speak. Just let me know if you were the one who gave my name to David."

Hank turned around to look at Luke, one lazy eye trailing off to the side. "SON, I DID NOT."

Heads turned. Lips pursed. Edith Lapp hushed them from across the room. Hank frowned at Luke and swiveled around to face forward.

Leaning forward, Luke put his hand on Hank's shoulder to whisper, "If you didn't, then who did?"

Hank batted Luke's hand away. "I DON'T HAVE THE FOGGIEST NOTION. BUT WHOEVER DID SHOULD HAVE HIS HEAD EXAMINED."

Luke heartily agreed. But that didn't help him in the slightest. He was trapped.

He shook off all those troubling thoughts. It really didn't matter who had whispered his name to David. All that mattered was his complete confidence in God's great wisdom. Certainly, the Lord God knew better than to guide him to draw the lot. He relaxed and dropped his chin to his chest, praying for the poor soul who would open the hymnal and find the piece of paper that would drastically change his life. There were four other choices, all good picks. Any one of them would make a fine deacon.

One hymnal opened. No lot. Second hymnal opened. No lot.

Luke glanced across the barn and caught Izzy's panicked look. He shook his head slightly to reassure her. Not a chance, he silently mouthed. Third hymnal opened. No lot.

Oh no. Oh Lord, please no. In case you need reminding, I am barely gaining some respectability. In fact, it's only because Izzy finally agreed to marry me that my reputation has improved a little among the church. Please, Lord, not me. Please don't make me do it.

David motioned to both Luke and Teddy Zook to step forward and claim their hymnals. *Lord, pardon my advice giving, but Teddy's the man you want.* Teddy Zook would be an outstanding deacon. In fact, he was the one Luke had nominated to David. Teddy Zook had a big heart, a great reservoir of patience, and an admirable tolerance for difficult people. Luke had none of those qualities.

He let Teddy reach out to pick a hymnal first, praying— pleading—all the while for him to grab the one with the piece of paper in it. Teddy picked up one hymnal, closed his eyes, and then put it down again. He picked up the other one. At that moment, Luke expected Teddy to open the hymnal and find that slim piece of paper, but no. Teddy didn't budge. Holding the old book against his chest, he waited for Luke to pick up the last hymnal. David cleared his throat, a gentle nudge.

Luke's heart started pounding, so loudly he was sure everyone in the church could hear it. A drumbeat, an audible warning.

A barn swallow darted overhead and disappeared into the rafters. He'd never envied a bird before, but at this moment, he wished he could sprout wings and fly out through the hay door. His eyes shifted to the open barn door. Could he make a break for it? Run for his life? No. That was the old Luke. He was the new and improved Luke. A happily married Luke, who wouldn't dare embarrass his Izzy with such childish behavior. She told him once that she had married him because of his potential. What kind of potential was he showing now? A pathetic lack of it, that's what kind.

He needed to man up. When he became baptized, he knew this day might come. He sucked in a deep breath, let it out. He should do this. With God's help, he could do this. But he did send one more silent, begging prayer upward. *Not me, Lord. Not me. Don't forget what I promised Amos, Lord, just before he passed. Amos gave me a big project. A huge undertaking. Not me, Lord. Choose Teddy.*

With a shaking hand, Luke reached out for the lone hymnal. He could sense the entire church sitting with bated breath, waiting to see who had drawn the lot. Teddy gave him a solemn nod, and they both opened their hymnals at the same time. A sudden coldness trickled down his spine.

Oh no.

Mollie Graber had to cover her mouth so she didn't laugh out loud at the look on Luke Schrock's face when he opened the hymnal and found the paper. He looked utterly stricken, as horrified as if he'd just witnessed a grisly murder. Next to her on the bench, sitting stiff as a grave marker, was his pretty wife, Izzy. Mollie heard her gasp, then exhale as if she'd been kicked in the stomach. "It's not possible," she said. "It's just not possible."

But it was. Luke Schrock was the new deacon for Stoney Ridge. Mollie thought it was an outcome so unexpected that it sent the most spectacular chills down her spine. But then, the drawing of the lot for ordained officials had that effect on her. Think, just think. The almighty Lord was directing a man's hand to choose the lot and accept the mantle of lifetime leadership. To her it was a rippling of wonder that ran through the church. Evidence of the sovereignty of God, right in their midst. Astonishing.

She had to admit, though, that her own pick had been Teddy Zook.

All around her was the sound of sniffles and tears, sorrowful mumblings. It was always like this. Only twenty-one, Mollie had been through four lot drawings for ministers or deacons that she could remember, and each time was the same. When names were called out to draw the lot, everyone acted like it was a burden of enormous proportion. While she didn't know how she'd feel if she were a man, newly facing a lifelong obligation, she just didn't think that God wanted everybody to have such safe, comfortable lives. She thought he wanted to shake things up a little, get folks aware of how fragile life could be, how precious it was. The deacon role was an honor. Special.

If she were a man, and if her name was ever thrown in the drawing for a lot, she'd want it to be for deacon. Not so much a minister or bishop—that would require too much brainy Bible study. But a deacon? She'd love it. Deacons had the reputation for having the most difficult job of all three ordained officials. But how hard could it really be? Helping others, figuring out their problems, making sure folks in need were taken care of. And then there was the *Schtecklimann*, the go-between when a couple wanted to marry. The bridegroom would speak privately to the deacon, and the deacon would then go speak to the bride's parents to make sure nothing stood in the way. If all went well, the bishop would then announce the couple's engagement in church. Fun.

She knew there were some other pieces of the role that were less appealing—washing everybody's feet during communion, or being sent by the bishop to sniff out transgressions, or the worst of all, the very worst, bringing the message of excommunication to someone who had strayed off the straight and narrow path. How *awful* an errand that would be. Ghastly.

And yet, she didn't think that happened all that often. At least, not in the churches she'd been in. In fact, never once that she could remember. She'd seen plenty of folks—mostly young men—sit with remorse on the sinner's bench, heads hung low, feet shuffling nervously, but she'd never known a person to turn completely away from the faith.

The fellowship meal took place right after the church service. Today was so pleasant that the men moved the benches to the lawn and quickly rearranged them to form both tables and benches. The women and children ate separately from the men, and they always served the men first.

Sam Schrock, Luke's younger brother, was seated at the table where Mollie was serving. The men were squished together, with little elbow room. She placed a basket of homemade sliced bread and a jar of peanut butter in the center of the table, trying to catch glimpses of Sam while his chin was tucked to his chest. Oh my, that face of his could make a girl feel weak in the knees. A pair of creases between well-shaped brows. A knife-straight nose and a fine mouth. His face was long and lean, like the rest of him, with blue eyes that worked hard to keep the expression out of them. Same with his voice. Quiet-spoken, that described Sam Schrock. He didn't talk much. Or smile, not much.

She brought a pitcher of coffee to the table and started to fill the cups, one by one, casting furtive glances in Sam's direction. He lifted his head and startled in recognition when he saw it was Mollie filling the cups, so much that he spilled his coffee. "No problem, no problem," she said, whipping out a dishrag tucked into her apron belt. She dabbed at the spilled coffee, tucked the rag back at her waist, and took his cup to refill it.

Smiling down at him, noting the pleasure in his eyes, she thrilled at the realization that she had put it there. Sweet.

Heaven's sake, what a smile did to Sam Schrock's face—eyes crinkled up at the corners, prominent cheekbones lifted, lips softened, that emotionlessness gone. Normally he kept that face taciturn and reserved, serious to the point of solemn, which only added to his appeal. No one could figure him out. In church, she saw how girls stole looks at him. Sam Schrock, relaxed and smiling, made a fetching sight, no question about it. She was charmed.

As Mollie moved around the table, filling cups with coffee, men walked up to offer Luke condolences, like a family member had died. She heard Luke murmur back a woeful response, something about how he couldn't believe this had happened, no idea how he could do the deacon job, and something stirred inside her until it bubbled up and overflowed. "Luke Schrock, you'll do this the way every other deacon does it. By depending on God. That's how."

Luke's head snapped up when he realized who had spoken. "You! Mollie Graber. Are you the one who whispered my name to David? I heard that only one person voted for me. Did you play a prank on me?"

Sam's eyes had been following her as she moved down the table. "Mollie?" he said softly, as if he couldn't believe she would do such a thing.

"Me?" Mollie said. A laugh burst out of her, then more giggles. "No. Not me." She stopped behind Jesse Stoltzfus and tipped her head. "Just one vote? Oh Luke . . . that's so . . ." Sad.

"Pathetic! I know! That's why I have no business being deacon."

She shrugged. "Apparently God has a different point of view on that."

"Mollie's right on two counts." David Stoltzfus had walked up to the table and squeezed in next to Luke. "Mollie was not the person who whispered your name, and the drawing of the lot is God's business. Not man's."

"But David, hold on," Luke said, shifting over to make room. "Teddy pulled his hand back from that one hymnal. You saw him do it. Everyone did. My guess is that he saw the paper. He wasn't about to claim it."

Teddy, digging his knife into the jar of peanut butter, looked up when he heard his name mentioned. "I saw no such thing, Luke." He took a piece of bread from the basket and spread the peanut butter back and forth, back and forth, then took a corner bite. "But I did feel something. Like a hand had been placed on top of my hand, making me put that hymnal down." With the back of his sleeve, he wiped his mouth. "Somehow, I just knew that one book wasn't meant for me." By now, others had gathered around the table to hear the conversation. Teddy pointed his peanut-buttery knife at Luke. "I did not see that slip of paper."

Alice stood behind her husband, a swaddled baby in her arms. "I'm thrilled Teddy isn't deacon. We've got enough on our plate."

Alice and Teddy had a newborn baby with the worst colic in history. So said Alice, anyway. That baby never stopped crying. Even now, his little body would go rigid in his mother's arms, and he let out little mewling shrieks, like a kitten with its tail stepped on.

"Glad it wasn't Hank Lapp in the lineup," Edith Lapp said. She stood behind Luke, arms crossed, a scowl on her face aimed in Mollie's direction meant to hurry her along with the coffee. She knew she didn't move fast enough for Edith Lapp, but when wasn't there a frown or scowl on that woman's face? "Hank's got a to-do list a mile long." Jeering laughter followed.

Luke leaned forward on his elbows. "Well, I've got a lot to do too."

"Like what?" Mollie asked. She didn't mean for it to come out sounding as blunt as it probably did, but she didn't think Luke had too much to worry about. Newly married, they lived rent-free at Windmill Farm. They didn't have any children yet. What could possibly make him think he had more to do than anybody else?

Luke frowned. "Well, for one, I promised Amos Lapp

that I would empty out the foster care system in Lancaster County."

"You did *what*?" Izzy said, coming to the table with a basket of freshly sliced bread.

Luke snapped his head up. "It was Amos's idea," he said quickly, eyes fixed on his wife. "Something he had wanted to do for Fern. He and I talked about it a lot, especially when he knew his time was growing short. I promised him I'd do my best, Izzy. Get those children into Amish homes." Meekly, Luke looked around at all who had gathered around the table. "Anyone interested? Any takers?"

That question had the effect of a drenching of rain on the group. Men and women who had been standing nearby, eavesdropping, slipped away. The few still seated turned their attention to their plate of food, as if it was suddenly the most delicious meal they'd ever had.

Mollie remained near the table. This notion of making a difference, of meeting a need head-on, of taking on life as a grand adventure—it was the very reason she had uprooted her life and moved to Stoney Ridge. "Count me in," she said with a big smile. "I'd love to have a foster child. Maybe two. Siblings, perhaps?"

Sam Schrock stared at her like she had just sprouted horns.

$\mathcal{T}$WO

Most every morning, Sam Schrock beat the sun up. Not today, though. Today, he was missing his usual get-up-and-go. On this foggy September Monday morning, it had got up and gone.

Typically, Sam hurried through the early morning chores to care for his stepfather Galen's Thoroughbreds: fed them hay, filled their water buckets, turned some out to pasture, mucked out stalls. Later in the morning, the serious training of preparing horses for buggy work would get started. But in between, if he timed it just right, he could fill the last water trough in the pasture that sat across the road from the little schoolhouse . . . at the same time that teacher Mollie Graber arrived for the day. She would wave cheerfully to him and invite him in to share a cup of coffee from her thermos.

These "accidental" meetings had begun innocuously, a month or so ago, back in late August when school had just started for the year. A horse, recently purchased straight off the racetrack and still skittish, had broken through the fencing and run off. Sam had been up since dawn tracking the horse down and finally found him out near Blue Lake

Pond. He was walking the horse back to Galen's farm, past the schoolhouse, just as Mollie was unlocking the door. He'd noticed her at church throughout the summer—a cute new girl was hard to miss—but she was the one who called out to him to come on over for a cup of good coffee.

That's how it always was between them. Mollie described him once as a man of mystery and reserve, but he knew better. It wasn't mystery or reserve that kept Sam in the shadows. Long ago, Sam had learned that his best path was to try to be invisible. It had to do with being a Schrock in a town that, for very good reason, didn't think much of Schrocks.

Sam's father, Dean Schrock, had been in the financial investment business, helping Plain People plan their retirement. It went well until it didn't. His father made too risky an investment and it all fell apart. His clients placed the blame squarely on his shoulders. Never mind that the economy had tanked. Never mind that people should have been paying better attention to their money.

On top of being Dean Schrock's youngest son—and the one who most resembled him—Sam also had the distinction of being the younger brother to Luke, considered for years as the worst of the worst. Luke had repaired his reputation with admirable fortitude, but the Amish had long memories. Sam was viewed with suspicion, guilty by association, simply because of the blood running through his veins.

But Mollie Graber held no such assumptions. New to Stoney Ridge, she had no history with the Schrocks and that was one of the best things about her. Mollie was getting to know Sam for who he was, not who his family was. She saw him the way he wanted to be seen. He liked being around her. More than liked. He loved being around her.

He'd never felt about a girl the way he felt about Mollie Graber. Luke liked to jab that Sam had been struck by Cupid's arrow, and although he ignored his brother's teasing, he didn't disagree.

Throughout the days, Sam found his thoughts returning often to Mollie, wondering what she was doing, how the school day was going, if the children were behaving themselves. There was a group of headstrong boys in her class and he worried they might be challenging for her to manage. Especially Rudy Miller. He was a steadfast admirer of Luke, for all the wrong reasons.

Of course, Sam never told Mollie any of those thoughts. After all, he really had no idea how she felt about him. She was friendly with everyone, and he'd heard the fellows talk about her. More than a few had their eyes on Mollie. How could they not? She was pretty and kind, and unfortunately for him, she showed the same warm interest in everybody. And her voice—low, soft, kind of husky. He loved her voice.

Yesterday, he was *this* close to asking if he could drive her home from church—he had searched for the right words during the service and mentally practiced saying them—but by the time he gathered his courage to approach her, another fellow cut in. A missed opportunity.

That was another problem of Sam's. When nervous, he fumbled for words. Girls made him extremely nervous, so as a result, he didn't speak much.

Ha. Mystery and reserve. More like, awkward and insecure and tongue-tied. What he really wanted to say, he could scarcely formulate as thoughts, let alone put into words. Certainly not words he could ever voice aloud to this wide-eyed girl, who gave him the same shaky-excited feelings he got listening to crashes of thunder in the night or watching young colts gallop around the pasture.

Sam yawned, stretching his arms over his head, as his thoughts wandered to church yesterday. How in the world did his brother Luke end up drawing the lot for deacon? It was . . . mind blowing. His brother had matured in the last few years, all thanks to a combination of David Stoltzfus's and Amos and Fern Lapp's steady pressure on him and belief that he could do better. Izzy, too, was a wonderfully maturing influence on Luke. Still, a deacon? Sam loved his brother, and he'd come a long way from the guy he was, but he felt a little guarded around him. Sam sure would never ask Luke for help. Besides, he was working for Galen, who didn't want Luke anywhere near his Thoroughbreds. Long memories, these Amish.

The cock crowed and Sam threw back the covers. He needed to get the day started. The heavy rain last night eliminated his excuse to fill the water trough. As he dressed, he tried to cobble together another reason to be near the schoolhouse, but nothing seemed logical on this cold gray morning. Nothing seemed quite right.

No, it was him. He was out of sorts.

He replayed Mollie's eagerness to take on foster children, and his stomach started churning. What was that all about? Was it him? Or was it her?

Mollie spoke up without hesitation, she moved so confidently, faced the future with boldness. He admired such qualities in a person—male or female—but rashness also unsettled him. Sam liked life to be predictable, to be manageable. Mollie strode headfirst into a gale. Act now, think later. The very opposite of Sam's nature. And yet. . . foster a child?

He'd heard terrible stories about foster children—setting homes on fire, killing their foster parents in their sleep. After all, these children were from troubled homes. They were troubled children! It made no sense. Mollie was only twenty-one, single, a schoolteacher, and lived in a tiny cottage. All alone.

His eyes narrowed beneath the deep shadow of his hat brim while he thought about it. As he put his boots on, he simply couldn't come up with a valid reason to walk by the schoolhouse, so today, for the first day in a month's time, he skipped his chance to have morning coffee with Mollie. It saddened and worried him. Both.

Early the next morning, Mollie unlocked the schoolhouse door. Two blue jays were having an argument in the towering elm tree that shaded the school. She walked inside and inhaled, savoring the smell of lemon-waxed floors, books, woodsmoke. She loved the welcoming scents of the schoolhouse each morning, but she loved even more its clear association with children. Cheerful drawings lining the walls, an alphabet banner hanging along the window, books stacked on the counter, boxes of battered toys for rainy days. Lots of learning and plenty of recesses, Mollie thought, could cure most of the ills of the world.

She set her thermos on her desk and took out two mugs, one for her and one for Sam, and poured one mug to the brim with hot coffee. She didn't pour coffee into Sam's mug. Something told her he wasn't coming like he usually did. She hoped it was only because his early mornings were extra busy lately, training horses for the buggy. Getting Sam to talk was like priming a rusty pump, but once she got him started on horse training, he lost that guarded look, his normal reserve, and out spilled story after story. She relished each one. Treasures.

She took a sip of coffee, thinking back to the fellowship lunch following Sunday church, just after Sam's brother Luke had asked who might be interested in fostering children and Mollie volunteered. She hoped Sam's recent absences had nothing to do with her telling Luke that she wanted to foster a child, maybe two. Nothing was going to change her mind about that. Set in stone.

As her desk clock struck eight, she set the mug for Sam back on its hook by the sink. She liked Sam Schrock, liked him quite a bit, and at times she thought there might be something brewing between them. But maybe she'd been wrong about that, and maybe that was for the best. After all, as her mother continually reminded her, loving Mollie brought complications.

But you didn't come across many Sam Schrocks, that was for sure. Special.

The sun had burned off the morning fog, and it turned into such a pleasant day that Izzy took some freshly laid eggs over to her half sister Jenny's and stayed for a picnic lunch. Their mother, Grace Miller, who worked in a hair salon in nearby Lancaster, had dropped by unexpectedly, which she did frequently. They spread quilts to sit beneath the shade of a big elm tree, and ate egg salad sandwiches.

With a pang in her heart, Izzy observed the easy camaraderie between Jenny and their mother. Even Rosie, Jenny's fourteen-month-old toddler, was at ease around her. For

28

almost two years, since her mother had been released from Mountain Vista rehab facility and decided to stay in the area, Izzy had been determined to grow closer to her, to find a way to connect to her. She hadn't lived with her since she was five years old, when her mother ended up in jail and she was made a ward of the state. She spent the next fifteen years trying to find her. When she finally did, she had such high hopes.

Before each visit with Grace, Izzy would think, this time, there'd be a breakthrough. This time, they'd slip into those cozy mother-daughter chats that she'd seen other girls have with their moms. But as soon as Izzy was alone with her mother, her hopes would vanish. Long awkward silences, uncomfortable glances, that was the best they could do with each other. She still didn't know her mother any better.

Rosie snuggled in Grace's lap and let her run her fingers through her downy hair. Oh, how Izzy wished Rosie were hers. Another baby was already on the way for Jenny and Jesse. Izzy had hoped to be pregnant by now. She and Jenny wanted to have babies together, raise cousins together, watch them grow up together. Month by month, Izzy kept hoping. So far, nothing.

Izzy couldn't quit watching her mother's hands. It was one of those things that twisted her insides. She wondered if her mother had ever touched her so gently, so softly. Maybe long ago, but she had no memory of ever being touched by Grace. None at all.

Tears blurred her eyes and filled her throat. She wanted so badly to talk with her mother, simply talk to her the same way Jenny did—about diaper rashes or new recipes or a knitting project. But sitting there with her arms wrapped around her drawn-up legs, she could think of nothing to say, and her mother returned little interest in her. It was always that way. She and Grace remained polite but distant strangers.

So many questions were piling up inside that Izzy wanted to ask her mother. Mysteries in her childhood, gaps and holes only her mother could fill. Sometimes she felt as if she needed to go back with her mother in the past so that she could sort out the present. But as much as she wanted to know some answers, she couldn't bring herself to be the first to talk so candidly. It wasn't her nature to be direct or forthcoming, but even more importantly, she was fearful that her mother would interpret her questions as blame and accusations, and withdraw from her. The wedge between them would grow bigger.

If only she could say the words that were on her heart: *Did you know how much I missed you? How much I still miss you?*

Izzy squeezed her eyes shut, annoyed with herself. Good grief, here she was a grown woman. Yet there was a part of her that could not resist an overwhelming urge to be loved, to be wanted, by her mother.

When it was time for Rosie's nap, Izzy excused herself to head home. She walked along the road that led to Windmill Farm, barely noticing how the tips of trees were starting to change color. Her mind was still back at Jenny's house.

A V-shape formation of honking Canada geese flew overhead, startling Izzy back to the present with their rusty-nail-pulled-by-a-hammer sound. As she reached the long driveway of Windmill Farm, her thoughts shifted abruptly as she caught sight of her woollies, bunched nervously together in the sheep pen. Hank Lapp had given Luke an old trampoline. They had no idea why and no idea what to do with it, until Luke suggested using it to provide shade for the sheep in the pen. She'd been asking him to build a shelter for her sheep since last spring.

To Luke, it had seemed like a perfect solution. "Two birds, one stone," he told Izzy as he dragged the trampoline into the sheep pen. The sheep thought differently. The trampoline frightened them, and they huddled fearfully, far away from it.

Luke walked down from the fix-it shop to join her at the gate. "They'll get used to it, Izz. Give them time." He dropped a kiss on the top of her head and went back to the shop.

He was probably right. Sheep were frightened of anything new. They were frightened of everything. They had reason to be. They were utterly defenseless animals.

Izzy checked on them three times a day, always bracing herself for some horrible discovery. The worst of all was when she found her two favorite ewes, Lucy and Ethel, cast down, dead in the field, with vultures already working on their carcasses. It took her days to get over it.

Amos was still alive when that particular tragedy occurred and gave her a stern warning. "If you keep falling in love with your sheep, you're going to get your heart broken over and over again. Sheep get themselves into so much trouble. Some folks say sheep are born looking for a way to die."

And wasn't that the truth? Nearly every single day, there was a threatening situation one sheep or another got itself into. Still, she loved them. She loved being a shepherdess. She loved being out in the pasture, early in the morning, late at night, fussing and caring over each one of them as if they were her babies.

Even Luke, who helped her throughout the year with shearing and spring lambing, often questioned her attachment to sheep. "Did you know that nearly every animal cleans itself? Dogs, cats, raccoon. Birds take baths. So do elephants. But not sheep. They are dirty as can be."

"I know," she would reply.

"Did you know they're considered the dumbest animal on the earth?"

She nodded. "I know."

"Did you know sheep can barely focus two feet in front of them?"

"Yes, I know they're nearsighted."

He would smile and shake his head. "Izzy, why do you love them so?"

"I don't know. I just do."

How she loved those sheep. She loved the sweet lanolin in their wool, she loved their unique personalities, the wide-eyed looks on their faces, their skittish behavior. She "got" them.

Her mother referred to them as "Izzy's needy beasts." Like they were annoying or burdens. They weren't annoying or a burden to Izzy. Now, the neediness part, that she had no argument for. Sheep were needy. They needed her. She considered it a privilege to care for them. Her mother would shake her head at that, thinking Izzy foolish to put herself in a situation where she was responsible for vulnerable, dependent creatures. That's exactly why Izzy loved them. It felt as natural as breathing to her.

There was something she would never admit to Luke, and especially not to her mother. She loved sheep because they loved her too. Yes, they were animals, and probably had a different version of love than she did. But love was love.

As soon as school let out for the day, Mollie went straight to Windmill Farm to talk to Luke. She hadn't stopped thinking about the idea of fostering a child, and she couldn't wait to get the ball rolling. She'd even spent some time reorganizing her little cottage last night. She definitely wanted to foster girls, maybe age six or seven. She imagined hushed conversations lasting late into the night, getting ready for school together in the morning, braiding hair, baking cookies. The whole notion felt so . . . wonderfully right to her.

She scootered up the hill that led to Windmill Farm, one foot kicking against the road, trying not to think of how much she missed her old bicycle. It was so much easier to get to places on a bicycle than a scooter—but that was Ohio and this was Pennsylvania. That was part of her old life and this was her new life. She had desperately wanted a new, unencumbered life, so she shouldn't complain when things were . . . new.

Her mind was wandering again. She blinked, swaying the scooter dizzily. She shifted her thoughts to how happy she was to be here, how glad she was to have accepted Aunt Fern's offer to move to Stoney Ridge and become the new schoolteacher. Her mother didn't want her to go. She fretted constantly, to the point where Mollie felt she needed to leave Ohio. As much as Mollie loved her home, surrounded by friends and family, she was oversheltered by a protective mother. Even on her best days, her mother had never been a calming influence. Mollie felt as if she were suffocating, shadowed by the past. She just couldn't live with that constant worry in her mother's eyes anymore, nor pity in anyone else's.

She zoomed around a corner, past the phone shanty shared by Windmill Farm, and noticed Luke Schrock was coming out of it. She swiveled her scooter handles around to come to an abrupt stop. "Luke! Just the one I wanted to see. When can I get my foster children? I'd like two girls, sisters, if possible. Age six or seven years old. Five or six would do, I suppose. No older than seven, though. Eight, tops."

A crease appeared between Luke's eyebrows as he frowned at her, a look that reminded her of Sam. She had never seen much similarity between them, which, for some reason, pleased Sam to hear.

"Mollie," Luke said in a cautionary tone, "I'm pretty sure it's not that easy. It's not like picking out a rescue dog."

"No, I suppose not." That made sense. She should know, of course, but she felt a little disappointed. Naïve. She was way too naïve. "But I want to get things started. What should we do first?"

"We?" Luke let out a big weary sigh. "Honestly, I have no idea. Izzy might know. She's up at the big house, doing something with Fern. Want to come up with me? We can ask her what we should do."

Mollie hopped off her scooter and the two started up the steep driveway. "I love this idea, Luke. I think it's wonderful. Just the kind of thing our church should be doing more of. Making a difference."

He gave her a sideways glance. "I'm glad you think so. Not sure too many others agree with you. Did you see how many slipped away from the table? Other than you, not a single person showed any interest in fostering."

"It's just a new idea. Everyone was focused on you being the new deacon, and then you declared your first mission.

34

I think you took everyone by surprise. You'll see. They'll warm up to the concept."

His eyebrows lifted. "My first mission as deacon? Is that what I did?"

"Yes. That's what you did."

From the kitchen window, Izzy had seen them coming up the hill and came out to the porch to greet them. "Come on in. Fern and I just baked some apple cider doughnuts."

"Yum," Mollie said, inhaling. "Is that what smells so good?" She set her scooter down on the bottom step. "I stopped by to ask Luke some questions about foster care. He said you're the expert."

Izzy shot a glance at Luke, then spun around and opened the door. "I'm not."

"I didn't use the word 'expert,' actually," Luke said, following them both into the kitchen. "I said that you might know more how to get started. Mollie is interested in fostering a child."

Mollie said hello to her aunt Fern, who was peeking in the oven at the next batch of doughnuts and lifted an oven mitt in a greeting.

Chin tucked, Izzy pulled out a dinner plate and set four doughnuts on it. She filled two glasses of milk and handed one each to Luke and to Mollie. "Help yourself. I've got to go check the honor jar on the farm stand. I meant to when I came back from Jenny's but got distracted by the sheep."

"Izzy," Luke said quickly. "Slow down. We wanted to ask you some questions. Mollie came all the way to Windmill Farm to get some information."

At the door, Izzy stopped and turned to face them. "I really don't have any information to offer."

"But you must have an idea about how someone gets started as a foster family."

Firmly, she repeated, "I have no idea. None." Her eyes narrowed, but only slightly.

As Izzy left the kitchen, Luke turned to Mollie. "I'm sorry. I'm not sure what's got her bothered."

Fern pulled out a tray from the oven. "Might have something to do with the fact that she grew up in foster homes and doesn't want to remember them."

"Oh," Luke said, rubbing the trim black beard that framed his chin. "Oh."

"Izzy wasn't born Amish?" Mollie said, amazed. "She speaks Penn Dutch without an accent." She sat down at the table and took a bite of a doughnut. Delicious.

"I forget you're new here." Luke reached out and took a doughnut. "She became baptized a few years ago. Learned the language and traditions from Fern. Learned how to cook like an Amish woman from Fern too." He stuffed half the doughnut into his mouth, and his dark eyebrows wiggled in approval. Pointing to his mouth, he mumbled, "Whoa. These are amazing."

Mollie examined the doughnut's dusting of cinnamon and sugar. "How'd you get so much flavor into them?"

"Reduce the apple cider down until it's practically a syrup." Fern glanced out the window. "Might be nice if you took a doughnut or two out to your bride, Luke, and apologize for putting her on the spot in front of Mollie."

Luke took two doughnuts, then reached out for a third, and said, "Good thinking." He nodded at Mollie. "I'll do a little homework and get back to you about fostering a child."

"Siblings," Mollie said quickly, before he got out the door. "Don't forget that I'd like to foster siblings. Preferably around the ages of six or seven. Eight, tops." As he crossed the threshold, she added, "Soon, Luke? You'll call the right people soon?" She was eager. She hadn't felt so excited about a project since she decided to move to Stoney Ridge just a few months ago. Or maybe when school started. She felt excited about a lot of things.

"Soon," Luke said around another mouthful of doughnut.

"Good," Mollie said. "I'll check in with you tomorrow."

Luke gave her a feeble wave and hurried down the steps.

Mollie walked toward the screen door and peered out. "Izzy said she was going down to the farm stand, didn't she? I just saw her go into the Stitches in Time yarn shop. And didn't Luke say he was going to talk to Izzy?" She turned around to face her aunt. "He's heading over to his fix-it shop."

"Hmm," Fern said with a frown. "Hmm."

"Yup. That's just what I thought." Mollie sat down at the table and helped herself to another doughnut.

THREE

If Luke had been entirely truthful with Mollie, he would tell her that he really did not want to do any homework on this foster children project. He did not want to move forward on it at all. Prior to church, if someone had asked him about it, Luke might have felt he could tackle it, give it a good try, for Amos's sake. Maybe he'd have success placing one or two children in foster homes. Definitely, Mattie and Sol Riehl would take in a few children; they'd had some experience fostering. Frankly, he might have felt that was good enough. He'd done what he could. Amos would've understood that.

But like a lightning strike from the sky, out of the blue, Luke was now the church deacon. He had to finish things he'd started. Be an example to others. Suddenly, he had all kinds of nameless responsibilities that he couldn't get his head around. The truth kept hitting him in the gut, over and over. He felt thoroughly, completely, totally overwhelmed. In over his head. Drowning.

He couldn't even face Izzy. They'd been having some tension over their current living situation. They lived in two tiny rooms behind the fix-it shop at Windmill Farm. Most of Luke's time was spent overseeing Amos's orchards, but there was a steady stream of customers who needed small household repairs: harnesses, furniture, tools. Living behind the fix-it shop had been comfortable enough when Luke was single, but after he and Izzy married last year, it was much too small. One of the rooms—and to call it a room was a very generous description—was the kitchen. It was about the size of a narrow bathroom or closet, with a sink and a counter and a tiny refrigerator that fit underneath. Only one person could fit in it at a time, so their meals were taken at a corner table in the repair shop.

Amos's illness had been a consuming focus for the first year of Luke and Izzy's marriage. They had spent most of their time up at the big house, helping Fern with round-the-clock caregiving. But after Amos had passed away in late June, Fern had encouraged Luke, in her no-nonsense way, to get on with living. Luke wanted to make the fix-it shop feel less like a temporary abode and more like a real home for Izzy. She'd never had her own home. Fern gave him her blessing to remodel it.

"I couldn't have managed this last year without you and Izzy," she told him. "You've been better to me than any son or daughter could be. So now it's your turn. Turn that old outbuilding into a home."

Izzy had been thrilled. She and Luke spent a week designing the additions they wanted to make. She wanted him to add a baby's room first, so it would be all ready and waiting, but he insisted on redoing the kitchen. After all, they needed to eat, and as far as he knew, there still wasn't a baby on the horizon. Reluctantly, Izzy agreed, and even seemed to get excited about the plans for the kitchen.

And so, well over a month ago, he started the remodel. The demolition part, to be exact, which was always the fun part. Luke tore through the walls, convinced it would only take him a few weeks to frame the new addition and drywall those bare studs. But he'd underestimated what a hot, dry summer was doing to the orchards. The fruit started to ripen, one variety after another, weeks ahead of schedule. Luke was busier than a one-eyed cat watching nine mouse holes. The remodel ground to a halt.

Izzy dismissed that excuse. "You've been working Amos's orchards for three years now. How could you not have considered the timing of fruit ripening before you started tearing walls down? Why wouldn't you just wait until the orchards were done for the year?"

Excellent question. He had no answer for her.

"I know why," she said, hands on her hips. "Starting things is exciting for you. Finishing . . . not so much."

True.

She wanted him to ask Teddy Zook for help, because any time Teddy was involved in a project, it was not only done correctly, but it got finished. Consider the Stitches in Time yarn shop, she reminded him, just in case he'd forgotten.

He knew, he knew. "I can't ask Teddy for help right now, Izzy. That baby of his has the colic and Teddy says they haven't slept more than an hour a night in months. He's exhausted. Last time I saw him, he fell asleep midsentence." He dropped his chin to his chest in an exaggerated motion and feigned a snore or two. When he dared a peek at Izzy, he saw her smile. A little.

Resigned, Izzy put a wide board on top of two sawhorses to use as a makeshift kitchen counter. That just happened on Friday.

Today was Monday. And now he was the deacon. He had no business being a deacon! He hadn't even had a chance yet to discuss what this new role might mean to the two of them, how it might change their life. As if he had any idea. He didn't.

He was hoping they could talk it over last night. Lo and behold, David arrived before supper to say Luke was needed to go to the hospital with him. One of the sisters from the Sisters' House had fallen and broken a hip. First night of deaconing and he was already on duty. He and David didn't get home until after eleven, and Izzy was sound asleep. And then the morning started at dawn and there was no time to talk. And just a few minutes ago, he'd said something that bothered her and she slipped away to the yarn shop like a barn cat. She did that whenever she wanted to avoid him.

Luke had assumed most of the storms he and Izzy had weathered in their courtship would've prepared them for smooth sailing in marriage. Not so. The problems, they kept on coming.

Without meaning to, he would often disappoint Izzy or annoy her. Either way, when she was upset, she withdrew. She went silent.

He didn't mean to upset her like he did. Living with a woman in a small space required a great deal of sensitivity and self-awareness, two qualities Luke was particularly short on. After he did something stupid, *then* he could see what he'd done or said that was insensitive, especially if Izzy or Fern pointed it out. In the moment, though, he had no such awareness.

Last Saturday came to mind. Stitches in Time had reached its first anniversary after an impressive year. Long ago, Edith

Lapp had been the one to suggest that Stoney Ridge could use a yarn shop, and she was spot on. Stitches in Time filled a need in Stoney Ridge for knitters, and it filled a need in Izzy too, helping her feel as if she truly belonged to the church of Stoney Ridge. Luke was pleased for his wife.

Fern had wanted to have a celebration on the shop's first birthday. She made her incredible homemade peach ice cream and a ginger cake. And Grace Mitchell Miller, Izzy's mother, had been specially invited. Four times the invitation was extended. Once by Izzy, once by Luke, and followed up by Jenny. And then a reminder was issued by Luke.

Izzy had knitted a warm winter sweater for her mother and planned to give it to her at the party as a surprise. Grace had picked out the pattern and even chose the color of the wool—her favorite shades of light blue and navy blue. Izzy had stayed up late Friday night to finish it, sewing on special wooden buttons that she knew her mother liked. "Stitched just in time," Luke had quipped as she finished the last button and wrapped the sweater in a box and tied it with a bow. "She'll love it."

Izzy shrugged, as if it didn't matter, but it did. Luke knew it did.

The party started happily enough, with lots of church members and customers coming through. The shop grew crowded with well-wishers. But no Grace. About midway through the party, Jenny slipped out to the phone shanty to call Grace, but she returned without an answer. "Her phone just kept ringing," she told Luke. Grace never did show.

Luke knew how her mother's absence hurt Izzy, how it churned up memories of disappointments. He knew that.

So why did he then say such a dumb thing?

Before cutting the ginger cake, Fern took a moment to silence the crowd. "Stitches in Time is more than a yarn shop," she told everyone. "It's become a hub of our community for the women."

"JUST LIKE THE BENT N' DENT IS FOR THE MENFOLK," Hank Lapp said. Everyone chuckled at that, because Hank Lapp spent most of his days loitering there.

Fern looked at Luke to say a few words. There were so many affirming things he wanted to say about Izzy, things like how hard she had worked to bring her vision of a shop into reality. How many women circled through it in a week's time, Amish and English, and how those tour buses made regular stops all summer long, and how many knitting classes had been started, and how highly respected Izzy was. That once she made up her mind to do something, she was invincible. All those compliments, he could have easily, earnestly said.

Instead, he announced to everyone that the yarn shop was such a success, ha, ha, ha, that he might just retire from the fix-it shop and let Izzy be the breadwinner. Ha, ha, ha. He could just sit in a rocker at the Bent N' Dent and play checkers with Hank Lapp, all day, every day. All the men chuckled along with him. Izzy turned away.

Dumb, dumb, dumb.

⁓

Izzy opened the door of her yarn shop and took in a deep breath. She loved being here. The sweet scent of lanolin in the air, the rainbow colors of yarn in crisscross shelving against the wall, the circle of chairs waiting for knitters. Being here was so much better than being in the half-demolished fix-it shop, staring at bare wall studs. Why, last week Hank Lapp had come into the shop and yoo-hooed to her through open framing of two rooms, all while she was pinning together her dress!

But this wonderful yarn shop, it was all hers. She sat down at the spinning wheel, set the bobbin into the flier, and screwed on the whorl. She inserted the flier into the mother-of-all, popping one string on the bobbin, one on the whorl, and checked to make sure the bobbin spun freely inside the flier. She'd made that mistake before.

She tested it first to make sure the yarn took up on the bobbin and adjusted it by tightening it up. Satisfied, she sat down to split the roving in half lengthwise, then split it again, and grabbed her lead yarn. She started the wheel spinning with her foot and let the roving twist onto that strand of start yarn. She held the roving loosely in her right hand, and her left hand gently pushed and drew the roving as it twisted into yarn and filled the bobbin. The inchworm method, she called it. There were different methods to spin, depending on the spinner's mood and the type of roving she was working with. The inchworm method went slow, but it was relaxing for short stints of spinning.

It amazed her, this spinning. To take a basketful of carded fleece, almost like large cotton balls, and turn it into hand-spun yarn, with fibers joined so tightly together that they couldn't separate. A miracle, in a way, and she was part of it. She liked to sit here and think of the first shepherd, long ago, who came up with the notion of shearing a sheep and using its wool to create yarn. No, not a shepherd. A shepherdess. That's who must have first conceived of such a good idea. It seemed like something a woman would think of.

The door opened and in walked Luke. The sight of him

still made her catch her breath, even when she was bothered with him, which was often. Her feet came to a stop on the treadle. The spinning wheel gave a final whirr and then settled into silence. Through the open door, off in the distance, she heard the bleating of a lamb and then its mother answer back.

"I said something up in Fern's kitchen that seemed to have annoyed you. I didn't mean to make you mad." He closed the door behind him. "Did I say something stupid again?"

"No, not really."

"Is the half-finished house getting to you? I'll be back at it soon."

"Half finished?" A corner of her lips tugged upward. "Half started, don't you mean?"

He rubbed his forehead. "Yeah, I suppose you're right."

She looked at him thoughtfully. She had some complicated things to tell him and she wasn't yet sure how. "Luke, another month has gone by."

"Right. That's true. October will be here soon." He squinted. "Is that what you meant?"

"Another month. It's passed."

He had a perplexed expression on his face, a common look. "Okay, I get that time is passing. But I'm not exactly sure what you're hinting at."

She sighed. She loved him dearly, but he could be so impossibly dense. "Another month. No baby."

"Oh." His eyes dropped to her belly. "Oh!"

"It's been over a year now. You said not to worry until a year had passed." She turned away and started straightening chairs, one by one. "Jenny and Jesse are expecting their second baby. Jenny and I, we wanted to raise babies together."

Softly, he said, "Honey, it's not a race."

She finished straightening the last chair. "Now that you're deacon, you'll hardly ever be home. Look at what happened last night. That's the kind of life I'll have to expect."

He approached her, wrapping his arms around her, pinning her close against him until he felt her relax. "Izzy, you lived with Amos and Fern while he was the deacon. Amos was around plenty of times. Last night was just a chance for David to take me along with him, show me the ropes. I don't think it'll be like that very much." He kissed her on the neck. "A baby will happen for us when it's meant to happen. Worrying won't do any good."

She felt the ache in her throat. He didn't understand how this issue frightened her. More than that. It terrified her. She'd always had a strange sense that she might not be able to get pregnant. Her cycle was irregular at best. When she was living on the streets, barely getting enough to eat, a year or more had gone by when she had no cycle at all. All those years of abuse had taken a toll. Being unable to have a baby was her greatest fear, and now it was coming true.

She knew he was trying to console her in his own clumsy way. She straightened, turned around, and their eyes met.

"Mollie's enthusiasm is kind of catching. Maybe if we take in a foster child, it'll help get your mind off this."

She broke free from him, took a step back, and glared at him. "Oh no." She wagged a finger in the air. "I am not having a foster child. End of discussion."

"Why not? I would think you of all people should be leading the charge on this, not Mollie. She's a single schoolteacher. Why wouldn't you want to help out a child in need, the way others helped you?"

She shook her head. "Luke, you have no idea what you're doing. What you're asking of others! No clue! I don't know how you could have made a promise like that to Amos. What were you thinking?"

"He asked me, Izzy. I owed him a yes." He reached a hand out to her. "That's why I need you to help me. We're a team."

She looked down at his hand. "I'm not the one who made a promise to Amos. You did." She swept past him and out the door.

"Izzy, we're not done talking about this," he shouted from the store's open door.

Oh yes we are, she thought, as she strode toward the woollies in the pasture, her babies. *Oh yes we are.*

Mollie glanced at the ticking clock on the wall of the schoolhouse. It was nearly half past eight and the scholars would be arriving soon, galloping in from all different directions. As hard as she tried to stay away from the window, she kept veering toward it, hoping to catch sight of Sam, climbing over the fence railing, crossing the road to stop in and say hello . . . the way he used to nearly every morning. The rope that pulled the big school bell that sat in the roof's cupola was old, clumsy, and hard for her to pull. Not for him. He could do it one-handed, and she smiled as she thought of the pleased look that would cover his face as she admired how easily he could manage it. Strong.

She had seen him yesterday at the Bent N' Dent. She was carrying a big box of groceries, heavy and clumsy. As she struggled to open the door, it suddenly opened and the box was lifted out of her arms. Magic. And there was Sam, standing tall at the open door with her box in his arms, helping her out again. She could feel her mouth open in shock. "S-Sam!" she sputtered. "Where've you been?"

Before he could respond, twelve-year-old Rudy Miller bolted up the store's steps and stopped abruptly, peering at the two of them with a cat-that-ate-the-canary look on his face. "Yeah, Sam, where ya been?" He slipped behind Sam, making an obnoxious loud kissing noise as he darted into the store.

Under Sam's black hat, two red streaks flamed up his cheeks. "I'll put this in your buggy for you." And that was all he had to say to Mollie. He never did answer her question.

Oh! That reminded her. She picked up a piece of chalk and wrote on the chalkboard: *Rudy—clean out outhouses.* She smiled. Effective.

Spirits lifted, she grabbed her shawl to head outside to ring the big bell. With or without Sam, the day had begun.

There was a new mare in Sam's life. Galen had sent her up from Kentucky after buying her for a song. "She'd been run in one race, just one," he explained to Sam on a phone call. "Apparently, she's frightened by loud noises." When the gun went off to start the race, she reared, tossed the jockey off, and ran the opposite direction of the rest of the horses. "If anyone can work that skittishness out of her," Galen said, "I think it's you," and Sam's chest swelled with pride. "But watch out," he had added. "Don't let her fool you. She's a saucy one."

The trailer arrived with the mare late in the morning, and Sam was instantly smitten. She was a beauty, a glossy

black-haired two-year-old Thoroughbred with perfect conformation. A long, arched neck, a white blaze down her nose,
and four even white socks. Her gait was graceful and athletic.
Normally, he rested new horses in the pasture for a few days
to give them time to settle in. But he kept checking on the
mare throughout the day, and she seemed to take the move
in stride, so he finally decided to take her for a ride. Just the
two of them. It was a big vote of confidence for Galen to
send a horse all the way from Kentucky. He wanted to prove
to Galen that his confidence had been well placed. And he
really wanted to know what this saucy mare was like.

He put the mare in crossties and saddled her up, placing
a gentle bit in her mouth. She took everything well, and he
felt encouraged. He rode her around the pasture for a long
time, to tire her out and see how she acted under the bit. If
Galen were here, that's all the riding they'd do for the day.
But Galen wasn't here, and this horse seemed eager for more.
He decided to go down the road, just down and back. But she
rode so smoothly that when he got to the end of the road,
he decided to make a circle to head back.

He trotted the mare slowly past the Sisters' House, and
then past the group home of Stoney Ridge. Two girls were
hanging on the fence, smoking cigarettes. Seeing them made
him think of Mollie, and he wondered again why she would
consider fostering children. Before the thought was finished
in his mind, suddenly—*CRACK!* An almighty explosion
rocked the very air around him. Every bird in the county
took flight. The mare panicked and reared, dancing on her
rear legs, but Sam held his seat. As if time slowed down,
he saw one girl strike a match to light another firecracker,
but before it could ignite, he turned the mare around and

headed back down the road, straining to keep the horse in a controlled trot. He braced himself for what he was pretty sure was coming, sat deeper in the saddle, pushed his feet farther down in the stirrups, gripped the reins tautly. He was passing the Sisters' House when the second *CRACK* erupted, bouncing off every house from here to kingdom come, followed by the two girls' joyous laughter. This time the mare took off at a full gallop, and all he could do was hang on.

Saucy, yup. Full of vinegar.

$\mathcal{F}$OUR

L ater in the week, Luke drove by the Bent N' Dent one afternoon and slowed the horse. David's buggy was there and, happily, Hank Lapp's was not. It might be a good time to talk to David, tell him what he'd been thinking about since Sunday. He walked inside the dimly lit store and nodded to Jenny at the cash register. "Is he here?"

"Back at his desk," Jenny said. "But he's on the phone, so don't interrupt him until he's off."

Luke liked Jenny. She was no nonsense, much like Fern. It was still nearly impossible for him to get his head around the fact that Jenny and Izzy were half sisters. Jenny looked like her mother, Grace—petite, blonde, delicate. He wondered about Izzy's father, whoever or wherever he might be. Izzy would never speak of him, and Grace wasn't exactly the type to offer any information. Luke had tried and gotten shut down.

Luke had a tenuous-at-best relationship with his mother-in-law. He didn't like Grace, and he certainly did not trust her. But those feelings didn't really matter. It was how she treated Izzy that irked him. Like she was a distant niece rather

51

than a daughter. Grace oozed over Jenny's little girl, offering to babysit, holding the baby every chance she got. He was amazed that Jenny and Jesse would even let Grace babysit. He sure wouldn't want her to be alone with his baby. He'd worry the whole time that she would fall asleep or drop the baby or both.

Babies. Hmmm. Maybe that's why Izzy was so overly focused on having a baby—to get her mother's attention.

Luke looked forward to being a father one day, but he was barely keeping up as it was. It wouldn't bother him if fatherhood were a long way off. Marriage, it took more out of him than he had expected.

What had he expected? Mostly, to be honest, the pleasures of intimacy with Izzy. They'd waited through their courtship for intimacy and were both hungry for that special closeness. Sharing a bed was all he'd hoped for and more, but it didn't solve other problems they had, like communicating clearly without misunderstandings. Resolving conflict in a healthy way. And they seemed to have plenty of both: miscommunication and conflict.

Standing outside David's door, Luke heard him say goodbye to whomever he was talking to and hang up the phone. He knocked and walked in. David looked up and smiled.

That greeting of a welcoming smile, it meant the world to Luke. No matter what Luke had done, David always kept an open heart toward him. Luke couldn't remember a single time when David didn't greet him with a smile.

"Sit down, Luke. What's going on?"

"I've been giving this a lot of thought. I'm not qualified to be a deacon. I think I should resign. Or be fired. Or be replaced. Is that possible?"

David pointed to the chair. As soon as Luke sat down, he calmly asked, "Any particular reason?"

Oh, plenty of them. He'd been called out every single night this week. Hospital visits twice, delivering a death message another night—and he didn't even know the elderly lady who had died. He'd just received the call and was told to relay the news of her death to her daughter. Last night, he was called out to Teddy Zook's house to help with their crying baby. "Here." Teddy handed the baby to Luke. "Alice and me, we need some sleep."

Luke walked that baby down the road and around the barn and back up the road again for more than three hours. Is that what a deacon's life looked like? He couldn't handle it. "Don't you agree that only one vote might be an indication that it was a mistake? Isn't there some kind of rule in the Ordnung about that?"

"No. None that I know of."

"Could you talk to other bishops? See if there's any precedent to replace a deacon due to a massive shortage of votes? Think about it. The entire church has a lack of confidence in me. There must be some kind of rule for that. There's rules for everything!"

David looked as if he was trying very hard not to laugh.

"But you have to admit that only one vote is pretty pathetic."

"That one vote led you to draw the lot. I would say that's not at all pathetic. I would call that the hand of God."

"Maybe God wasn't thinking about what being a deacon might do to a man's marriage. Not good." He shook his head. "I've hardly had a chance to speak to Izzy all week. Each day I'm in the orchards, each night I'm called out to deacon duty."

"It's a big adjustment, that's for sure. It'll take time for you both to get accustomed to some added responsibilities."

It was more than an adjustment. Luke leaned forward in his chair. "My own wife didn't vote for me."

David settled back in his chair, gazing at Luke in that way he had, as if he was peering into his soul. "Birdy wouldn't have wanted me to be a minister or deacon. Everyone knows what it's asking of a man."

Luke took off his hat and set it on his knee, eyes fixed on it. "So you think that's why a man's wife wouldn't vote for him?"

"Absolutely. If she loves him."

Luke turned his hat brim around and around and around. Maybe that's why Izzy hadn't voted for him. She had lived at Windmill Farm as Amos became a deacon. She would've seen up close the way much of Amos's life was taken up by deaconing, how much was transferred to Fern's shoulders.

"So, Luke, you've been married a year now. How's it going?"

"It's uh . . . it's, well . . ." His voice dropped off. He couldn't lift his eyes to look at David.

"Let me take a guess. It's a lot more work than you'd ever thought."

Luke's head snapped up. "Yes." How did David know that? "Is it that obvious?"

"One thing about you and Izzy—you both didn't have childhoods filled with day-to-day examples of a healthy marriage." He lifted a hand as Luke started to protest. "I'm not saying you both didn't observe good marriages. But there's something about the day-in, day-out realness of married life that you missed. The burnt-toast moments. The dad who forgets anniversaries."

Oh no. Luke thumped his palm against his forehead. No!

He'd forgotten the thirteenth monthiversary with Izzy this week. It was a celebration he had started on the one-month anniversary of their wedding date, and she had seemed so pleased, so touched. He'd done a great job remembering to celebrate monthiversaries for most of the year, until . . . until this deacon job took over his life.

"Without seeing how day-to-day troubles were normal, how they can be resolved, it seems that the two of you might have huge expectations of what a marriage should look like."

Eyes still cast down, Luke said, "Yeah. It's . . . hard." So much more difficult than he could have imagined.

"Just because marriage is hard doesn't mean it isn't right. Every single marriage is made up of two sinners. Marriage is a refining tool God uses to shape our characters."

The scoff that came out of Luke didn't sound like himself at all. "A sharp tool."

"Thankfully, the Lord is in the midst of marriage, and that makes all the difference."

Luke leaned back in his chair and stretched his legs out, one ankle over the other. "Any advice?"

A mellow grin reached David's eyes. "Try to do the opposite of what comes naturally. Listen more than talk. Ask questions more than spout answers."

Do the opposite. Deceptively simple, yet surprisingly good advice. "I'll give it a try. Thank you, David." For being the father I've needed. For showing me how to be a husband. And now, to be a church leader. For everything. "I still think I shouldn't be the deacon."

"If it helps, I still think I shouldn't be the bishop."

That's where he was wrong. David was a fine bishop. The best a man could be.

As Luke rose to leave, David said, "Oh, one more thing. Tomorrow is the gathering. It'll be held at my house."

"Huh?"

"The church leaders in the area. Our annual gathering. You need to be there."

"But Amos never had to attend those meetings."

"Well, he wasn't well, for one thing. And Stoney Ridge is hosting this one. I think it's good to have our full church leadership in attendance. There'll be a lot of wise, experienced ministers whom you should meet. I think there's a lot you can learn."

The brief settled feeling in Luke's heart was gone. It felt like David had just given him a hard kick to the stomach.

Mollie had completely reorganized her tiny cottage, eagerly preparing for the day when her foster daughter would come to live with her. It was a two-bedroom cottage, though neither bedroom was much bigger than a shoebox. Her bedroom had a double-sized bed in it, but that meant little room on either side of the bed and she couldn't fully open her closet door. The second bedroom fit a twin-sized bed, and it was no small task to get it around that hall corner and into the tiny room. It took her most of the afternoon, but she finally did it, and now she felt confident her cottage would pass the inspection of whatever government agency it needed to pass. All she was waiting for now was for Luke Schrock to get things rolling—my, oh my, he was slow—and then for her foster daughter to be assigned to her. She couldn't wait for that day. She simply could not wait. As she finished washing her dishes, she imagined how fun it would be to have someone to wash dishes with, to cook with, to talk to. Someone little who really needed a home. Someone who needed her.

For the next few afternoons, Sam rode the saucy mare past the group home, past those two wayward girls who hung out on the fence smoking cigarettes when they should've been in school. Each day, the two saw him coming down the road and set off firecrackers, whooping and laughing at him. He probably did seem ridiculous to those two. Who would keep coming back for more of the same abuse?

He would. Sam was a skilled horseman, and he knew exactly what he was doing.

By day four, the mare didn't rear when the firecracker exploded. By Friday, day five, the mare danced on her hooves, but she didn't panic, and although her ears went forward, her nostrils flared, and her eyes went wide, she kept her wits about her. He was able to trot her home at an even pace, even when a third firecracker went off.

Unbeknownst to them, those two wayward girls were helping him condition the saucy mare to traffic noise, working the skittishness right out of her.

Luke should've just slept in last Sunday morning. Should've feigned an illness. Gone to see a distant relative. Skipped the whole drawing of the lot. If he'd been smart enough to think of it, he wouldn't be on his way this beautiful Saturday morning to David's house for the ministers' gathering when he'd rather stay home. He tried to remember what last Saturday felt like, his last day of freedom, before this whole deacon business got dropped in his lap. It felt like a lifetime ago.

Today was the annual meeting of the Old Order Amish church leaders of eastern Lancaster County. They met once or twice a year to discuss the changes or difficulties the congregation was facing and share ideas of how to manage those concerns. Not three or four years ago, he was probably a topic in the meeting. How a church should handle a troublemaker like Luke Schrock.

Three or four years ago, Luke might've enjoyed knowing that he was causing the ministers to wring their hands over him. Today, the thought shamed him. It was just one of the two reasons he didn't want to be going to David's today. The other reason was that the meetings were mind-numbingly boring.

As a young teen, he and his brother Sammy had once handled the horses for the host family who opened their home for the annual event. It had lasted most of the day, with lunch served by the women. The two boys had eavesdropped on the ministers by sneaking up in the hayloft, then Luke had a stellar idea. With string and a couple of handkerchiefs, he fashioned tiny parachutes. He gave Sammy the job of finding mice. During a particularly dull bishop's talk, they parachuted the mice down on top of the bishop, one by one. As Luke recalled, it went terribly wrong, and they were quickly found out.

Today, he planned to say nothing, not a single word, to listen and learn, to hope that the dull bishop was not in attendance.

His strategy evolved last evening as he helped Izzy hunt down one of her sheep. She called the ewe Houdini, because it was constantly escaping the pen. Luke nicknamed it Phooey, as in why bother? That one ewe created more trouble than the entire flock. He'd send it off to the slaughterhouse, if it were up to him. Not Izzy. She would not give up on that stupid ewe. They finally found her stuck in a gully. If it had been a rainy day, she might've drowned. Luke picked her up and helped her over the edge, while Izzy patted her and stroked her and checked all her limbs for damage.

"You know this ewe will only do it all over again tomorrow," he said. "You know that, don't you?"

Izzy gave him one of her direct looks. "Not if you move the trampoline to the center of the pen."

She blamed him for Houdini's latest escape and she wasn't wrong this time. Luke kept forgetting to move the trampoline. Hank Lapp was always bringing junk over to Windmill Farm that he didn't know what else to do with. He treated Luke's fix-it shop as his own personal dump. Luke didn't want that old trampoline, until he realized it might be a cheap and fast solution to bring shade to Izzy's sheep.

He thought it was a pretty brilliant idea until Izzy pointed out that he had set it too close to the fence. Houdini climbed on top of it and bounced right out of the pen. Well, no one actually witnessed the escape, so maybe she didn't actually jump and bounce—but she did figure out how to get from the trampoline to the fence and out of the pen. "I'll move it." Like he should have done from the start.

Izzy was oohing and aahing over her poor stupid Houdini. "She's the prettiest ewe I've ever seen."

"Pretty is as pretty does. She is a pain."

"She just needs a better shepherd."

"Oh, honey. You are a good shepherd."

"I'm a shepherdess. You're the shepherd I was talking about."

"Ouch." He watched Houdini butt her head against a little innocent lamb, just minding its own business. "We should sell her." *Better still, enjoy her for Sunday supper.*

"Never. Houdini's wool is exceptional."

Wool was wool. "How do you know that?"

"Edith Lapp. She says so. She knows all about sheep."

Luke couldn't disagree. Edith Lapp was the prickliest person in Stoney Ridge, but she was the go-to person in town. She read voraciously, remembered details, never exaggerated, and had a reputation for being the expert on just about everything. The very opposite of her husband, Hank Lapp, in every single way. Hank limited his reading to the headlines of a newspaper, couldn't remember anything of importance, exaggerated all things, and had a reputation for being a man with a surfeit of spare time. He enjoyed most everyone, while Edith disapproved of most everyone.

For some reason, Edith had developed an inexplicable fondness for Izzy. She'd spent long hours helping Izzy design and set up Stitches in Time, and she sent droves of people into the store.

Izzy had started walking up the hill toward the orchards. "And another thing. Houdini has beautiful lambs."

He caught up with her. "Izzy, she's going to start teaching those lambs how to escape the pen."

"I'll deal with that when I have to. One thing at a time. One day's troubles are enough for anybody. Right now the thing I need to tend to is to get those woollies in the pen before dark."

Aha! That was it. Unknowingly, Izzy had just delivered the

advice he needed to face the leaders' gathering. He would handle things one at a time. He wouldn't allow himself to be overwhelmed by thinking of a lifetime of deacon service. Good grief, he was only twenty-five. His life stretched out in front of him, and it terrified him—*No! No, no, no.* New policy. He shook his head and stomped his feet as he followed his wife up the path. He wasn't going to borrow tomorrow's troubles. He had plenty for one day.

But that was yesterday and this was today, and his insecurities swirled around his head like bees around honey. He did not want to be at this meeting, did not want to be the recipient of countless skeptical looks from the other ministers and bishops and deacons. He pulled his buggy up to David's house and stopped at the end of a very long line of buggies, but he couldn't quite make himself get out of his. He noticed the horse's reins were quivering and realized that was because his hands were trembling. He squeezed his eyes shut, trying to gather his courage to go inside.

Thoughts of how church members had reacted to him on the day of the lot drawing swirled through his head. He knew many—most—had serious doubts about his ability, his worthiness, to be deacon. Freeman Glick was the one he had trouble shaking off. He was a bishop who had been Quieted, a thoroughly humiliating experience. Of all people to show a little compassion to a new church leader, it should've been Freeman Glick. Just the opposite. His mind was made up about Luke, and once it was made up, nothing could change it. On the Sunday morning when Luke drew the lot, Freeman had come up to him with a troubled look in his hard, dark eyes, neck veins throbbing. All he had said, in a voice so loud it felt like the earth trembled, was, "This is impossible to fathom." The whole church could've stayed home and heard his verdict.

His brother Levi peered over his shoulder. "Impossible," he echoed, though not quite so loud.

They shook their heads, muttering, "Impossible. Unfathomable."

What did *that* mean? Luke had a pretty good idea: the system had broken down. A wolf had slipped into the fold.

As Freeman and Levi walked away, Fern had quietly slipped up behind Luke. "Prove them wrong, Luke Schrock. You've done it before. You can do it again." By the time he turned to face her, she had disappeared into the crowd.

Okay, Luke. Okay. Pull it together, man. You're making too much of this.

"What's wrong with you?"

Luke opened his eyes to see Rudy Miller staring curiously at him. "What do you mean?"

"You sick?"

"No."

"You look sick. Your face is pasty white. Blotches of red on your neck."

Annoying. "Rudy, what do you want?"

"I'm handling horses today. Are you going in or you just gonna sit here all morning? Ready or not?"

Was he ready? No, not at all. He slid open the buggy door and put his feet on the ground. "Take good care of my horse. His name is Bob."

Rudy took the reins from Luke and patted Bob's long nose. "I know Bob. I'll put him in the pasture with his friends."

Luke shook his head on the way to the barn where the gathering was held. A horse didn't have friends. It sounded like something Izzy would say, always putting human feelings into animals. As he neared the barn's open doors and heard the hum of men's voices, he braced himself. David saw him and waved him over, eager to introduce him to other ministers and bishops. White bushy eyebrows shot to the barn rafters when David said Luke was Stoney Ridge's new deacon. He was the youngest one here, by a mile, which confirmed to him that he needed to keep his mouth tightly shut.

He soon discovered that wouldn't be a problem. He wasn't expected to say anything. The men sat on backless benches for most of the morning, listening to different ministers rattle on and on and on about the need for unity. They all had the same message, the same intent, but no one had any solutions. Unity, unity, unity. Luke wanted to stand up and shout, "But what does that mean? What does it look like? How do we get there?"

Of course, that would be foolish. He sat, listened, and said nothing.

The barn was warm, and where Luke sat, the sun was beaming at him through the open doors, hitting him right in the face. He felt himself grow sleepy. An old bishop rose to speak, so old that his wiry white beard covered his belly, and his voice was thin and warbly. Luke felt his eyelids grow heavier and heavier. He tried sitting on his hands, he tried pinching himself, biting on the inside of his cheek. Nothing worked. He forced himself to concentrate on the old bishop's words, to pay attention.

"I have found," the old bishop said in his trembly voice, "the more I pray, the more things happen."

A jolt of lightning shot down Luke's spine. Not once had he prayed about this new role as a deacon. Not one time. He had worried over it, felt overwhelmed by his responsibilities, tried to talk David out of it, wondered how humiliating it would be if he just quit. Never once had he thought to pray, to ask God to provide all he would need to be a good deacon. Because the thing was, underneath all his insecurities, he really wanted to be a good deacon. A very good one.

Wide awake now, Luke sat up straight.

"I start every morning with a question—'Lord, what do you want me to do today?'" The old bishop paced down the center aisle, pivoted, turned, paced back, all the while peering at the men. He pointed a long finger at them. "Let me warn you. It's a dangerous question." His eyes caught Luke's and held on. "But it's more dangerous not to ask."

Luke's life as a deacon had just found its footing.

FIVE

Luke took the old bishop's words to heart. Each morning, he started the day by asking the Lord, "What do you want me to do?" So far, there wasn't much in the way of a response. None that Luke could discern, anyway.

Mollie Graber should try asking the Lord the same question. She was relentless. Every single day, she stopped by Windmill Farm to ask Luke what her first step should be to start fostering. That girl would not let this topic rest. This morning, just to have something to tell Mollie when she stopped by later in the afternoon, he called the town office of Stoney Ridge and learned there was a privately run foster care agency that managed a group home.

Check. He'd done *something* today to tell Mollie. He exhaled a sigh of relief.

As he set down the phone, the slip of paper with the foster care agency's phone number fell to the ground. He bent down, picked it up, and sensed a strange pressure. He couldn't even say where the pressure came from; it wasn't a bad or frightening feeling, but it left a definite impression. Like when he gently poked his fingers in a loaf of rising

bread—that kind of impression. He had started the morning by asking the Lord what he wanted Luke to do today. He
sensed he shouldn't ignore that odd impression.

He picked up the phone and dialed. It took three transfers
until he reached the right person: a social worker named Roberta Watts, clearly experienced, abundantly intimidating,
even through the phone.

"And you want to do *what*?" she asked him.

Luke repeated the story: his church had some interest in
fostering children.

"And you haven't started the licensing process yet?"

"I thought this was the process. I call in, and you send
over a foster child." He knew it was a stupid comment the
moment he uttered it.

Roberta Watts did not find him amusing. "Son, you trying
to be funny?"

Of course he knew there would be paperwork involved;
he was trying to make a joke. "Sort of."

"Mm-hmm," she muttered under her breath. "That's what
I get for answering the phone. Crazy folk . . . all the livelong
day."

Quickly Luke added, "But I am serious about fostering.
Our church is, I mean. Ready and willing."

Big longsuffering sigh. "Then you tell your church members to fill out paperwork online, then get a clean bill of
health from the doctor, get fingerprinted, then we do a home
study. Then there's training. Then, and only then, do *we*
decide if y'all are qualified to be licensed as foster parents."

"I see." But he didn't. That sounded like it could take
months and months. He pictured Mollie bugging him every
single day. "Is there any way to speed up the process a little?"

"Son, do you have any idea what you're getting into?" Roberta Watts spoke in a tone of voice that could scorch a fellow's eardrums.

No. No, he didn't. But Izzy did. "My wife, she was raised in foster care."

That information caused Roberta Watts to pause, ever so slightly. "Tell me about her."

Luke explained that Izzy had been placed in a foster home at the age of five, and that the court had severed her mother's parental ties so that Izzy was made a ward of the state.

"So she aged out?"

"What does that mean?"

"She left foster care without any tie to a forever family?"

"She ended up connected to an Amish family. Amos and Fern Lapp of Windmill Farm. And me. Now I'm her family."

Another long pause. Luke sensed a shift starting to take place, ever so slightly.

"Where'd you say you live?"

"On a farm. Most everyone in our church is on a farm."

"Mm-hmm. Any chance that Mattie and Solomon Riehl are part of your church?"

"They are." Luke brightened. He thumped his palm against his forehead. He should have started out the conversation by way of Mattie and Sol. They'd fostered lots of children.

"Carrie and Abel Miller?"

"Sure are." Another forehead thump. Carrie and Abel had fostered some city children during summers. *Luke, why do you always do things backward?*

"And they can vouch for your character?" Roberta Watts said, low and threatening. "Offer a good reference."

"I think so."

"You *think* so?"

There it was again. That tone of voice that implied Luke might be feebleminded. "I know so. Yes. Absolutely. Of course they can."

"Mm-hmm." Big inhale, big exhale. "Hold on a minute."

Luke heard Roberta mumbling to someone in the background. Then he heard a high, tinny voice—the opposite of Roberta's deep and skeptical one—shout out a loud, "Thank you, Jesus!"

Instantly, the hair on the back of his neck stood up. What was going on?

More mumbling, then Roberta took her hand off the receiver to talk to Luke. "We have a group home for some sweet, dear children right there in Stoney Ridge."

Luke knew it. It was next to the Sisters' House. The group home for wayward teens. Whenever he drove by, he saw mean-looking girls outside, defiantly puffing away on cigarettes. He hoped they were just cigarettes.

"Normally, we don't expedite the process just because someone calls out of the blue to ask. We're not giving away kittens and puppies here. Son, we clear on that?"

"Yes. Crystal clear."

"Any of you people know CPR?"

"Actually, yeah. A lot of us just got certified for CPR. Dok Stoltzfus gave a Saturday class at the Bent N' Dent a few weeks back. Someone nearly choked to death at a church fellowship, and Dok thought it was high time we knew CPR for emergencies."

"Dok Stoltzfus? You know her?"

Luke's spirits lifted another notch. "Very well."

"Son, this might be your lucky day. We've got a . . . situation on our hands. Just this morning, the state inspector found some black mold in the walls of the group home in Stoney Ridge. We need to find homes for ten children. Pronto. By the time they get home from school today. But it's short-term. A week or two. Only until the group home is repaired." She paused. "So, what do you say to that?"

Luke swallowed. Oh boy. "The church, I'm sure, would be willing to take in ten children." He squeezed his eyes shut. Why in the world did he say that? He had no idea if anyone, other than Mollie Graber, would be willing to take in a foster child . . . even for a week or two.

"Son, the question isn't whether you be willing. It's whether y'all can pass muster to get licensed for emergency short-term foster care. I'll head over to Mattie and Sol's this afternoon. One o'clock sharp. Get everybody there. My assistant Mavis and I will be bringing a doctor and nurse along with me, and a lot of paperwork. A ton of paperwork. And a police officer to take fingerprints. We got to run those through the database lickety-split. No felons allowed, got that?"

"Got it."

"Tell all your families that I am sending out social workers to their homes this very afternoon to do inspections, and they need to be ready. If it all looks good, if everything and everybody checks out"—her voice took an aggressive turn again—"and I am not cutting corners on any single one of you, just because we have a *situation* on our hands—well, then, you'll soon be temporarily fostering ten dear, sweet children." She exhaled. "One o'clock sharp. Mattie Riehl's house." And she hung up.

Luke sat back down on the phone shanty stool, stunned. What in the world just happened? What had he promised, without any right to do so? He felt his heart start to hammer. *The more I pray, the more things happen.* But he didn't know exactly what was happening.

Mollie had woken today with the funniest feeling, as if Christmas morning had arrived. Or her birthday. But it wasn't Christmas and it wasn't her birthday, and yet she couldn't shake the feeling of excitement. Even the children seemed to sense there was something special in the air today. Six-year-old Elizabeth Baker asked if it was going to snow today, though the sun was shining brightly. Birdy arrived to take the scholars on a bird-watching expedition and whispered to Mollie that today was the day she was sure they would spot a red-tailed hawk. "They migrate later than other hawks, you know."

No, Mollie didn't know that. She didn't pay much attention to birds, but she did share Birdy's sense that something special was going to happen today.

Fifteen minutes after Luke hung up the phone with social worker Roberta Watts, he burst through Carrie and Abel Miller's back door, only because no one answered at Mattie and Sol's house. "I need your help."

Carrie was in the kitchen, stirring a hot cookie pan filled with granola. She looked up in surprise, then calmly went back to the granola. "Good morning to you, Luke."

Rudy, Carrie's son, was curled up in a chair, reading a thick book. He looked curiously at Luke, and closed his book, eager to listen in. Rudy had a little bit of spit and vinegar to him, which Luke liked in a boy. "What're you doing out of school?"

"Sick." Rudy pointed to his nose. "Bad cold."

Luke turned to Carrie. "Roberta Watts is coming to Mattie's house at one o'clock today."

"Roberta Watts? The social worker?"

"Yes, the very one. Is she as frightening in person as she sounds on the phone?"

"Worse." Carrie spooned granola into a large container, then set the cookie pan in the sink. She hung her thick oven mitts by the stove and put on the tea kettle.

"No more foster children, Mom," Rudy said, returning to his book. "We all agreed after last summer, when that boy put poison ivy in all our beds." He scratched his neck, remembering.

Carrie didn't pay him any mind, which Luke took as an indication that she might be open-minded to having a foster child. Today, with virtually no notice. He leaned against the doorframe and tented his fingers together. "What would you think about taking ten children in?" He held a finger in the air. "Oh wait. Hold it. Only seven. Mattie, I think, will take one. Mollie wants two."

"Seven?" Carrie stopped washing the cookie pan, just froze perfectly still. "What are you talking about?"

Out of Luke spilled the whole story—his promise to Amos to empty the foster care system in Lancaster County (which, the more Luke learned, seemed like an impossible request—he had no idea there were so many children who needed homes), the conversation he'd had with Roberta

Watts, the group home with black mold. "Carrie, can you take in seven children?"

"No way," Rudy said. "Mom, I'm leaving home if you say yes."

Carrie shook her head. "Don't worry, Rudy. That's not going to happen."

Luke gasped, panicking. "But I don't know of eight other families who would take in a foster child!"

"I thought you were the deacon," Rudy said. "You're supposed to know everything."

"I've been a deacon for barely more than a week. And I know nothing about being a deacon. Less than nothing."

By now Carrie had recovered. "Calm yourself down, Luke. Let's have a cup of tea and talk this over." She picked up the kettle.

"But tea isn't what I need. I need you to say yes to seven foster teens."

Carrie poured herself a cup of tea and sat down. "That might solve your problem. But it would create enormous problems for us."

"Enormous," Rudy echoed.

"And you're the one who made the promise to Amos."

"Carrie, do you have any idea how many children are in the foster care system in Lancaster County? I had no idea! I made a promise without knowing what I was doing."

Carrie leaned back in her chair, sipping her tea. "Imagine what would never happen if we had a full idea of what lay on the other side of a decision? Take marriage, for example. Did you have any idea what marriage would really be like?"

Oh, that was a whole different kettle of fish. If Carrie was trying to discourage Luke, she was doing a fine job.

"I'm never getting married," Rudy said. "Too much trouble."

Luke frowned at him. "If you're sick, shouldn't you be in bed?"

"I'm sick. I'm not dying." He opened his book and went back to reading.

Luke shook his head and turned to Carrie. "Roberta Watts will be at Mattie and Sol's in three hours, expecting lots of families to be there."

"She can be rather difficult to say no to."

Rudy snorted. "Dad calls her a not-so-silent steamroller."

His mother frowned at Rudy, then turned to Luke. "You look a little . . ." She tilted her head.

"Blotchy," Rudy chimed in. "Sweaty."

Carrie shot Rudy a look of exasperation, communicated clearly enough that he put his nose back in his book. "I was going to say . . . you look a little stressed. Why don't you sit down?"

The room was bordering on oppressively hot. Either that or Luke was close to a panic attack. He sat at the table, sweating, while Carrie calmly gazed at him. "I don't know what to do."

"First, you need to stop panicking."

Rudy looked up from his book. "Deacons shouldn't panic."

Luke let out a loud sigh. Unsolicited advice from a twelve-year-old was especially irksome when it was correct. "Okay. I will stop panicking. Then what?"

"Tell me again what Roberta Watts said about the group home."

Luke explained the black-mold-in-the-walls problem.

"Okay." Carrie nodded. "Okay, then. It's a short-term situation."

"Yes! I should have started with that. One week, maybe two."

"That makes it easier. Let's make a list of families who might consider opening their home on a short-term basis." She took a piece of paper and pencil out of a basket. "Who are you thinking of?"

"None. I can't think of anyone. Not a single family."

Rudy put down his book. "What about Esther and Joe Blank? Their oldest two sons just went to Indiana to work in an RV factory." He sat up in his chair. "Those boys told me they plan to make big bucks. Me too. I want to move to Indiana and make big bucks."

Luke shifted in his chair to look at him. "Working in a factory?"

"Yup. Big buckaroos, they said." Rudy rubbed his thumb and fingers together. "Boatloads."

Luke resisted the temptation to straighten Rudy out about the limitations of minimum wage and turned his attention back to Carrie's list. "Okay. That's one family. Esther and Joe Blank." He tapped the table. "Write their names down." He felt himself starting to relax, ever so slightly. "Who else? Rudy, any other ideas?"

He gestured for Rudy to come forward, but he needed no invitation it seemed. He was already on his feet, acting ten feet tall. "Hmmm . . . maybe . . . Teddy and Alice Zook. So long as the foster children don't mind snakes. Or a crying baby."

"Put their names down." He doubted Alice would agree to it, but he was desperate.

"What about you?"

"Me?"

"Fern took you in."

That Rudy could be a little too wise for his years. Cheeky, that boy. "I'd have to see how Izzy felt about it."

Carrie set the pencil down. "I would think she'd be all for it. She, more than anyone, knows how important a stable foster home is to a child."

"Yeah, you'd think so. But . . . I'm not so sure she is." Not at all. When Izzy didn't want to talk about something, there was no way to change her mind. Luke had learned that much about marriage. He had to wait until she was ready to talk. Most men and women seemed to have the opposite problem. It was yet another piece of marriage that baffled him. He liked to talk things through. Izzy, not so much. He kept his focus on the jiggly lines of the design on the tabletop, but could feel Carrie's eyes on him. "So, then, who else?" Think, think, think. "Birdy and David?"

She squinted. "They have a very full house."

"Wait. What about The Inn at Eagle Hill? It's big and empty. Sammy's living over at Galen's house, taking care of the horses."

"That would mean Patrick and Ruthie would be the foster parents. Think they might say yes?"

Patrick, definitely. Ruthie, he wasn't so sure. "Put their names down." *Think, think, think.* "Sadie and Gideon! He's a minister. He's got to take in somebody."

"How old is Sammy?"

"Twenty-two."

"He could be a foster parent."

"Oh, I don't know. He's not very . . ." He's not very . . . what? Talkative, for one. Bold, for another. "He's got a really big job taking care of Galen's horses. You know how particular Galen is. Sammy's got a lot of responsibility on his shoulders."

"Luke, don't underestimate people. They can surprise you. It's worth asking. Give a person the chance to say no."

"But that person is my little brother." He thought he knew his brother pretty well.

"You might be seeing Sammy only as your little brother. There's a lot of growth to come, given the chance." She set the pencil down. "That's the whole point of foster care. It's not just to give a child a place to sleep and eat. Good fostering means opening your heart to them, to help them heal." She picked up the pencil and wrote down a few more names.

Oh boy. Luke hadn't even considered the heart.

Carrie put down the pencil. "Did Roberta Watts happen to mention if they were all boys or all girls, or some of each?"

"All girls."

"Ah." She picked up the pencil and scratched out a name. "That would eliminate Sammy." She set the pencil down again and tore the paper in half. "I'll go talk to these three families." She handed Luke the torn paper. "You take the rest. And we'll let the Lord do his work of changing minds and hearts."

"Yes, but . . ."

"Luke, God is at work. Don't mess it up by interfering."

He inhaled sharply. Amos had told him that same thing, many times. Lesson number one of deaconing.

Carrie cupped her chin with her hand, elbow resting on the table. "One other thought. You've run this by David, right?"

David? As in . . . the bishop? Argh! A knot formed in Luke's stomach. How could he have forgotten to check this out with David? Well, because Roberta Watts had taken hold of him to ramp up his day. He didn't have time to stop and talk this over with David. He had to keep moving.

She smiled. "You're allowing Roberta Watts's urgency to overwhelm you. I realize she's a difficult person to say no to, but it's important to slow down. Take a breath. These are people's lives you're dealing with. Do this in the right way."

"But, but, but . . ."

"Go. Talk to David. Ask for his blessing. Then go talk to these families."

Okay. Good advice. David and Birdy's name was on his half of the list to talk to, anyway. He gave Carrie a nod and opened the door. As he started down the steps, he heard Rudy's voice float through the open window: "Mom, how in the world did Luke Schrock get to be deacon?"

Indeed.

Sam Schrock was crossing from the barn over the path that led to the Inn at Eagle Hill when he saw his brother Luke's horse and buggy go tearing down the road, slowing only as the horse pulled the buggy up the long steep driveway that led to the bishop's house. He stopped for a moment, watching Luke jump out of the stopped buggy to bolt to the house, not even bothering to hitch the horse's reins to the post. This sight, he thought to himself, was one that will probably become very familiar. Deacon Luke, in a panic, rushing to Bishop David's for problem solving.

It was still hard for Sam to get his head around his brother as the new deacon. Luke had always been such a cutup, always seeking attention, whether good or bad. Mostly bad.

Sure, his brother had come a long, long way, but . . . the deacon? Sam had known only old men to be deacons. Wise, experienced, seasoned men. Luke? He was the opposite. It was like trying to burn fresh-cut wood in the fireplace. It just didn't make sense.

Head down, thinking about his brother, Sam took the steps to the house two at a time, not noticing that the door had opened. When he reached the top step, he lifted his head and stopped abruptly at the sight of Mollie Graber, standing at the threshold. Looking so pretty, she took his breath away. And his words too.

"Hello there, Sam. I haven't seen you in a while. You haven't come by for morning coffee."

Blank. His mind was a complete and total blank. He opened his mouth to talk, but felt the familiar knot in his throat block his words. "School," he blurted out at last.

"School? You mean, me? I should be at school? Well, yes, that's true. Birdy took the children on a bird-watching expedition this morning. It's migration time, you see, and she wanted the children to observe a flock of red-winged blackbirds before they left. I had to drop something off at Ruthie's, so I decided to pop over while the schoolhouse was empty." She stopped and waited for him to say something.

So . . . say something, Sam. What could he say? Things like, *I sure have missed starting the day with you over coffee at the schoolhouse, Mollie. I've missed the effect of your happy nature. Each time I'm with you, my whole day lifts considerably. I've missed you. And I was hoping that you might miss me a little too. Maybe I could start coming back for morning coffee. I'd like to. I regret that I stopped coming. It was foolish of me . . . but I got scared with that foster parenting talk.*

Did he say any of that to her? Nope. Like a jerk, all he said was, "I was looking for Patrick."

Her face fell. Why did he have to be so aloof? Knowing he had disappointed her with his cold response made him cringe. Why couldn't he show his feelings to her? It was like he was holding tight reins on himself, reluctant to let Mollie know how he really felt.

Luke's horse and buggy came charging up the driveway. He circled the buggy so that he was facing Mollie and Sam from the driver's side. "Mollie. One o'clock. Mattie and Sol Riehl's. There's a lady coming to check everybody out for foster care. Tell Patrick and Ruthie to come. We need everybody."

Mollie let out a gasp.

Sam snapped his head from Luke to Mollie, back to Luke. "What in the world are you talking about?"

"Mollie can explain everything. But you're not eligible, Sammy."

"Call me Sam, like everyone else. And eligible for what?"

"For being a foster parent."

Good. He didn't want to be one.

"Isn't it wonderful news, Sam?" Mollie clasped her hands together. "I'm hoping for a little girl. Two."

Luke held a hand in the air. "Hold that thought, Mollie." He seesawed his hand. "Maybe, not such a little girl. But a girl, definitely. They're all girls."

"Mollie, you can't be serious," Sam said.

"Oh, I've never been more serious about anything in my life."

Luke jammed his hat down on his head. "Sam, do me a favor and cover for Mollie at the schoolhouse so she can come to the meeting." He flicked the reins to get the horse going.

"I'm off to talk to Teddy and Alice. One o'clock. Don't be late."

Sam watched Luke's buggy bob down the driveway.

"Oh, Sam," Mollie sighed. "Your brother Luke . . . he's just remarkable. This church, why, we are so . . . *blessed* . . . to have him as our deacon. If you could come to the school-house around half past twelve, that would be very helpful." She squeezed his arm before she went back into the house to find Ruthie.

Blessed? The church was *blessed* to have Luke as deacon? His brother, he was *crazy*. Sam had planned to ask Patrick if he could feed the horses for him during the noon hour so he could go to an auction. Apparently, he was going to be a substitute schoolteacher instead.

Six

Out in the pasture of Windmill Farm, Izzy walked among her sheep, her skirts swaying in the wind. Her sheep. They were truly hers. Amos had gifted them to her, long before he was bedridden. "They know your voice, Izzy. Better than mine. I see how they run to you when they hear you coming. They've already decided that they're yours."

In the pasture, a couple of ewes suddenly jumped up and started butting heads and blatting protests. She watched for a moment, ready to intervene if necessary, but the ewes suddenly lost interest in their argument and went back to munching their way around the pasture. "Silly girls," she said.

Amos was absolutely right about how the sheep responded to her. All she needed to do was to open the fence and call out—just one call, sung in a special way—and her woollies' heads would lift, bleats would begin, and each would hurry to be the first to reach her.

When she told Luke they came to her quickly because they loved her, he dismissed it by saying they came to her because she was the one who fed them. All they loved was their food. "Animals aren't created to love, Izzy. Their devotion goes to the one who feeds them. Stop feeding them, and their loyalty will go to any other shepherd."

Maybe, but she preferred her way of thinking.

She heard the clip-clop of a horse along the road and tented her eyes to see who was coming. She recognized Luke's horse pulling the buggy, and her heart skipped a beat. She wondered when that feeling might stop, the thrill of knowing her husband was coming home to her. This wonderful life she had fallen into, it still amazed her. If only she could get pregnant, it would be a perfect life. More than she ever dreamed possible. She patted the head of a lamb and hurried down the hill to meet Luke as he turned the horse and buggy up the driveway to Windmill Farm.

"I have news." He pulled the horse into the shade and jumped out, holding his arms wide for her to fall into, which she did. He scooped her tightly against him, almost crushing her beneath him, speaking quietly into her ear. "There's a social worker coming to talk to everybody about taking in foster children."

Izzy squirmed out of his embrace. "What?"

Luke repeated what he'd said. "I sure didn't expect it to happen quite this fast." He looked up at the house. "Is Fern here? I need you both to come to the meeting at Mattie Riehl's house at one o'clock."

She backed up a few steps. "I can't, Luke. The yarn shop is open this afternoon."

He tipped his head. "You can put a sign up. You've done it before."

She shook her head. "Only once, and that was because

one of my woollies fell into a ditch. Don't look at me like that. You know that my sheep are important to me."

"This is important too."

"Tour buses count on making a stop at Stitches in Time. Consistency is important."

"I can watch the shop for you."

Fern's voice caused both Izzy and Luke to startle. She had a way about her, Fern did, of appearing out of nowhere. Izzy still wasn't accustomed to it. "Thanks anyway, Fern, but it's my responsibility."

Fern gazed at her with those inscrutable blue eyes, then turned to Luke. "Then I'll be at the meeting. One o'clock?"

"Yes, one o'clock," Luke said. "At Mattie's."

Izzy turned to head down the path to the store, to open it up for the day's customers. She expected Luke to follow her, to try to persuade her to come, but he didn't. Instead, he hopped in the buggy and tore off like he was heading to a fire.

Before she turned the lock on the door, she watched him go. She could not join him in this venture. She simply could not. He should know better than to ask. If he truly loved her, he would know not to ask more of her than she could give.

She closed the door behind her and walked inside the shop, inhaling the scent of wool. She picked up a tuft of carded fleece and fed it into the spinning machine, pushing her feet slowly against the pedal, feeding the roving with her fingers so that it twisted and turned into nubby yarn.

She cherished time alone in this little shop. It was the only place that had ever been truly hers. She almost felt guilty about it. At times, she'd rather be here, all by herself, than with Luke. She loved him so much, but living day to day with him was so much harder than she thought it would be. She knew she was too defensive. She was working on that, but her wall went up so quickly. Before she knew it was happening, before she could even stop herself, she'd retreat into silence. And that silence drove Luke crazy. Once, he'd told her that he thought she used silence as a weapon. He was right. She did.

But it was one thing to acknowledge a weak character trait; it was an altogether different thing to try to change it.

The door opened and in walked Fern. "Are you all right?"

Fern's face was full of worry, and that made Izzy want to cry. "I'm fine," she lied.

Fern knew. "Shouldn't you go to this meeting and hear what the social worker has to say about fostering children? Go and support your husband?"

Izzy sputtered for words, trying to harness one or two of her spinning thoughts. "Fern, I can't. I just can't. Please don't ask."

Fern closed the door behind her. "He won't stop, you know. I know Luke. For all his flaws, he is a man of his word."

Izzy tucked her chin. "I'm not interfering with his promise to Amos. But that doesn't mean it has to be my promise to fulfill. He's the deacon, not me."

"I don't think this is about deaconing, though it is his first big effort. It would be a good thing to help him see it through. You know as well as I do how most everyone feels about him drawing the lot."

Izzy kept her chin tucked to her chest, trying to hold back a smile. Most folks were horrified that Luke Schrock drew the lot. She knew what they thought about him and it didn't bother her one bit. They underestimated Luke. For a very long time, she'd certainly underestimated him. He had been determined to win her over, and he finally did. She was pretty sure he could do anything he set his mind to.

Oh, but this? Why this? Of all things. Why not start a food bank or homeless shelter? Why did he have to want to bring a foster child into their home? "I'm sorry, Fern. I know I'm disappointing you and Luke. I just can't."

Fern watched her for a while, thin arms folded across her chest. Then she gave a nod and reached out to grip Izzy's arm, give it a gentle squeeze of reassurance. "Honey, you can never disappoint me." She walked to the door and turned back. "I suspect you've got your reasons for not coming today."

As the door closed behind Fern, Izzy felt her eyes sting with tears and squeezed them shut. It wasn't often that Fern called her a term of endearment like "honey" or "dear," but when she did, she felt deeply moved. It always gave her a little glow inside that changed the day for her—the way a small candle, once lit, could illuminate even the darkest room. It almost felt like she had a real mother. Not quite, but almost.

⌒

Roberta Watts was not exactly what Luke expected. First off, she was as tall as he was, weighed considerably more, and had a look in her eyes like she could take on a grizzly bear and win. Her skin color was the darkest mahogany he'd ever seen on a person. It made her piercing brown eyes all the more intense. She scared him, flat out.

Seated next to her on Mattie's green sofa was a skinny woman with pointed glasses. Mavis Connor was her name, a social worker who couldn't stop smiling. Or talking, either, in a high-pitched squeaky voice. She went on and on about how today was the biggest answer to prayer she'd ever seen, in thirty years of social work, a miracle! As big to her as the parting of the Red Sea must have been to Moses. And wasn't this just the best thing, ever?

Roberta Watts did not seem nearly as enthusiastic as Mavis Connor. She sat on the sofa without much expression, eyeing each person up and down, side to side, as she let Mavis do all the talking and make all the introductions.

Seated around the room were Carrie and Abel, Mattie and Sol, Teddy Zook—Alice was home with the baby, he said, and Luke was relieved because that baby cried nonstop—David and Birdy, Gideon and Sadie, Ruthie and Patrick, Mollie, of course, and Fern. Faithful Fern. Luke kept a seat free next to him, hoping Izzy might change her mind and come, but he doubted it. She wasn't one to change her mind. Luke had driven from farm to farm asking others to come too, but most everyone turned him down flat.

The door opened again and he had a glimmer of hope that Izzy might've changed her mind and come. Alas. So wrong. To his dismay, Hank Lapp swept in, robust and big-voiced, booming a hello to everyone before he plopped down next to Luke in the empty seat saved for Izzy.

Hold on. Luke did not invite Hank to this meeting. He purposefully did not invite him. Hank's involvement in anything meant he would gum it up. Luke had watched Hank make a mess of things time and time again. *En Schparre zu viel odder zu wennich.* That man had one rafter too few or one too many.

"OKAY! LET'S GET STARTED!"

Roberta Watts lifted an eyebrow—the only movement on her face so far. Even Mavis quieted down at Hank's bellow.

Luke had to stifle a smile. Hank was a sight to behold. White, wild hair, stuffed under a worn-out straw hat; long, lean body; and a very loud mouth. A good heart, though. A very good heart.

Roberta tried to get out of the sagging sofa, but she was stuck. Hank sprang from his chair and yanked on her arm. "HOLD ON THERE, MADAM." He only made everything worse. Luke took one arm, Sol took the other, Hank sputtered directions, and they pulled Roberta up and out of the sagging sofa. She harrumphed and smoothed out her dress. Then she turned in a circle, lifting her nose, as her piercing gaze swept the room. She filled up every space, even in this large room. "Ladies and gentlemen, we have a situation at our group home in Stoney Ridge and I hear you have a desire to help."

"WHAT ARE YOU TALKING ABOUT?"

Luke jabbed Hank with his elbow. "Let her do the talking."

Hank jabbed him back. "I AM."

Roberta stared at Hank until he settled down. *Wow.* Luke had never seen Hank stared down before. He was impressed.

"Let me give it to you straight, people," Roberta continued. "The group home down the road here has black mold in the walls. The county has red-tagged it until we figure out how to fix it. We need homes for eleven youths, pronto."

"On the phone you told me you needed ten," Luke said.

"One more came in this morning." Roberta pivoted on her heels, arms akimbo. "So, can you help?"

Silence. Utter quiet. Finally, Mattie raised her hand. "How long do these youths need homes?"

"Not sure. Until we get that house fixed. And then there's inspections. County's as slow as molasses on a cold January morning."

"Oh, not so long as that," Mavis interjected. "I'm sure it'll all go swimmingly. Sail right along! A week, maybe two." She clapped her hands against her knees. "And they're the sweetest, dearest children. You'll just love them."

Roberta gave Mavis a sideways glance. "Mm-hmm." She waved one hand in the air. "Mavis is more optimistic 'bout most everything than I am. Nicer too. These youths come from troubled homes."

"SO THEY'RE ALL PROBLEM CHILDREN?"

Roberta Watts sent Hank a sizzling glare, long and hard. "They're *not* problem children. They come from homes that have problems." Hank shrank, though only a little. "They need stability, they need discipline, they need love."

Mavis waved her hand. "Most of the news focuses on negative stories, but for every negative story, we can give you two positive ones." She held two fingers in the air. "Maybe three." She added a third finger.

"SO HOW OLD IS A YOUTH?"

"Their ages run from eleven to fifteen," Mavis said.

"WHAT ARE YOU GOING TO DO IF WE SAY NO?"

Well, one thing Luke had to admit, Hank was able to ask questions that everyone wanted answers to.

Roberta focused her eyes on him until he shrank down a few inches. "Mister, I'm going to be honest with you. It's hard to place teens. Especially minorities." She made a clucking sound. "And we are a private agency. If the state of Pennsylvania was running this group home, I can guarantee there's no way we could be talking to y'all today about this emergency situation." She planted her fists on her big hips. "So if you can't do it, if you don't feel the call to help, get up and walk on out. I need to get busy and find people who will answer the call. People with real hearts." She pointed to the door. "Go on. Get up and go." She walked around the entire circle, making searing eye contact with each person.

No one budged. They just looked back at Roberta with blank faces. Luke felt a bead of sweat roll down his back. What now? What was he going to do if no one was willing to provide emergency foster care?

Finally David rose to his feet. "Roberta, don't misunderstand our silence. It's just our way." He cleared his throat. "Could you explain what requirements you have? I realize this is an emergency, but I'm sure you need to fulfill certain expectations before placing a child in a home."

"Yes, we do. A clean bed in a good, safe, loving home. That's what we expect. Doctor Stoltzfus is coming over soon with her nurse to get some vitals on y'all. Make sure everyone's healthy."

"Doctor Stoltzfus is my sister," David said.

One of Roberta's eyebrows arched. "Dok? She's your sister?"

"And her nurse is my daughter." He pointed to Ruthie, across the room. "I think that piece will be easy."

The corners of Roberta's lips lifted, ever so slightly, a subtle sign of approval. "Good. That's good to hear. And the sheriff is coming by to fingerprint all of you."

Eyebrows shot up.

"So . . . assuming y'all check out, who is willing to be a foster parent?"

"Oh, I will, I will!" Mollie said. "I'd like a girl, aged five to seven. Maybe two. Sisters, if possible."

Roberta nearly smiled as she handed Mollie a packet of paperwork. "Miss, let's start you with one." Maybe it was a smile. Hard to say. In Luke's opinion, it was not the smile of someone who wanted to be friendly, nor was it the smile of one who did not care for you. It was the smile of someone who thought this was a crazy idea, but she was out of options. "Mm-hmm," she said. "Who else?"

"Sol and I," Mattie said, "we'll take one."

Mavis breathed a deep sigh. "Oh, thank you, thank you, thank you."

"Thank you, Mattie. You've always been someone we can count on." Roberta kept walking around the circle, sizing each person up with a deadpan glare. "Who else? We have eleven children to place. Who else is willing to step up?"

Patrick Kelly lifted his hand. "We'll take one."

"Fine." Roberta looked half satisfied. "That's fine." She bent over to get more folders out of her briefcase.

"We'd be willing to foster a child," Teddy Zook said. "Someone who isn't fearful of snakes."

"Snakes?" Roberta's voice shot up an octave.

"Snakes," Teddy said. "Safely in cages. I raise them for farmers." He lifted his eyes upward, as if something just occurred to him. "Oh, and someone who doesn't mind a baby with a—" he squeezed two fingers together—"with a tiny bit of fussiness."

"A TINY BIT OF FUSSINESS? THAT BABY CRIES LIKE A SQUEALING PIGLET."

Luke jabbed Hank with his elbow again. Offended, Hank jabbed Luke back.

"Chloe!" Mavis said, holding a finger in the air. "She's cucumber calm. Don't you think she'd be just the one for them, Roberta?"

"Mm-hmm. Four down, seven to go." Roberta gave each one a thick bundle of paperwork to fill out. "Who else?"

Luke saw Birdy give David an elbow nudge. He whispered something to her and she only smiled back at him. "We can only host a girl," David said. "And she'll have to share a bedroom."

"No problem," Roberta said. "The group home is only for girls."

A collective sigh of relief went through the room. "WHY DIDN'T YOU SAY SO?" Hank bellowed. "BOYS SCARE FOLKS. ESPECIALLY AFTER LIVING THROUGH LUKE SCHROCK'S ADOLESCENCE. WE'RE ALL PERMANENTLY SCARRED."

Luke frowned at Hank.

"Him?" Roberta asked, pointing to Luke.

"HIM!" Hank thumbed Luke. "AND WOULD YOU BELIEVE HE JUST BECAME OUR DEACON?" He slapped his knees in amusement. "WONDERS NEVER CEASE."

Roberta took that in for a moment. "Well, now. That just shows what can happen when a child gets what he needs."

Luke was mortified. He kept his eyes on the tips of his boots. Good grief, these people had memories like elephants.

Abel Miller, sitting next to him, sensed his discomfort and put a hand on his shoulder. "If someone can turn out like Luke here, to be a young man who's devoted himself to the care and well-being of our community, then we'd like to be part of that someone's story."

"Count us in," Carrie said. "We have room for one more."

Mavis let out a deep exhale. "Oh good. Good, good, good."

Roberta handed a packet of information to Carrie and Abel. "Five more, people. I need five more hearts to open wide."

Gideon and Sadie whispered back and forth, and then he raised his hand. "We'll take one."

The door opened and in came, ever so slowly, three old sisters from the Sisters' House. There used to be five. One was gone to Glory, one was in the hospital with a broken hip. Sylvia stood at the edge of the circle, leaning on her cane. "What have we missed?"

Luke found three seats and helped the sisters into their chairs. My, oh my, they were so fragile. A strong gust of wind could knock them over.

Hank jumped up. "SISTERS, I'M AFRAID WE ARE TOO OLD FOR THIS VENTURE."

Roberta pointed a long finger at Hank. "That is not true. If you're in good health and can provide a good home, you can't be too old." She glanced at Mollie. "Nor too young. Twenty-one is the age to become a foster parent. You don't have to be married. You don't have to own a home. You don't have to have a college degree."

"THAT'S GOOD. CUZ NONE OF US DO."

By now, Roberta had figured out what Luke and everybody else knew to do: ignore Hank. "You just have to open your heart, provide a stable home, and have a good sense of humor."

"And get qualified," Mavis whispered.

Mollie beamed. "If that's the case, then, I'll take four!"

"Mm-hmm."

Luke was learning to read Roberta's murmurs. Mm-hmm = No way. Not a chance.

"Roberta," Mavis said quietly, "we do have a couple of sibling pairs I'd like to try to keep together."

Mollie clasped her hands together in delight.

Roberta cocked her head at Sylvia and you could see her whole self soften. "Miss, you really interested in becoming a foster parent?"

"Our house is next to the group home. We're very familiar with it. Some of the girls have even worked for us now and then. We have the room to spare, and our hearts are open."

Roberta turned to Mavis. "The O'Henry girls?"

Mavis's face lit with a smile. "Oh, they'd be perfect for them. Very sweet girls, extremely helpful and thoughtful. Yes, yes, yes. An ideal match."

"Y'all in good health?"

Sylvia nodded. "We're old, but we're vital."

"You got room for two?" Roberta asked.

Sylvia looked at her two sisters. She had to repeat what Roberta said, twice. Then they all nodded in agreement. "Yes, we have room."

"Mavis, who else?"

"Eleven-year-old twins. Tina and Alicia. Just the cutest girls in the world."

Roberta looked around the room, until her eyes landed on Mollie. "You said you're a schoolteacher?"

Mollie nodded.

"And you really want sisters?"

"Oh, I do!"

Roberta clucked her teeth with her tongue, then sighed. "All right. We'll give it a try. Mavis, give the twins to that tiny little wisp of a schoolteacher."

Fern sucked in a gasp of air. "Oh Mollie, are you sure?"

Mollie's head nodded with conviction. "Absolutely."

"It ain't for long. Mavis thinks just a week or two." But Roberta didn't look convinced. "Mavis, how many left?"

Mavis counted with her pencil on her pad of paper. "One to go. Cassidy. She just arrived this very morning."

Roberta looked at Luke. Stared at him. Waited for him to cave in. "Just one more."

He gulped. Izzy wasn't budging on this. She'd said no, more than once. He knew her well enough to know she wouldn't give an inch.

"WHAT ABOUT ME?"

"You married?"

"SURE AM."

"How does she feel about this?"

"I HAVEN'T TOLD HER YET."

"Well, then, that says quite a bit, don't it?" Roberta passed Hank over and drilled down at Luke. "Just one to go."

Luke glanced down at his hands, cupping his knees. They were trembling and he wasn't sure if it was his hands or his knees. Both, maybe. How could he refuse to take in a child? He had started this whole thing. He had promised Amos. He was the deacon now. This was the moment he needed to show his backbone, what he was made of. And the truth was, he wanted to become a foster parent. He wanted to show the church that he had an open heart too.

But all he could think of was how angry Izzy would be with him for ignoring her wishes. She had made it abundantly clear to him that she did not want to be a foster parent. It was hard for him to understand why she was so adamant about the topic.

He wanted to say yes, to raise his hand and give that last

child a home. But he couldn't say yes without Izzy's agreement. It wouldn't be fair to her, and the repercussions in their marriage would be enormous. That much about marriage, he'd already learned.

Good grief, was he scared of his wife? Yes. Yes he was. He felt like a mouse of a man, but any way he looked at it, he was stuck in a hard place. Roberta's glare was like being under a spotlight. Sweat trickled down his forehead. The room was starting to spin. Oh boy, was he going to pass out? Add yet another humiliation to his long list of embarrassing moments.

Fern popped her head in between Roberta and Luke. "I'll take her," she said.

SEVEN

Mollie had never been so happy in all her life. Ecstatic. The morning had started out as such a typical day, just an ordinary autumn day, and it ended in a miracle. She was now a foster mother to two young girls. Twin sisters, aged eleven. She had hoped for younger girls, but she trusted God's plans over her own. Around five o'clock that afternoon, Roberta Watts delivered them to Mollie's cottage, two sweet, angelic-looking sisters. They were coffee colored, with thick long brown hair, and the most beautiful doe-like eyes. Bright smiles. Goodness, they never stopped smiling.

The two sisters studied Mollie carefully, their gaze moving slowly up over her prayer cap, her lavender dress and black apron, then back up to her starched white cap again. Still smiling. To be honest, there was something odd about their smiles, Mollie sensed. Although she could say what it was not, she couldn't necessarily say what it was.

Roberta went through each paper in the stack of forms, rarely taking her eyes off the girls for more than a few seconds.

Mollie's mind wandered as Roberta went through the

paperwork. She was eager to get to know the girls, to be alone with them in her house, to start mending the holes in their hearts. She wondered how much they'd endured in their young lives, how much they'd suffered, what their stories involved. Finally, Roberta came to the last piece of paper. Mollie signed it and handed it back to her, jumping up from the table, hoping the social worker would soon take her leave. Roberta rose from the table, reached down to speak in a gruff whisper to the girls on the sofa, something that Mollie couldn't overhear, and then nodded to follow her outside.

On the way to the car, Roberta said, "I gave you two girls because you said you wanted siblings. I figured you're young, and you're a schoolteacher. I figured you're accustomed to kids and their shenanigans. But you sure you can handle two?"

"I'll do my best."

"Mm-hmm," she said. "Start slow. Let those two prove themselves to you. It's hard to take away privileges. Easier to give them when they earn them."

"I like to give everyone the benefit of the doubt. Especially children."

"Mm-hmm." Roberta's mouth pursed from side to side. "Call me or Mavis if you find yourself sinking fast in quicksand."

"I'm sure we'll be fine. Just fine." Roberta's advice seemed excessive. Stern.

"Mm-hmm."

Roberta's mm-hmming, Mollie concluded, was her way to say "I'll believe it when I see it."

After she drove away, Mollie walked back to the cottage steps where the twins waited for her inside, still sitting on the sofa. She clasped her hands together. "Well, girls, let me show you around."

The girls didn't budge. They stared at her, eyes gleaming in the lantern light, still smiling, but there was no longer any warmth there.

"What are you?" Tina said. "Some sort of nun?"

Mollie laughed. "Goodness, no."

"Then why do you wear that funny hair thingy?"

Mollie touched her head. "I'm Amish. This is a prayer cap. It's a symbol, a reminder to always submit myself to God's will. Women wear these prayer caps during the day, and we've other caps for night as well."

"What's your name again?" Alicia asked. "Mary Lou?"

"Mollie. My name is Mollie Graber."

The girls got up off the sofa to circle Mollie. For a split second, Mollie knew what a lamb might feel like as it was surrounded by a pack of wolves. Ridiculous. They weren't predators. They were little girls, only eleven years old!

"Why do you wear such a frumpy dress?"

Frumpy? Mollie looked down at her lavender dress. "I dress this way because that's the way Plain women dress."

"But why?"

"It's always been that way. It's part of the *Ordnung*, the rules for living." She tipped her head. "Didn't Roberta explain that you'd be living with the Amish until the repairs in the group home are done?"

The girls looked at each other and shook their heads. "She only told us that you were a witch."

Mollie gasped.

Alicia nodded. "And she warned us that you might try to kill us in the night."

A witch? Shocked, Mollie thought of Roberta's gruff whisper to the girls. Ridiculous. Roberta would never say such a thing. But why would the girls think such a terrible thought? Frightened. They must be frightened. Mollie couldn't imagine how it might feel to not know where you were going to sleep at night. "Rest assured that I have no intentions of killing anybody. Goodness gracious, I've never killed anything. Not even a fly." She smiled, trying to pretend she was calm and relaxed. Just the opposite! Her stomach was doing somersaults.

She gave the girls a tour around the small cottage, which took less than a minute, and helped them unpack. That took two more minutes. The girls didn't say much during supper, but maybe that was because Mollie couldn't stop talking. She had all kinds of plans in the making. "On Saturday morning," she told them in a hushed voice, "we'll make cookies. Later in the afternoon, we're going to a knitting comfort." When the girls exchanged a confused look, she quickly added, "You'll love it! And it'll give you a chance to meet other girls."

"Girls from the home?"

"Maybe. I suppose I was thinking of girls from our church."

The girls exchanged an eye roll. "We'll pass."

"Don't you want to meet other girls your age?" Mollie had already chosen a few especially nice girls from school whom she wanted Tina and Alicia to meet. She envisioned having slumber parties for them.

"Nope," Alicia said. "We aren't staying that long."

"A week or two, at least," Mollie said. "Maybe longer, knowing how slow construction projects can be."

For some reason, that comment made the girls burst out in giggles.

Strange. This wasn't going as well as Mollie had hoped. "Girls, do you have any questions for me?"

Tina lifted her head. In an accusing tone she said, "Just how old are you?"

"I'm . . . old enough."

Alicia snorted. "You seem awfully young to be a foster mother."

Tina smiled, but it didn't reach to her eyes. "Don't you worry, Mindy. We'll help you."

"Mollie. My name is Mollie." They kept getting her name wrong. Poor girls. They must be confused by all the changes they were facing. Bewildered.

And help me . . . do what? Mollie wasn't sure what *that* meant. Did she seem so very young and inexperienced? Even to eleven-year-olds?

They peppered her with more questions, odd ones that flustered Mollie. Did she color her hair? No. Highlights? No. Would she consider trying eyeliner and mascara to make her eyes pop? No. Instead of that pinned-up hairdo, could they give her a messy bun? No. Did she have a boyfriend? No. Had she kissed many boys? None. Stunned into silence, they looked at her with wide eyes. Then they doubled over in laughter, hooting and howling over Mollie's innocence. It went downhill from there.

Opening herself up to questions from the girls made Mollie feel like a pincushion. Poked. Sharp pins. She hopped up to start cleaning up the supper dishes, expecting the girls to help, but by the time she had the sink full of sudsy hot water, the girls had slipped off to their bedroom. No matter. It was their first night.

As she washed dishes, she looked out the window at the

gray dusk, catching the last pale light of the day. *This is the day the Lord hath made.* And what a day. Oh, what a day it had been. She thanked God for the surprise of this momentous occasion and asked for his help with patience and understanding. And love. An abundance of love.

Mollie packed the girls' school lunches and helped them lay clothes out for the morning. The county sent a small school bus to pick the girls up for school each morning, in front of the group home. Roberta Watts was clear that the children had to attend their regular public school in Stoney Ridge, not the Amish school where Mollie taught.

To be truthful, keeping the foster children in their own school made the days easier for the Amish families. There was a place for the girls to spend the day, especially the older ones, as the Amish school only went up to grade 8.

When the clock struck nine, Mollie said good night to the girls and took the oil lamp with her. They had flashlights by their bedsides if they needed light. In the front room, she plopped down on the old hand-me-down sofa Aunt Fern had given to her. She was beat. After the meeting at Mattie's house, she had raced back to school to relieve Sam from substituting—and he seemed eager to go—then as school was dismissed for the day, she hurried home to get her house ready for the social worker's inspection. She'd been worried that she would need twin beds for the girls, but since they were sisters, a double bed passed inspection. She thought about the events of the day, dozing off for a while.

A hard knock at the door jolted her awake. She glanced at the clock. Midnight? Already? She rose from the sofa, disoriented. "Who's there?" she asked.

"Stoney Ridge sheriff."

Mollie's heart started to pound. What was the sheriff doing here? She opened the door a crack to find a stern-looking police officer peer down at her.

"Are you Mollie Graber?"

"I am."

"Any chance you're missing two girls?"

"Goodness, no. They're sound asleep. They've been asleep for hours."

Another policeman walked up the path with Tina and Alicia. "We found them hitchhiking along the highway. They said they're on their way to Las Vegas."

Oh dear. Oh no.

⌒

After the UPS driver dropped off a package at the fix-it shop, Luke took the box into the yarn shop. "This just came for you."

"Good timing," Izzy said. "It's cashmere yarn that Edith Lapp ordered. She's been stopping by each day for it."

"Not so fast," Luke said. "Handing over this box will require a kiss."

Izzy smiled, lifting her face to him. "You're always stealing my kisses."

He leaned over the box to kiss her once, then twice. "Wer en Schof schtelt, is ken Bockdieb." *Stealing a kiss doesn't make you a thief.* He handed her the box. "Cassidy's a nice girl, don't you think?" Fern's foster girl had been with them for a few days and seemed to be fitting in well. Quiet, helpful, polite. But Izzy stiffened as soon as he mentioned her name. He saw her back straighten as the smile left her face.

She set the box on the table, looking for scissors to open it. "Nice enough for Fern."

"Fern's an older woman, though. And always busy, never still. She doesn't have much time for Cassidy. I see how Cassidy watches you. I have a hunch she'd like to have some of your attention."

Izzy was paying him no mind. She was focused on counting the skeins of cashmere yarn. "Perfect. Just what Edith ordered."

"Izzy, sweetheart, can't you tell me why you won't even look at Cassidy?"

Izzy glanced up with a frown on her face. "I look at her."

"Not really. I think you know what I'm talking about. She's practically invisible to you."

Izzy put the skeins back in the box and closed it up. She walked over to the window and stared out at something.

Luke was just about to start talking when David's advice floated through his head: Do the opposite. He came up behind her and carefully, oh-so-carefully, put his hands on her elbows. "What's running through your mind?"

"This whole foster child thing."

"What do you mean?"

"They're everywhere, those teens. I see them every single day. Sadie brought her foster daughter over for cooking lessons from Fern. Alice wants Chloe to have knitting lessons. I can't get away from them."

"Why do you want to get away from them?"

"Because."

"Honey, why? Tell me. Why won't you spend a little time with Cassidy?"

"I'm busy."

He turned her around and tipped her chin up. "Iz . . . come on." He looked closely at her.

The moment hung in time, until Izzy said, "Each time I see Cassidy, I see me. I keep wanting to move forward with my life, and you keep grabbing my heels, pulling me backward."

"I'm doing that to you?"

"You started this."

He moved closer to her, hoping to see her soften. He tucked a loose strand of hair behind her ear. "Amos and Fern started this. They brought you home. They brought me home. Where would we be if we hadn't had them? That's what I'm trying to do. To give back. Not pull you back."

Slowly, she leaned into his embrace, until her face rested against his shoulder. "I know. It's just hard to . . . remember. I want to forget all those foster homes. I want to forget that I was once a child in those homes. When I see a certain look in Cassidy's eyes—a hungry look, so insatiable—it takes me right back. Hoping, hoping, hoping, and always feeling disappointed. I can't do it. I can't handle going back there, even in my mind."

"But Cassidy's story isn't yours."

She pulled away, rolling her eyes. "It's close enough."

"Maybe it's close, but the ending might be close too. Wouldn't it be wonderful to be part of her happy ending?"

"I just want to start our own family and keep moving forward. Make new memories."

"It'll happen. I'm confident of that."

"You don't know that, Luke. What if it doesn't happen?"

"What I'm confident about is that it'll happen when it's meant to happen. But not until then. Maybe there's a reason God's held this up for us."

She stiffened again. "What's that supposed to mean? I don't have what it takes to be a good mother because I didn't have one?"

There. This was it. The core of her insecurity. As remarkable a woman as Izzy was, as loving and caring and faithful as everyone else knew her to be, as beautiful as she was, this profound sense of inadequacy was always lurking around, ready to pounce. Deep down, she saw herself as an unwanted child, as unlovable.

Luke had been in enough counseling to understand this dynamic. No matter how damaged Grace Miller was known to be, how incapable she was to be a good parent, Izzy felt she was to blame. She wasn't enough to keep her mother on a clean path, at home, willing to work hard for her daughter's sake. It wasn't true, of course, but it was hard to shrug off those deeply ingrained feelings. Luke's childhood was much different than Izzy's, but he had a father with all kinds of issues. He grew up with that same core insecurity: he wasn't good enough.

He slipped his arms around her waist. "That's not what I meant. Honey, do you remember David's sermon a few weeks ago? Those thoughts are the hiss of the snake. The devil wants you to doubt the goodness of God."

"What did you mean, then?" She kept her eyes lowered. "About God holding things up for us."

"I wonder if God wants to heal something inside of you, of me. The timing of this fostering—I didn't expect it. It seems like God has engineered this right into our church, and we all need to be open to what he might be trying to teach us."

"And you think I need a lesson?"

"You do. I do. We all do. There's a lot to learn in this life.

I'm just asking you to open up a little." He squeezed her shoulders gently, until she relaxed and gave him a slight smile.

"You're starting to sound like a deacon."

"Ha! First time anyone's told me that. Mostly, they wonder when I'm going to quit and run for the hills."

She slipped her arms around him. "You're a lot of things, Luke Schrock, but you're no quitter."

He hugged her against him, loving the feel of her body against his. It fit into his body like they were made for each other. "Speaking of not quitting, maybe tonight we can get back to work on that baby-making project."

She laughed, and he laughed, and something shifted: they felt a sweep of love for each other. It had been a while since being together had been easy between them.

Another lesson of marriage that he needed to remember. Things could get good again.

Sam Schrock was astounded by the bravery of Mollie Graber. Of all the foster girls placed in homes, it sounded like most had pretty decent, accommodating teenagers. The two O'Henry girls at the Sisters' House sounded amazing—they were taking such good care of the old sisters that the one sister who had broken her hip had been allowed to go home and rehabilitate there. Cassidy, over at Fern's, was quiet as a mouse. Luke said you'd hardly know she was there. She made no demands and fit in like a glove. Teddy and Alice had the best situation of all—their foster daughter, Chloe, knew of a special way to hold the baby high against her shoulder, walking with sort of a sway step, so that he suddenly hushed. His colic eased up. They had such a sense of appreciation for Chloe and her calm, pleasant disposition that yesterday, when Teddy had dropped by to see about a new buggy horse, he'd hinted Alice wanted to adopt her.

Sam hadn't heard much about the other girls, but that in itself told him things were working out. Bad news had a way of traveling fast, like a river running downhill.

As for Mollie's girls . . . when he saw them walking down the road to the schoolhouse one afternoon, alarm bells went off in his head. Or maybe they were explosions. He recognized those two girls. They were the firecracker girls.

Sam had grown up in the shadow of his brother Luke. He was wise to the way some minds worked—devious, sneaky, mischievous. He felt increasingly worried about Mollie. She was so trusting. So naïve. He wondered if she was even safe with those two hoodlums in the little cottage. Could they cause her bodily harm, like those stories about foster children that Hank Lapp spread around town? Sam was in the Bent N' Dent earlier this afternoon and overheard Hank tell a horrific tale about a foster boy who had set the house on fire. "KILLED EVERYONE IN IT," he said in his ordinary bellow. "AND THE BOY WAS OUTSIDE, LAUGHING THE WHOLE TIME, HOLDING AN EMPTY GAS CAN IN HIS HAND." Hank let out a weird laugh that still rang in Sam's ears.

On the way home from the Bent N' Dent, he couldn't stop thinking about Mollie. It was only the third time he'd placed the saucy mare in buggy traces, just short trips on very quiet country roads to help her grow accustomed to pulling the weight of the buggy. So far, so good. She handled the buggy well. He drove slowly past the schoolhouse to see if Mollie was still there. The sky was a menacing greenish-gray, and he knew he should get the mare home, but he noticed the glow of a buttery light inside the schoolhouse. The mare must have read his mind or felt the slack in the reins, because she slowed to a crawl, then to a full stop.

Sam jumped out and tucked the reins around the hitching post. He stopped to stroke the horse's velvety nose. "You think you're pretty smart, don't you?" The mare gave him a nose bump, pushing him toward the schoolhouse. "All right, all right."

This saucy mare was something special. If he was ever going to keep a horse for himself and not just train it for someone else's benefit, it would be this one. Unbidden came the thought: *Nope, not going there. Never going to love an animal again. No way.*

He brushed off his pants, tucked in his shirt, straightened his hat, and knocked on the schoolhouse door. He opened the door and peered inside. "Mollie?"

"Sam! Come in, come in."

She smiled at him as she approached him, and it felt as if the sun had pushed the thick gray clouds away. Her happiness and warmth were that palpable. When he saw her like this, he'd think, *You sure look pretty today, Mollie.* But he could never say those particular words. They got stuck in his throat. The only words that could get through were dull ones. "I was just passing by and saw a light on. Rain is coming. Thought you might need a ride home." He took off his hat and brushed a hand through his hair. She followed his movements so carefully that he wondered what she was thinking. Did he have something on his face? Was his hair sticking straight up?

"That is so incredibly thoughtful, Sam. I'm waiting for

Alicia and Tina to meet me. The school bus drops them off around the corner, in front of the group home, and they walk here. If you don't mind waiting, I think the girls would love a buggy ride. They've never been around animals much. I think it would be good for them to see how you handle your horses. You're the expert, everyone says. Down at the Bent N' Dent, they call you the Horse Whisperer. Masterful."

He dug his chin deeper into his chest at that compliment. Mollie was always doing that to him, making him feel like he was one of a kind, really unique, when he wasn't. He felt his cheeks grow warm. *Change the subject, Sam. Get your mind off yourself.* He heard drops of rain start on the roof and glanced out the window. "Here it comes. My new mare will be getting a bath from Mother Nature."

"Oh, well, you go on ahead, Sam. Better get your horse out of the rain." Her voice held a tinge of disappointment.

He whipped his head around to face her. "She needs to get used to rain. It's part of training a horse—getting them accustomed to all kinds of inclement weather. She's a good horse." He cleared his throat. "The best one ever." Almost the best. There'd been only one that was even better.

Mollie relaxed. "Really? The best horse you've ever trained? Tell me more. What makes this one so very special?"

That was all it took, and suddenly Sam was telling her all about this horse and what a fine, intelligent beast she was, details about her conformation, her carriage, how quickly she had grown accustomed to loud noises. He didn't say *which* loud noises, not today, because he didn't want to accuse the girls of mischief. Mollie had enough on her plate without worrying about firecrackers. Ten minutes must have passed before he realized he'd done all the talking. There was something about Mollie, the way she listened to him, asked him questions, kept her eyes on his the whole time. He ended up saying more than he ever intended to say.

A high squeak of brakes pierced the air. "That's the school bus," she said. "The girls will be here soon. They'll be so excited to meet you."

Excited wasn't the word Sam had in mind to describe those girls. More like explosive, volatile, unpredictable. "Is it going . . . okay?"

She nodded, a little too vigorously for him to really believe her. "I mean, it was a little rocky at the beginning, but I think we're finally on our way. Things have really taken an upturn lately."

"Really? They've only been with you a week."

"Yes, well, the adjustment is quite immense for them, you see. It's quite a significant one. They've been in foster care for years now." She fingered one of the capstrings that rested on her shoulder. "Would you believe that the reason they're in foster care is because their parents are famous movie stars? Apparently, they're living and working in Hollywood. All the way out in California."

He had to seal his lips to keep from laughing out loud.

"Apparently they can't care for their own girls while they shoot their movies. Big jobs. Important."

"The girls told you that?"

"Yes. Last night at dinner. I think they're really opening up to me."

So sweet, Mollie, but can't you see they're lying to you? Watching her, the way she would lock her hands behind her back as she spoke and lean forward on her toes; listening to her, that husky voice as gentle as a whisper, he became entranced. Mollie had such an unexpected effect on him. He felt dazzled by her, like all he could do was to blink, the same way he felt after he'd spent hours in the dimly lit barn and walked straight out into the bright sunshine.

"But it's sad, isn't it? To put work above your children like that? To just leave them in foster care so you can chase dreams of fame and fortune?"

"Huh?" He snapped to. "Uh, Mollie, maybe you should check out that story with the social workers."

"Oh Sam, I believe them." She clasped her hands over her heart. "They're good girls at heart. Maybe a tiny bit rough around the edges. Nothing that love and understanding can't fix."

There was an odd noise outside, and Sam turned his head toward the door, alert, on guard, checking for the source of those sounds. "Hold on, that's not what I think it is . . ."

"Oh no," Mollie said. "Please don't let it be *that*!"

Sam bolted to the door, opened it, only to see his horse and buggy gallop down the road.

Mollie came up behind him and released a surprised breath. "Oh dear. Oh no."

EIGHT

Dinner was silent. Mollie was appalled that Alicia and Tina took Sam's horse and buggy for a joyride, and she hadn't decided how to handle the situation yet. She just didn't know what to do, or what to say, to get through to them. She had told Sam that they were good girls down deep, but she was no longer convinced of that, only hopeful. Could their hearts be touched? Or was it too late?

And if it was too late, what was she doing, trying to manage them? What other tricks might they have up their sleeves?

Amazingly, the two girls seemed to sense her exasperation with them, because they were contrite during dinner—none of the usual eye rolling or elbow jabs or inside jokes like they usually did. They even helped clean up the dishes afterward. And then they said good night and went quietly to bed. Still, Mollie said not a word. She needed to pray about how to make things right from this afternoon's mischief.

Mollie believed in the Bible's words about guardian angels. The guardian angels for those girls—oh, they must be worn out! They must have been hovering over them this afternoon, because those two girls had no idea what they were doing. They'd never held a horse's reins in their hands, never even touched a horse. A horse that had only been in buggy traces three times.

And the rain! It was pouring. The girls had put themselves in a dangerous situation, not to mention endangering Sam's horse. His favorite one too. Minutes before they absconded with her, Sam's face had practically glowed as he described the horse's talents to her. It was the longest conversation he'd ever spoken to her without any need for her to keep him talking, to prompt him with continual questions. She kept losing track of his words. She'd been studying his face and noticing the sun-squint lines around his eyes. His hat was in his hands and his hair curled around his collar in a way she'd never noticed. It was probably helped along by the humidity, the way hers grew even curlier before a rainstorm.

Getting words out of Sam Schrock was always a worthwhile challenge, but today, she had finally seen that side of him that she knew was in there. And then the moment was gone.

But it could have been worse, Mollie reminded herself. Much worse. The horse was nearly home when the girls jumped in the buggy and screamed at it to go, slapping its rump with the reins. Sam's barn was around the corner, and that's where this smart horse took those two girls. To the barn.

Sam took off after the buggy, and Mollie ran full speed behind him, though she couldn't keep up. By the time Sam had caught up with them, the girls had tumbled out of the buggy, visibly dazed, but the horse—*thank you, Lord*—was just fine. Patiently waiting by the barn for her master to arrive and bring her supper of oats and hay.

That's what Sam did, after checking to see that the girls were unharmed and running a hand over his horse's legs. Without saying a word, he focused his attention on unbuckling the buggy traces and getting the horse out of the rain. With a set jaw, he led the mare into the barn, passing through the sliding double doors.

Standing in the rain, Mollie didn't know how to react. The girls had done a terrible thing. They'd scared Mollie. Sam too. And while at first they seemed shaken, then they were giggling over the entire thing, like it was a big joke.

Sam had come out of the barn, not even looking at the girls, only at Mollie. The rain was tapering down now, but she was soaked, head to toe, and shivering. "Let me take you home." He didn't mention the girls.

"No, Sam. Thanks. A walk will do us good."

"Mollie," he said, under his breath, and it said much. *What have you gotten yourself into, Mollie? What were you thinking? Give them back, fast.* She could read his thoughts in that one word, because those were her thoughts. *Dear God, what have I done?* she asked herself.

But at that moment, it wasn't his problem to solve, it was hers. "I'm sorry, Sam. We'll make this up to you. I'm not sure how, but we'll make this right."

They had stood there for a moment, eyes fixed on each other. Finally, he said, "No harm done."

But there was.

⌒

Luke was working on Hank Lapp's broken chair leg in the fix-it shop, and the unfortunate thing was that Hank was there too, watching his every move, offering up a steady

stream of advice. "SON, THAT'S EDITH'S FAVORITE
CHAIR."

"I know, I know. You told me, Hank."

"IT'S BROKE TWICE NOW. YOU NEED TO FIX IT
PERMANENT-LIKE. THE JOINT DON'T HOLD."

It had broken twice because it was not a chair designed to
hold the considerable poundage of Edith Lapp. But to try to
explain that to Hank or Edith seemed like a worse solution
than trying to fix this chair leg for the third time.

"I SHOULDA BROUGHT MY SLEEPING BAG."

"Why?"

"I'M NOT LEAVING WITHOUT THAT CHAIR. I
THOUGHT I'D JUST STAY HERE IN CASE YOU NEED
SOME HELP FIXING IT."

This was the tricky part of the fix-it business. People
didn't understand the law of entropy. Most everyone in
Stoney Ridge thought that nothing should ever break in the
first place, not ever. Luke knew that everything was wearing
out—everything!—and he could only do so much tinkering
and jerry-rigging.

Luke took the broken leg over to the open door for better
lighting, and of course, Hank followed right behind him.
"WHAT'S THE MATTER WITH THOSE SHEEP?"

Luke glanced over at the pen. The sheep were running back
and forth, back and forth. "They're nervous about that trampoline you dumped here, without asking if we wanted it."

"I FIGURED YOU'D FIND SOME WAY TO USE IT.
AND LOOK AT THAT! YOU DID."

Luke sighed. "A while ago, I put it in there for shade, but
I set it too close to the fence. Izzy wanted me to move it,
but the sheep had finally gotten used to it, so I kept putting

it off. This morning, I moved it to the center of the pen and those stupid sheep think it's new. A monster or wolf or something." Staring at the chair leg, turning it around and around, he found the problem. The leg had a slight, almost imperceptible crack running along one side, just enough to make the joint give way. He returned to his workbench with the chair leg and Hank followed right along.

Fern appeared at the shop's open door, Cassidy behind her, with two glasses of ice-cold lemonade.

"FERN LAPP. YOU READ MY MIND." A big smile wreathed Hank's face.

Fern handed him a glass of lemonade. "That's not so hard to do."

Hank burst out with a guffaw as he lifted the glass with a thank-you nod. "AND WHO IS THIS? ANOTHER STRAY?"

"No such thing as a stray child, Hank. They all belong to God. This is Cassidy. She's staying at Windmill Farm for a while."

"WATCH OUT, CASSIDY. FERN WILL TURN YOU INTO A MINI-FERN. I SEEN IT HAPPEN."

Fern gave him her look. "And is that such a bad thing?"

Hank took a big sip of lemonade and wiped his mouth with his shirtsleeve. "NOT SO BAD AT ALL."

Cassidy peered at Hank as if he was an oddity, which he was.

"FERN, DID YOU SEE THOSE SHEEP? ACTING ALL TETCHY."

"I saw."

"They don't like the trampoline," Cassidy said.

Everybody was suddenly an expert. Luke tried not to roll his eyes. "They just need to get used to it."

"Give them time," Fern said. "Sheep don't like the unknown. It causes them to panic. Their natural impulse is to run from it."

That's exactly what was happening to Izzy's sheep. They were in a panic, gripped by fear, just because of the trampoline. Something meant for their good. Something that had been in their pen for weeks, but just a few yards from where it was now. Stupid sheep, Luke thought to himself.

"MOB MENTALITY. SHEEP CAN'T THINK FOR THEMSELVES." Hank went outside to watch the sheep. Not a few seconds later, he popped his head in the door. "YOU ALL NEED TO COME AND SEE THIS."

Fern, Cassidy, and Luke went outside to see what Hank was crowing about now. Izzy had come out of the yarn shop and gone into the pen, singing her special call to the sheep. As the sheep realized their shepherdess was in their midst, they stopped their restless back-and-forthing they'd been doing all morning. Instead, they settled, went back to calm grazing, slowly spreading out around the corral. They could rest and relax. A few ventured under the trampoline, and others started to join them. They were once again a contented flock of sheep.

The four of them stood in front of the fix-it shop, side by side, arms crossed, transfixed. Cassidy turned to Fern. "How in the world did that happen?"

"Izzy," Fern said. "The shepherd's presence makes all the difference."

The four of them didn't budge, just stood watching those happy, peaceful sheep, until Hank had to go and ruin the moment with his big mouth. "THAT REMINDS ME. EDITH'S SERVING LAMB CHOPS FOR SUPPER."

With a look of disgust Fern took Hank's empty glass and went to the house. Luke went back inside the shop, with Hank at his heels. Cassidy stayed outside, eyes on the sheep and on Izzy. Luke wondered what she was thinking about and hoped Hank hadn't spoiled the extraordinary moment for her. It truly was an extraordinary moment. Luke had seen Izzy's sheep stop whatever they were doing when they heard the sound of her voice. He'd watched how a runaway sheep, once found, would follow behind her like a puppy. But this, today, was like no other. To see the way the sheep were able to lose their anxious ways and settle down contentedly, simply because their shepherd was in their midst. The Good Shepherd. This moment from nature gave him a new understanding of how the awareness of God's presence could—and should—deliver a person from fear. Should bring peace and contentment. Should bring the return of rest.

He wanted to close up the fix-it shop and hurry over to the Bent N' Dent, to have a long talk with David about this biblical concept he'd seen illustrated in the natural world. A month ago, he'd have done just that. But now he couldn't. Deacon work took up a lot of time, on top of his long to-do list. He couldn't stop, he had to keep moving. And whenever Hank showed up, everything slowed down.

Hank was still walking around the fix-it shop, picking things up and putting them in different places, muttering about how he wanted to get on home with his fixed chair and eat his lamb chops. "CAN'T YOU JUST GLUE IT BACK IN?"

"Hank, we tried that twice and it's not working. There's a fracture in the leg that causes the glue to crack. I think I need to get Teddy Zook in on this. Have him make you a new chair leg."

Hank threw up his hands. "THAT'LL COST TOO MUCH."

Luke sighed. "I don't think so. Let me see what I can do. Come back in a few days."

"EDITH WON'T BE HAPPY."

"She will be when her chair stops breaking out from under her."

A cackle burst out of Hank and he finally left the shop to go pester Fern, thank goodness. Luke put the chair leg on a pile to take to Teddy Zook's and picked up a broken harness clip.

"Lordy, she'd make some mother."

He glanced up to discover Cassidy at the doorjamb. He'd forgotten all about her. "Huh?"

"She'd make a good mother."

"Who're you talking about?"

"Izzy." She turned around to look out the door, talking to the sky as if he wasn't even there. "Always gentle voiced. Always looking out for the sheep."

Luke stopped what he was doing. He hadn't really thought about what Izzy would be like as a mother, just assumed it would come naturally to her like it did all Amish women. But Izzy wasn't like most Amish women, and yet Cassidy was right. If shepherding was any indication, Izzy would be a wonderful mother.

He sure hoped a baby was in their future. Normally, he didn't let Izzy's worries about not getting pregnant bother him, but lately he'd felt a little unsettled feeling stir in his soul, wondering if she might be right. Wondering if they might not ever be able to have a baby. She asked him just the other day if she should go see Dok about it, and he'd only shrugged, tossing the decision back to her. He wasn't sure he wanted to know the answer.

Cassidy turned back to face him, standing by the door, and he wondered what she was waiting for. Why did people think he was available at all times to talk? He wasn't!

But he should be. That's the kind of thing church leaders did. David allowed for interruptions. Luke knew that to be true because he often interrupted him. He thought again of the advice David had given him: Do the opposite. "Cassidy, is there anything you want to talk about? Anything on your mind?"

She looked down at her feet, then up again, and if he wasn't mistaken, he thought her eyes had grown shiny. "Nope," she sighed. "Nothing at all." She turned and left.

There was still so much Luke had to learn about women. Once again, he had read one all wrong.

Izzy was aware that Fern's foster girl was watching her walk among the sheep in the pen, so she purposefully kept herself turned away from Luke's fix-it shop. She waited until she saw the girl walk back toward Fern's kitchen before leaving the pen to return to the yarn shop. She didn't want to interact with her any more than was necessary.

Izzy knew the girl would like some attention from her. She was a nice enough girl. Nice for Fern. Izzy didn't want to have to think about this girl, or hear her sad stories, or have the girl put any expectations on her. As far as Izzy was concerned, that group home couldn't be repaired fast enough.

It was long after dark. Luke and David had made a visit to a family who had just moved to Stoney Ridge from another church district. They went to welcome them and to discuss some of the customs observed here, as Stoney Ridge was a more conservative church than the one this family had come from. The husband and wife had a handicraft shop and used a computer for his business. "It's not connected to the internet," he told David. "My other bishop allowed it."

"I understand," David said. And Luke knew he did. Each Amish church was a stand-alone, allowing for countless variations on what was acceptable and what was not. "We just haven't opened the door to computers yet."

The man persisted. "Then let's give it a try. See how it goes. After all, I need it for inventory and billing."

David explained that if he'd had some history with this fellow, he might bend on the issue. But to allow a newcomer to be the one to try out a new technology just didn't seem wise, nor was it fair to the rest of the church. "I'm a believer in taking the long view. As bishop, I've learned that I've had to look beyond, far down the road, to see how a decision might play out over time." Finally, he told the man to not use the computer for a year.

The man's jaw dropped. "You can't be serious."

"Just set it aside, for at least a year. Then we'll take it under consideration."

The man wasn't at all happy with David, and his wife looked like she was ready to pack up and go.

On the buggy ride home, Luke said, "They sure didn't expect that."

"This is a common occurrence," David said. "Folks move in, expecting the church to adapt to them, rather than the other way around. But if we bent and changed for everyone's whims, we'd soon be whittled down to nothing."

Luke kept his eyes on the road. "Would it be so very bad to give this new fellow's way a try? There's less and less farming. More and more businesses. To use a tool for work, like computer software, when it's not connected to the internet . . . it's no different than the solar panels on the Bent N' Dent roof. It helps your business stay solvent."

"Tools to help our work aren't bad things at all. But computers aren't the same thing as solar panels on the roof. Allowing the use of computers and all they bring with it is a decision that needs time and thought and prayer. Once something starts, it's difficult to stop."

Luke hadn't considered the consequences of a decision. It was a shortcoming that returned to bite him many times, and yet he still had trouble seeing how something could play out down the road. There was so much Luke had to learn about leading a church, about being a deacon, about making good decisions that benefited others. As he pulled the horse to a stop in front of David's house, he kept his hands on the horse's reins. "This deacon duty . . . Sometimes I feel as if I'm at the bottom of a steep mountain, looking up at the crooked path ahead. Steeper, harder, rockier than anyone had told me it would be."

David cocked an eyebrow and thought a moment. "Well said, Luke." He climbed out of the buggy and slid the door shut, then leaned through the window. "But just imagine the view from the top."

NINE

On a golden afternoon in early October, Izzy was in the yarn shop preparing to dye wool. She filled a tub halfway full of water and set it on the counter. She took a ball of yarn and started rolling it around her elbow to her hand, over and over and over, so that the yarn was untangled and could be held in a circle. She snipped two pieces of yarn and tied the circle at each end, so it wouldn't end up as a big tangled mess. She'd learned that lesson the hard way.

Next, she dunked the yarn into the tub, pushing it down so that it would absorb the water. Soaked yarn absorbed dye better. Izzy set an oven timer for ten minutes to let the wool soak. When the bell rang, she picked up the little ties and squeezed the excess water out of the wool, then stuffed it into an old large glass jar, a hand-me-down from Fern. She used to make sun tea in it, but after the lid cracked, she gave it to Izzy. It was the perfect size to use for sun-dyed wool. Through trial and error, she had discovered that the color in the yarn set better from the sun than from boiled water.

Grabbing rubber gloves (a lesson she'd learned through a mistake that had left her with bright orange hands for over a week), she took a packet of purple Kool-Aid and shook it into the leftover tub water, then swirled it all around with her gloved hands. As soon as the Kool-Aid dissolved, she would pour the purple liquid into the old tea jar, over the yarn, until it was full, and set it out in the sun. Edith Lapp was the one who told her about Kool-Aid. Izzy couldn't believe it at first, but it worked.

Edith had explained how the citric acid in the Kool-Aid helped the color set in the fibers. Izzy didn't really understand the process but she did like the price of Kool-Aid. Less than a dollar a packet. And the colors were bold, vibrant, especially the blues, greens, reds, and purples. Yellow needed a little boost of food coloring to make it pop.

Luke was the one who had asked Edith Lapp how to dye handspun wool. Izzy had just assumed she would send it away to someone to dye it, but Luke was confident that she could do it better once she had someone teach her what to do. He brought Edith Lapp over for an afternoon tutorial and that was all Izzy needed. Since then, she'd experimented with all kinds of colors and types of wool, including variegated coloring. She'd overheard a tour bus driver tell his group that Izzy was known in the area for her wool colors, which shocked her. Imagine that!

When she told Luke what the tour bus driver had said, he didn't seem at all surprised. "You've always had an eye for color and you have a knack for putting things together. Remember what you did with Amos's farm stand? Tripled sales in one summer."

Quadrupled them. But that was beside the point.

That's one of the things she appreciated most about Luke—he had such confidence in her. He continually pushed her to try and learn new things. She wouldn't have dared ask a single question to Edith Lapp, of all people—why, everyone was frightened to death of Edith Lapp—and yet Edith shared her vast knowledge generously.

Izzy still felt great reluctance to take risks, to put herself out there. Luke wanted her to put her past away and embrace a new way of interacting with others. She wanted that too, but he made it sound easy. It wasn't.

Luke couldn't understand what her upbringing had been like. How could he? His own childhood was safe and secure, food on the table and a bed at night. Hers was anything but. He had family, brothers and a sister. She'd had no one.

He kept pressing her to befriend Fern's foster girl, but she just . . . couldn't. The girl's very presence took Izzy right back to days and nights she wanted to forget. Even the way the girl kept her eyes averted reminded Izzy of the way she was when she first arrived at Windmill Farm. She couldn't look Amos—dear, sweet, grandfatherly Amos—in the eyes for the first six months.

Izzy and Luke ate most of their meals in the corner of the fix-it shop, but on Sundays they went up to the main house to eat with Fern. When Izzy sat across from the girl, she could hardly stand to watch her eat. The girl ate two to three helpings of every dish Fern had prepared. The way she gobbled food reminded Izzy of how she felt when she first lived at Windmill Farm. It took her a long time to get over feeling astonished at the variety of food, even more so at the quantity of food prepared for every single meal. Each and every day felt like Thanksgiving. That must be how Fern's girl felt, and it should make Izzy feel empathy for her, but instead it made her mad. She didn't want to go back to those days, not even in a memory.

She thought she heard a sound outside, someone shout out her name. She opened the door and saw Fern's girl over in the sheep pen, calling for help. Izzy's first impulse was, *My woollies! What's she doing, messing with my woollies?* Then she saw the problem and bolted across the driveway to squeeze through the fence. A sheep was cast on its back, legs up in the air.

The girl was pulling the ewe's legs, but it wasn't working. "I can't get her up!"

"Stop! Don't pull her," Izzy said. "We need to get her on her side."

Together, they pushed and pushed to turn the sheep over to her side, until she could get up on her feet. Startled, the ewe shook her head and scampered off, then slowed to eat. Crisis over.

Izzy sat back on her heels. "Oh my soul, that could have been a close call." She glanced at the girl. "How did you know she was in trouble?"

That particular ewe was always getting cast down. Sheep were the silliest animals. If they rolled over onto their backs, they simply couldn't get up. If left like that, they could die.

"I had a foster dad who was a vet. He taught me a lot about animals."

Izzy got to her feet and put out a hand to help the girl up. "Thank you."

"No problem." She looked at Izzy's hands. The dye had seeped through a hole in the gloves and made them a strange purple color. "Holy smoke. Do you have some kind of circulation problem?"

Izzy chuckled, looking at her hands. "No. I was dyeing wool. In fact, I'd better go finish up." She started toward the fence, then stopped before she bent down to slip through a board, remembering Luke's persistence to be nice to Fern's girl. She turned back. "Do you want to see the shop?"

The girl shrugged, like the offer didn't really matter, but Izzy knew it was a big deal to her. She knew that look, that careless shrug of the shoulders, that cavalier mask that covered real feelings. It mattered. Too much.

The girl walked around the yarn shop in amazement. "It's so beautiful. I didn't expect it to be stylish. So beautiful."

Izzy softened, feeling her resolve to be distant slip a little. "Luke built it for me."

"He told me you designed everything. Even the wall of yarn? The corner for classes?"

Izzy nodded.

"Most yarn shops, they don't look like this."

"What do they look like?"

"Old lady-ish. Musty. Boring. My grandma used to take me with her." She walked around the room and stopped abruptly when she saw the sweater Izzy had made for Grace. It was folded on the table, used as an example of cable knitting for Izzy's advanced knitting class. Cassidy picked it up, touched the wooden buttons. "This is the prettiest sweater I've ever seen in my whole life. Ever, ever."

Pleased, Izzy smiled.

Cassidy set it down and walked over to the spinning machine to examine it. She picked up the two carding handles and touched their tiny prongs. Then she bent down to the basket of wool to touch it, smell it, hold it against her face.

Izzy had to bite her bottom lip to keep from saying *Please don't touch my things.* She wanted to, but she held back.

"How'd you learn to spin wool?"

"A woman in the church, she taught me."

"Edith Lapp?"

"Yes. How did you know?"

"She comes by Fern's kitchen a lot. She has a lot to say."

A smile tugged at Izzy's lips. "You can learn a lot from her if you listen."

Fern's girl looked up. "Yeah. I didn't mean to sound snarky."

"You didn't. Edith does have a lot to say. Her husband has even more to say. And in a much louder volume too."

A laugh burst out of the girl, and Izzy noticed she had big dimples. Both cheeks. The girl went back to touching the wool. "Have you ever thought of using Merino wool?"

"Merino?"

"Yeah. It's the rage now. Crazy popular."

"How do you know that?"

"The vet's wife. She loved Merino wool. Her husband would barter his services to the shepherd in exchange for some fleeces each spring."

"Why didn't you just stay with that family? Sounds like you liked them."

"My dad got out of jail and so I got to go home with him."

"Why not now? Why not stay with the vet instead of going to the group home?"

"The vet and his wife ended up getting a divorce." She grinned, one that reached her eyes. "Turned out, he liked the shepherd's wife a little too much."

Izzy knew the rest of *that* story.

"The vet's clinic sends me a Christmas card each year. Isn't that a kick?"

Izzy had moved around so much during her childhood that it was hard to stay in touch with anyone, even if she'd wanted to. So many foster placements, all those new schools.

She carefully poured the purple dye over the yarn to cover it to the top. As she swirled the yarn in the dye, Izzy studied Fern's girl from the other side of the room. She was tall, as tall as Izzy, but bigger than her. Broad shouldered, broad hipped. Milk chocolate skin, thick dark wavy hair. Probably mixed-race, she guessed. A combination of Hispanic and African American. She was quite pretty when she smiled. Those big dimples.

The girl ran her hand to make the spinning wheel spin. Izzy knew exactly what she was thinking, what was right below the surface. The girl wanted Izzy to teach her to spin wool. But she knew the girl wouldn't ask, and Izzy wouldn't offer.

"It's funny about sheep."

"What's funny?"

"How many times sheep are talked about in the Bible."

Izzy stilled. "What do you mean?"

She started numbering her fingers. "There's Adam's son Abel, he was a keeper of sheep. And Moses. He was stuck out in the desert with sheep for forty years until he got rescued by a burning bush." Her eyes lifted to the ceiling, as if she was trying to remember. "There's others, I think. Sheep and shepherds are in the Bible a lot."

Izzy's mouth snapped open in shock. She'd never heard any of this. She tried to keep her voice calm and low. "You seem to know a lot about the Bible." For a girl in foster care.

"Nah, not so much. Just parts of it. My grandma made me go to Vacation Bible School each summer. The last summer I went, just before Grandma died, the whole week was about the Good Shepherd. You know that one. Everybody knows that one."

Izzy shrugged, emptying the leftover dye from the tub into the sink. "Go ahead. You can tell me anyway." She had no idea what the girl was talking about.

"Hmmm, let me think . . . something about Jesus being the Good Shepherd. They showed a video that was really funny. A bunch of sheep were on a hill, and these tourists thought they could call to them to try to get them down the hill. One by one, they gave a call or a whistle or a 'Yoohoo.' The sheep didn't even look up. But then the shepherd came and gave his own 'yoohoo' and those sheep, why they lifted their heads and their ears went up and one by one they all started to head down the hill to the shepherd." She clapped her hands together, grinning. "That was something else."

Izzy could imagine the sight of those foolish tourists, thinking sheep were so dumb that they would come to anyone who called them. In her mind, she saw the entire story played out, but the image that came to her was of herself as the shepherdess. She screwed the cracked lid on top, as tight as it could go with its crack, and waited to see if the girl would say more. When she didn't, Izzy asked, "So, what else did you learn that week?"

"In Vacation Bible School, you mean? Well, we learned a lot about King David. Writing that psalm about sheep that everybody knows by heart. We even had it at my grandpa's funeral, and he never went to church a day in his life."

Wait. What? This was all new information to Izzy. As her

mind spun, looking for a way to ask a question without it sounding like a question, Fern's girl climbed off the spinning wheel. "Oh, listen to me rattle on."

Izzy was just about to say that it was all right with her if she wanted to rattle on. She wanted to hear more about sheep in the Bible, she found it quite fascinating, but then the girl covered her face with her hands for a few seconds. Then she let them fall to her lap where they made a single, gripping fist. "I think . . . I need some fresh air," and she made a beeline toward the door, yanked it open, and went outside.

Izzy thought about just closing the door behind the girl and carrying on with her chores, but she could hear Luke's scolding voice in her head, asking which was more important: a girl in need or a to-do list?

Eek! Even in her head, he was turning into a deacon.

She poked her head outside the door and saw the girl doubled over. Izzy stood behind her stooping form. The girl had braced both hands on her knees, trying to catch her breath. Izzy reached out a hand as if to lay it on her back, but thought better of it and crossed her arms tightly beneath her breasts. The girl straightened, muscle by muscle, and blew out a shaky breath.

After a long moment, the girl wiped her face with the back of her sweatshirt. "Sorry. Just started feeling a little dizzy in there. When I don't eat enough, sometimes I get a little light-headed. My dad's the same way."

"Fern's made some fresh doughnuts. Baked apple cider, straight from the trees in the orchard."

The girl gave her a thumbs-up. "I'll go check them out now."

From the door of the yarn shop, Izzy watched her walk up

to the main house. At the top of the stairs, the girl turned to wave, as if she knew she was being studied. Embarrassed, Izzy gave her a quick wave before she closed the door.

⁓

Tina and Alicia had lived with Mollie for over two weeks. Three times, the sheriff had found them hitchhiking to Las Vegas in the middle of the night and brought them back. Four times, the school had called to report their absence. They had cut school after lunch and spent a few hours at a nearby shopping mall, then returned at three o'clock to hop on the school bus to get home. And then there was running off with Sam's horse and buggy.

Today, the sheriff stopped by the schoolhouse. The scholars watched, wide-eyed, as he asked to speak to Mollie privately, outside. Apparently, Tina and Alicia's PE teacher had sent the class off on a cross-country run and the two girls had taken a left when the class had taken a right. "Please don't panic," the sheriff told Mollie. "I'm sure we'll find them. I've got a deputy out looking for them, checking all the highways. "

Panic was not the feeling Mollie was experiencing. What she was feeling most deeply was a mélange of exasperation, discouragement. Overwhelmed. Growing weary. All those feelings and more. But she wasn't panicking and she wasn't at all worried, which struck her as strange. "Check the school bus at three o'clock," Mollie said. "I have a hunch they'll find their way back to school by then."

A little before four o'clock, she heard the squeak of the school bus brakes down the road. A few minutes later, Tina and Alicia came swaggering into the schoolhouse, looking all-around pleased with themselves, reeking of cigarette smoke, full of stories about their long day at school.

"How was PE?" Mollie said. "Anything unusual happen?"

"It was boring," Tina said. "We had a sub."

Alicia added, "We played dodgeball in the gym."

They played dodge, all right, but not with a ball and not in the gym.

Lies, Mollie realized just then. Even more upsetting: lies rolled off their tongues like butter.

Through the window of the yarn shop, Izzy saw Luke drive Bob the buggy horse up the steep driveway of Windmill Farm. He'd come home late last night from some kind of deacon duty, slept in this morning, and by the time she was done with her first knitting class, he was gone again. She closed the shop and walked to the barn, hoping to grab a few minutes with him. She hadn't had a chance to talk to him, really talk, in a few days.

As she went through the sliding double doors of the barn, she slowed, blinking, as her eyes adjusted to the dim lighting. It always amazed her to see Luke's careful management of the barn. Amos cared well for his animals and his orchards, but most of the buildings on Windmill Farm—especially the barn—he kept in a state of disrepair. No longer. Under Luke, this entire farm looked spit and polished. Izzy didn't think there was a spiderweb to be found, even in the barn. She felt a little swell of pride in her heart for her husband's diligence.

She found him clipping Bob's harness to the crossties in the barn's wide center aisle. "Luke, have you ever heard of King David?"

He looked over Bob's neck at her in surprise. "Well, hello to you too."

"Sorry. I've been meaning to ask, but we keep missing each other."

He smiled, looking tired. "I'm here now. So let's see. I assume you're talking about the King David in the Bible. Yup, I've heard of him. Sure have." He bent down to pick up a brush, and stayed bent over, running the brush along Bob's fetlocks to get the street mud off.

Izzy leaned around Bob's chest to peer at Luke. "So, what about him?"

Luke glanced over at her. "King David? He was the greatest king of Israel. Unified the thirteen tribes into one kingdom. Had a few slipups, big ones, like with Bathsheba, but he got back on track. Always did. God called him a man after his own heart."

"So what did this King David know about sheep?"

Luke dropped the ankle brush, then exchanged it for a curry brush and began to run it down Bob's neck and withers. "What did he know about sheep? Everything, I guess. Considering what he did."

She knew Luke was tired, but this was way too slow. She'd have to be more direct. She came around to Bob's right side and petted his velvet nose. "Tell me why. How did King David know so much about sheep?"

Luke paused, hands resting on Bob's neck. "David was a shepherd boy. Youngest son, a lot of older brothers, and probably treated like the runt of the family. In those days, being a shepherd was like being a fisherman. Not a highly desired position. But Samuel the Judge was told to anoint someone from Jesse's family to be the next king. So he went to their house to meet all Jesse's sons, and passed them right by, each one. Then he asked if anyone was missing. Samuel knew there had to be another son around there someplace. So his father sent someone to call David in from the fields."

Izzy listened carefully. She knew almost nothing about the Bible, other than what she had learned from sermons in church. "So, this King David, he wrote a psalm about sheep?"

"Oh, I'll bet you're talking about Psalm 23. It's considered one of the most beloved psalms in the Bible. I'll show you in my Bible tonight."

"No need," she said, stiffening. She turned to go inside. "I'll find it for myself."

But she wouldn't, because she couldn't. The Amish read from the Luther German Bible, and while Izzy could speak and understand Penn Dutch fluently, an oral language—which suited her just fine—she was at a complete loss to read or understand high German. She wasn't much of a reader in English, so the German Bible was an impossible hill for her to climb. It embarrassed her to be ignorant, even to Luke, but she simply didn't know what to do. She was the wife of the deacon and she couldn't even read the Bible.

TEN

The weather was changing. When Izzy got out of bed in the morning, the floorboards were bone cold and the windows were frosty. She shivered as she dressed in the dark and wondered when Luke would have time to start putting walls up. Soon, she hoped, as she added a log to the woodstove in the fix-it shop. The warmed air all but floated away in this open-walled building.

There were no knitting classes scheduled today, and the tour buses had slowed down for the season, only coming on Fridays and Saturdays. A good day for Izzy to visit Jenny. She hurried through the morning tasks and took the scooter to head over to Jenny's. She found her out in the yard, hanging laundry on the line. From a distance, she dropped the scooter and paused to study the scene covertly, noting the round bump of her sister's belly as she rested a hand on it.

Jenny was so small and petite that her belly bump couldn't be hidden under a loose-fitting dress and large apron, as it could be on many Amish women. They were so private about such matters, so modest. Most women never discussed their pregnancies, and you'd certainly never ask anyone if she might be expecting. Even at the yarn shop, where women chatted about all kinds of things, pregnancy was rarely discussed. Izzy knew of families whose children never knew their mother was going to have a baby. One morning, a baby just appeared in their mother's arms. Like it was easy.

Little Rosie sat on the grass by Jenny's feet, hindering her mother's movement. The baby clung to her skirt, sucking her thumb, until at last Jenny reached down to pick her up. Rosie buried her face in her mother's neck. A spiral of envy curled up inside Izzy. *When, Lord? When will this scene be mine? How much longer do we have to wait?*

Jenny set the baby down next to her and returned to the task of hanging clothes. Izzy approached them with a hello, bending down to kiss her niece on the top of her feathery blonde head.

"An unexpected visitor!" Jenny held a bright green dress up and shook it, then stretched it, before she hung it carefully to minimize wrinkles. A trick she'd learned from Fern to cut down on ironing. "So what brings you here today?"

"A question. Do you read Jesse's German Bible?"

"Jesse reads devotions from it each morning. Why do you ask?"

"I don't know German. How did you learn?"

"Just by listening at church, I suppose. It's different from Penn Dutch, but the same too."

Izzy picked up a wet black apron and smoothed it out, then passed it to Jenny. "It's so easy for you."

"No, not really. I was just so much younger than you when I lived among the Amish. It was easier to pick up, to gain an ear for the language. Don't forget, I'd attended Amish schools too."

"I need to read the Bible," Izzy said, bending down to pick up a wet sock. "There's something about sheep in it."

"I'll say. There's a lot about sheep in it."

"Someone told me about a fellow named King David."

"David the shepherd boy."

"And Moses."

"That's right. I'd forgotten that he was a shepherd."

"And Abel."

"Abel, as in Cain and Abel? I guess that's right too."

"Are there more shepherds and sheep in the Bible?"

"Tons more."

"Old Testament? Or New?"

"Both."

Izzy let out a defeated sigh. She had to know what the Bible said about sheep. "What am I going to do?"

Jenny laughed. "Get an English Bible."

She looked over at the back of the Bent N' Dent store. "I'm the deacon's wife now. Seems like I should be good at German."

"What? Like, you're supposed to be instantly perfect? Hardly! Birdy is always trying to stop folks from putting her and David on a pedestal. She says they'll topple right off. She'd rather be firmly on the ground, with low expectations."

"Still . . ."

"I don't think there's a single person in our church who would discourage you from reading the Bible in your first language. Good grief, Izzy. You make being Amish so much harder than it needs to be."

Oh my soul, isn't that the truth? Izzy made everything harder than it needed to be. Marriage, especially. She knew she was too hard on Luke. A few nights ago, she asked him if she should go to see Dok about not getting pregnant, and he seemed so disinterested that she didn't speak to him for the rest of the evening. She didn't think he even noticed.

"Do you have time to come inside? I need to put the baby down for her nap, and then I'll make us some tea."

"You put the baby down and I'll make the tea." Izzy bent down to pick up the baby and held her close against her, loving her baby smell, the feel of her soft cheek. She felt such a bone-deep ache, such a longing.

Jenny picked up the empty laundry basket and paused a moment, watching the two of them. "It'll happen, Izzy. It will."

Izzy startled. Sometimes it seemed her sister could read her mind. Jenny slipped her arm through Izzy's and pulled her toward the house. In the small kitchen, she handed Rosie back to her mother, a little reluctantly. Jenny disappeared into the back room with the baby.

Jenny and Jesse lived in a two-bedroom cottage behind the Bent N' Dent and Jesse's buggy repair shop. Izzy wondered how they would manage with two babies in this tiny cottage, but Jenny seemed to take things in stride. Plus, she did have walls.

She filled the teakettle with water and set it to boil. The mugs hung under a shelf near the sink. She took two down and then hunted for tea bags in the cupboard. By the time the kettle was whistling, Jenny had come back to the kitchen. "Can't find the tea bags?"

"No. Where could they be?"

"In a bag in the freezer. Keeps them from going stale."

Izzy laughed. "I should have known! That's where Fern keeps tea and coffee. You, Jenny Stoltzfus, are a miniature Fern."

Jenny laughed. "That's what Hank Lapp always says. Fern taught me everything I know about housekeeping. How to cook. How to clean. Once I learn something, I don't deviate from it."

As Jenny made tea, Izzy noted that she had purchased peppermint tea specially for her, and she was touched. She knew that Jenny and Jesse didn't like the taste of mint. Jenny was always doing that kind of thing: thoughtful gestures that made Izzy know she was remembered. The two women sat down with their tea on the front porch, watching the customers go in and out of the Bent N' Dent. From where they sat, they could see Hank Lapp over at the buggy shop, waving his arms around as he told Jesse a story. It was fun, this sight. Watching the life of their community.

"I'm glad you stopped by, Izzy," Jenny said as she sipped her own cup of tea. "There's something I need to tell you." Her smile was gone, and a crease had appeared between her pale eyebrows. "Mama's left town."

Izzy froze. "She . . . left?"

"She sent a note. I just got it yesterday. Said she'll be gone for a while."

Izzy set her teacup down. Eyes to her lap, she wrapped her hands in her apron and started to twist it. "Where did she go? Why?"

"I don't know. Either she didn't know, or she didn't want to say."

A panic gripped Izzy's chest so tightly that she thought her heart might stop beating. "Where? Where could she go? I didn't think the probation officer would let her leave the county."

"That much I do know. A month ago, her suspended sentence was lifted, so she could leave the area."

"So she did."

"Yes. So she did."

What Izzy really wanted to ask: Was she coming back? Eyes focused intently on the amber liquid in her teacup, she said, "Did she have any message for me in the note?"

Jenny shook her head. "It was just a few sentences long. You know Mama. She gets something in her head and she just goes with it."

Actually, Izzy didn't know their mother well. Not well at all. "So she didn't even tell me goodbye. Just you."

"She wanted me to say goodbye to the baby for her. To give her a kiss from Grandma. That's the only reason she sent me a note."

But they both knew that wasn't the only reason. Jenny was the only daughter who meant something to Grace.

"Do you think she'll be coming back someday? Did it sound like she was gone for good?"

"She'll be back. I'm sure of it. When . . . that I don't know." Jenny leaned over to put her hand over Izzy's, still twisted in the apron. "I've told you this before and I'll tell you again: if you want to have a relationship with Mama, you have to lower your expectations."

"To the basement."

Jenny laughed. "Just about. You take what you get and don't ask for more."

Or hope for more. That was the hard part for Izzy. She couldn't seem to stop hoping. "It must be nice, having Mama love you like she does. Like she loves your baby."

"Oh Izzy . . . I wouldn't call it love. Not the way you and I know love to be. Sometimes I think . . . Mama really only loves herself."

"She treats you better than she treats me. Buys you gifts and comes around to babysit. She pretty much ignores me." She glanced over at her sister. "Don't say it isn't true, because it is."

"Probably because I look the most like her, whereas you and Chris, you both don't take after her."

Izzy shrugged. That's what happens when you have three different men fathering your children. The three half-siblings didn't resemble each other in any way. Izzy was tall, with thick brunette hair and dark brown eyes. Jenny was petite and fine-boned, fair and blonde, most like Grace. Chris was a man's man, muscular and broad shouldered, with sandy brown hair and hazel eyes. Luke said if he closed his eyes and listened to them talk and laugh together, he could tell they were all related. Even Chris, he said.

"She likes you best." And that was the truth. Jenny was easy to talk to, forgiving by nature. Izzy knew she was stiff and uncomfortable around Grace. Jesse was more welcoming too. Luke? Not so much. He didn't trust Grace. "Chris said the same thing. She's always liked you best."

Jenny sighed. "Don't forget that Chris and I were left on our own too. When Mama was doing drugs, there was nothing in her life but getting money for those drugs. I remember one time when I made it all the way back to Ohio to meet her as she got out of rehab, and she ended up stealing my backpack and leaving me at a McDonald's. She did that kind of thing to us back then. Raised our hopes that she was doing better, ready to be a good mother, only to leave us high and dry."

"But you weren't made a ward of the state. You didn't spend your childhood in foster homes and group homes." The sharp tone in Izzy's voice surprised her. That ugliness within, that bitterness. She tried so hard to keep it hidden, yet it would slip through now and then.

"True. Chris and I had it easier than you. We were fortunate enough to have one foster mother take us in, for years and years. Old Deborah. And when she died, Fern and Amos looked after us. But Izzy, you and I, we're in the same place now. Doesn't that matter more than the past? Look where we are now."

If it were only that easy to let go of the past. "So then, you've really, truly forgiven Grace."

"I had to. I didn't want to live the rest of my life with resentment stirring in my stomach. But I don't expect anything from her. The problem with you is that you keep wanting something from her."

"That's what Luke's always telling me. I need to stop expecting something from her that she can't give."

Jenny smiled. "Luke can be surprisingly insightful at times."

Izzy's eyes returned her sister's smile. "At times." Other times, not so much.

On the way home, Izzy decided she would stop being mean to Luke and try—try, try, try—to quit worrying about having a baby. And she would find herself an English Bible. Her spirits lifted considerably, just like she knew they would after a visit with Jenny. They stayed buoyed up as long as she kept herself from thinking about her mother.

Sam didn't need to create an excuse to go to the schoolhouse this morning to talk to Mollie. He had a plan for those girls to make amends to him for stealing his horse and buggy earlier in the week.

When he walked into the schoolhouse, Mollie was bent over the woodstove, trying to snap a piece of kindling, and straightened in surprise. "Sam! I'm so glad you've come."

He was unprepared for her reaction. She looked so genuinely delighted to see him, as if she'd been hoping he would stop by, that he had to fight a smile that threatened to spread over his face. He walked over to her and took the kindling from her hands. She wore a thick black sweater over a turquoise dress this morning, his favorite dress of hers, the one that made her eyes the color of a tropical sea, and he felt his face grow warm though the room was downright bitter cold.

Quickly, Sam knelt down to build the fire in the woodstove. He broke wooden sticks over his knee, taking care to lay the kindling just so, the way his stepfather Galen had taught him. Galen King was a man who believed there was a right way to do things, and Sam was an apt student. On this morning he took his time, enjoying a reason to linger in the schoolhouse. He surprised himself. He wasn't the kind of guy who lingered without a reason, especially if a girl was around. But this girl was Mollie.

When he was satisfied with the structure of kindling he'd created, enough space between the sticks so the air could move around, he struck a match and watched the kindling flare. When the sticks had a hearty start, he added a thick oak log and extended his palms toward the heat. "There's frost on the rooftops this morning."

Mollie rubbed her hands together. "I noticed that on my walk to school. Winter's first calling card." She crossed the room to close the door that Sam had left open, to keep the warming air from escaping. Squatting by the woodstove, he watched her go, scanning her appearance, appreciating all the details of womanhood. The ringlets along the back of her neck that escaped her prayer cap, the curve of her spine, the shapely calves beneath her dress. He wondered what it would be like to hold her in his arms, to feel her soft curves against his body, to . . . *Whoa. Don't look at Mollie's curves. Don't look at her calves. If you have to look, look at her face. Not her lips. Just eyes.* "Anything else I can do for you before I go?"

She pivoted, turned, and walked back to the woodstove, wrapping her sweater across her middle, before she crossed her arms. "There's one thing. Sam, I want to apologize again for the girls' impulsive behavior. Stealing your horse and buggy."

He rose to his full height, dusting his hands on his thighs. *Land sakes, she's so pretty.* He towered over her, openly regarding her from such a close proximity. He had never noticed the sprinkling of freckles over her nose. She had a pair of the nicest lips he'd ever seen, full and rosy. Soft. He noticed a small thin scar line along her neck, and wondered what had caused it. A few seconds passed before he was smitten by self-consciousness and he glanced away. "You don't need to do any apologizing."

"Oh, but I do. I do! Those girls, they're my responsibility."

"Mollie, why have you taken this on?"

She snapped her head up so fast that her capstrings bounced. "What do you mean?"

"Why did you have to get involved? Luke could've found another family to take those two girls. He still can. You don't have to do this."

Mollie dropped her chin, as if she was trying to gather her thoughts. After a long pause, she lifted her head to look up at him. "Remember the chapter of the Bible that Luke read in church last Sunday?"

No, Sam didn't. He had found a perfect seat on the bench to watch Mollie across the room, without anyone observing him. He spent the better part of church noticing how earnestly she sang the hymns, and how her eyebrows furrowed together as she listened to the sermons. He'd never known anyone who took church as seriously as Mollie. She even liked to talk over the sermons on Sunday afternoons. Who did that? On any given Sunday afternoon that followed a church morning, his friends mostly talked about girls and horses and farming and weather. In that order.

Her enthusiasm shamed him a little. Sam considered time spent in church to be part of his duty. When it was over, he felt only relief, like he could check it off the list for two weeks. Like it drained him.

Mollie mentioned once to him that she went to church to be filled up. She said that she could tell in her spirit when the two weeks had elapsed because she was so parched for worship.

Parched for worship. Thirsty for worship. What did that even mean?

He realized she was waiting for him to respond about whether he had listened to Luke's reading of the Scripture. Hmm. Part of a deacon's role was to read the Bible aloud during church. It was his brother's first time to read, and Sam hadn't even bothered to pay any attention. How should he answer that so he didn't seem like the selfish fool he was? "Which part of the reading? The first part or the last part?"

"Oh, that's such a good point. You have such a way of clarifying things, Sam. Your mind, it's just a fine mind. Orderly."

His mind? Orderly? Fine? He felt his cheeks grow warm again. He wasn't just a selfish fool, he was a prideful fool. "Mollie, I . . ."

She looked at him with that open, honest, wide-eyed look of hers. "I know, I know. It was a wonderful church service, start to finish."

He took off his hat and raked a hand through his hair. "Mollie, what I mean to say is . . . what was it in Luke's reading that moved you so deeply?"

"Oh! It was about King David wanting to bring the ark back to Israel. First Chronicles 12:32, I think it was. There was one little verse, about a man whose family knew what Israel should do. One tiny little verse. I can't stop thinking about it. Wouldn't it be wonderful to be remembered like that? Mollie Graber knew what should be done to please the Lord." She clasped her cheeks with her hands. "Oh Sam, does that sound boastful? I don't mean it in a prideful way."

He didn't doubt that. Mollie Graber didn't have a proud bone in her body. He shrugged, while humor lit his face. "To be remembered? Why do you sound like you're a little old lady?" He was teasing, but she was all business.

"You must know what I mean. You do it with Galen's horses. You know what needs to be done to train a buggy horse so it's a dependable animal for a family. Imagine how others talk about you. 'Sam Schrock knew what to do to please the Lord.'"

"You think my horse training pleases the Lord?"

"Oh yes. Oh my goodness, yes. Think of the care you take with those horses, to make sure they keep each family safe. Don't you just sense God's pleasure when an animal is ready to sell? When off it goes to another family and you know they're in good hands?"

He'd never thought of his work other than it was work. Hard work, that required a disciplined, steadfast effort. Training an animal like a horse, it took enormous patience. They were high-strung, skittish animals. Only two years old, straight off the racetracks, where their first inclination was to bolt. That was what they'd been trained to do. It took time to condition a horse to new responses. Unlearning what they'd learned from the racetrack.

He felt a great responsibility to train a buggy horse well, mainly because that was how Galen had taught him. Sam was all about responsibility. But he'd never considered work from a spiritual perspective. He felt protective over the horses, cared for them like Galen had taught him. But to think he was pleasing the Lord with that hard work? It gave him an odd thought that he would need time to ponder: a sacred purpose to his day.

But to share all that with Mollie, that would be too hard. He'd stumble on the words, make a mess of them. And what would she think, if she got a glimpse of how shallow a fellow he really was? "Speaking of horses, I thought of a way that those two foster girls could make amends for taking off with my best horse."

Her eyebrows lifted in interest. "Go on. I'm all ears." She squinted. "By the way, what's the name of that best horse? I've only heard you call her a saucy mare."

"I don't name the horses."

"Really? Why not?"

Why not? Because he didn't want to get attached to them. He guarded his heart carefully after Luke had taken his most favorite horse of all time on a joyride and ended up injuring him. That beautiful creature had to be put down. Luke went off to rehab. Sam was brokenhearted. He loved that horse. He loved his brother. Losing both at once was too much. Just too much. He never wanted to feel that kind of loss again—sorrow and shame all mixed together. He'd never named another horse since. To him they were known by their coat color or markings: the sorrel with the blaze down its nose, the chestnut mare with a black mane, the gray with three white socks. Or this one . . . the saucy mare. Saucy because she had a mind of her own, something he admired in a horse. But to Mollie, he only said, "Best to let the new owners choose the name. Just seems like the right thing to do."

"I see," she said, nodding her head as if she understood his reasoning, though there was no way she could. "So what's the plan for my foster daughters to make it up to you?"

Her daughters. They weren't her daughters. They were somebody else's. Somebody who wasn't putting the time in to raise them. "I thought that they could clean out stalls for me on Saturday. As penance."

"Oh, Sam, you are a wonder. To think you'd bring them onto your property and teach them about caring for horses." She clasped her hands over her heart. "It's just the thing they need."

Exactly. Shovel manure.

"Empathy."

"Huh?"

"It's just the way to teach them empathy. Brilliant."

"Empathy?"

"Caring for an animal is such a wonderful way to teach empathy."

Say what? All he was thinking to do was to make those girls do a little hard, stinking labor.

"I just . . . Sam, I just don't know how to thank you. Extraordinary. That's what you are."

Extraordinary? *Me?*

The door opened and in burst Rudy Miller on a gust of cool air. He stopped short when he saw Sam and wiggled his eyebrows, grinning like a fool, as if he'd just interrupted something private. Sam scowled at him and tipped his hat at Mollie. "I'll be off then."

"Thank you again, Sam."

As he brushed past Rudy, the boy made kissing sounds and Sam was tempted to smack him. Obnoxious, that boy. No wonder Luke liked him so much. He was a Luke-in-the-making.

As Sam headed down the road toward his barn, he should've been thinking of a full day of tasks that lay ahead of him: he'd bought three new horses at auction yesterday and they were going to be delivered soon. Those days always brought new challenges, because the new horses were particularly skittish and somehow set off a chain of restlessness in the stable.

His mind should have been sorting out how he planned to manage those three horses today, and which stalls would suit them best, which equine neighbor would calm them down. But as he turned into his driveway, all he could think was, *She thinks I'm extraordinary.*

Eleven

Luke had spent the last two hours hammering stakes in the ground to mark the perimeters for Izzy's new kitchen. Once he had it all staked out, he could start digging the cellar. Then came the foundation, framing, and roofing. He wanted to get the addition watertight before winter hit. He paused for a moment, gazing at the trees that dotted the main house at Windmill Farm. Nearly leafless. When had that happened? He blinked, and autumn was nearly over. It was his favorite season too. The orchards were quieting down after a busy growing season, but not yet ready for the labor-intensive work of pruning. They'd usually get a few weeks of Indian summer, which was the best part of fall. Summer's parting gift. Last October, he and Izzy had been newly married, and they spent lazy Sunday afternoons at Blue Lake Pond, picnicking in the autumn sunshine.

That was before deacon duty landed on his shoulders, flattening him. He was hardly aware of what day it was, he was that busy. Deacon duty was all consuming, and on top of everything else he had to do too.

But he wasn't alone in this. David, Gideon, Peter. They all

carried the same heavy load. He'd never appreciated how hard church ministers worked. A man just didn't fully understand most things until he'd experienced it for himself. Funny, that.

He saw a horse and buggy drive along the road that bordered Izzy's sheep pen and squinted to see who it belonged to. The horse turned right into Windmill Farm's driveway and he didn't even need to wonder who was coming. He knew. David had come to collect him for another deacon task. He tossed down the mallet and stake and brushed his hands on his thighs. So much for finishing up the staking of Izzy's kitchen today. He walked over to meet David as the buggy pulled to a stop. He leaned against the buggy's open window. "Something going on?"

David gave him a nod. "Remember the couple who just moved here? They wanted to use the computer?"

"You asked them to hold off for a year. To allow time to consider the ramifications of allowing computers for businesses."

"The man called this morning to say they couldn't keep their business going without the computer. He's asked us to reconsider. Or . . ."

Luke looked straight at David. "Or?"

"He said they'll leave our church. Find one that will allow it."

This was the kind of thing that worried Luke. If they didn't keep up with change, families would leave. "So what do you think? Will you bend on this? Let him use the computer?"

"That's what you'd like me to do?"

"Seems to me that the man has a reasonable request. After all, he's trying to feed his family."

David's eyes were steadfast. "*Is* that the point, Luke? Or is he trying to shape the church to suit him?" The horse shifted his weight and the buggy shifted with him. "It always comes down to the heart. Where is a man's heart in all this? That's what we're going to find out this morning."

Oh boy. Luke hadn't even considered the topic from that angle. Now that he did, he could see David's concern. The way the man had responded to his new bishop, almost belligerently, when he'd been asked to hold off using the computer for a year. And now . . . threatening to leave if he didn't get his way, those were red flags. Luke had completely missed them. A month of deaconing, and he still wasn't thinking ahead. Each day felt like it was his first. "Let me go clean up. I'll be out in a few minutes."

As he walked into the fix-it shop, Luke whispered a prayer of thanks that David continued to accompany him on these deacon errands. He hoped he'd never stop.

Izzy carried a lamb in her arms as she walked toward the corral gate. She called to the other sheep and they followed behind her, nose to tail, nose to tail. She saw the bishop standing at the gate and set the lamb down to wave at him.

"I never tire of that sight."

She looked over her shoulder at her woollies, making their way toward her. She felt the same way. "Sheep are such beautiful animals."

"Actually, I meant of sheep following their shepherd. Jesus picked up the same imagery in John 10. 'I am the good shepherd. They know my voice.'"

"I've been reading that sheep psalm a lot lately." She stole a look at David and saw a quizzical smile spread across his face.

"The sheep psalm?"

"The one about God being a shepherd. Psalm 23." She

felt a little pleased with herself for knowing the reference, being a deacon's wife and all.

David seemed pleased too. "It's a wonderful psalm, one of the most beloved in the Bible. There are other verses in Scripture that refer to people as sheep and God as our shepherd. Over two hundred, I believe."

Izzy's jaw dropped. "Two hundred?"

"Not all good comparisons, like in Psalm 23." He grinned. "But one of my favorites is from Isaiah."

"Isaiah?" The only Isaiah she knew was a one-eyed blacksmith in nearby Gap.

She must have had a shocked look on her face, because David quickly supplied a meaning. "Isaiah was an Old Testament prophet, a contemporary of Jeremiah, the weeping prophet. 'He shall feed his flock like a shepherd: he shall gather the lambs with his arm and carry them in his bosom, and shall gently lead those that are with young.'"

"Oh my soul." Those words escaped from Izzy's lips before she could stop them. To think of God caring so tenderly for his woollies, for the ewes that would be bearing spring lambs. The very thought of it overwhelmed her. She felt a rush of love for this God, who'd always seemed so distant, so aloof, so unpredictable. Like her mother.

"That's from Isaiah 40:11."

She glanced at him. "I've been reading from an English Bible." Adding quickly, "The King James version." David nodded and she felt relieved. Relieved that he knew, relieved that he didn't seem to mind.

David was watching her. "God made all languages, Izzy, not just German. English is your first language. You've done a fine job learning to speak Penn Dutch. Reading and understanding high German might take a long, long time." He raised a foot to the bottom fence rail. "You know, Psalm 23 was the first Scripture I ever memorized. My father taught me a few tricks." He held up his hand and splayed his fingers. "The. Lord. Is. My. Shepherd." As he spoke each word, he used his other hand to point to his fingers. "The. Lord. Is. My. Shepherd." He smiled, shaking his head. "I haven't thought of that in years and years."

"Why would you memorize it?"

David looked past Izzy to the sheep. They'd gone back to grazing around the pasture. "When you commit a verse to memory, it's like the sheep and their grass. They chew and chew and chew on the grass until it's ground down to a pulp, until it can be swallowed and becomes part of them. That's what happens with God's Word."

"Ruminates."

"Pardon me?"

"It's called ruminating. When a sheep chews its cud. That's what Amos used to call it."

"Ruminating. That's exactly the right word for it." A light shone in David's eyes. "Ruminating on God's Word is like nourishment. It's food for our soul." He pointed to his forehead. "And then it's with you whenever you need it." He folded his arms against his chest. "Izzy, you've given me an idea. Maybe our entire church should be encouraged to memorize Psalm 23 this autumn. Prepare their hearts for the advent season."

Oh no. She'd never been any good at memorizing. A door slammed. Izzy looked up to see Luke walk down from the fix-it shop.

David lifted his hand in a wave. "I dropped by to pick up Luke."

"Deacon business." She knew not to ask anything more.

Luke had made it clear that deacon business was between the bishop and the deacon. She felt annoyed with him when he told her that, as if she were a blabbermouth who couldn't be trusted. As if she asked many questions, anyway! She hardly ever asked questions of anyone. It was something she'd learned through her years in the foster care system. She had discovered that if she didn't show much interest in others, then they would respond in kind. But she actually was interested in what Luke was doing as a deacon, even what he was learning, but he acted like he was guarding state secrets. Often, he didn't even tell her where he was, or who he'd been visiting with David. This whole deacon business was making her feel very distant from her husband, and that was not a good thing. Expressing love, being intimate, it was difficult for her. But she didn't say any of that to David, of course. "He's trying hard to learn deaconing."

He smiled at her. "I see that, Izzy. He's taking this role very seriously. He's making a difference." He took his foot off the fence rail and pivoted, then turned back. "If you'd like me to, I'll write down some other references in Scripture about sheep and have Luke give them to you."

"I'd like that." Very much. Very, very much. That King James Bible, it was not an easy read. All she wanted out of it were the parts about sheep.

He nodded to her and walked off to meet Luke at the buggy. It felt good to hear David's kind words about her husband. Complimentary words about Luke were not commonly spoken.

She wondered who had cast the lone vote to David that drew Luke into the lot. It wasn't her. It never occurred to her that he might be a leader, and she suddenly felt a tinge of guilt. A wife, of all people, should believe in her husband. All she felt was a growing resentment for the time deaconing took from them. From her. From their baby project. Correction. Her baby project.

I can be so selfish. She knew it was wrong of her to want Luke all to herself. She knew it, but she just couldn't stop the feelings from coming.

⌒

Early Saturday morning, Sam kept an eye out for Mollie to arrive with those two girls. He was in the barn when he heard her voice, and ran his hands through his hair to give it a quick comb, then tucked in his shirt. He grabbed his hat and put it back on his head, feeling a little embarrassed. Since when did he care how he looked?

Mollie was outside, waiting for him. He stopped short when he saw her. The sun had just cleared the roof of the barn and was shining down on her, like a beam of light on an angel. That's what she looked like. An angel. Her curly hair framed her like a halo. She had a gentle beauty, almost fragile, and he was struck with the desire to protect her.

"Sam! Is something wrong? I got the right time, didn't I?"

That was the farthest thought from his mind. He ducked his chin. "Yes, sure. I was, uh, just finishing something up." He glanced at the girls. "Follow me."

He took them to an empty stall, handed them each a hayfork, and pointed to the wheelbarrow. "When it's full, give me a shout. I'll empty it for you."

"Full of what?" asked Alicia, the one who was actually taller and bigger.

"Very funny," Sam said.

Tina nudged Alicia with her elbow and giggled. "What do you think?"

Alicia shrugged. "I dunno."

Tina looked around. "Hey, there's no horses in here. Where'd they go?"

Mollie stepped right in. "Girls, we talked about this. Sam has some work for you to do to make up for taking off with his horse and buggy."

"Shovel this?" Alicia said. "You've got to be kidding! You said we were going to ride horses."

"Oh Mollie, you didn't," Sam said, giving her a horrified glance.

Her eyes were wide with shock. "No, I did not!"

"You two are not to go near my Thoroughbreds." He'd already taken the horses out to the pasture for the day, so the barn was empty. He wasn't stupid. "Let's get to work. I left some gloves for you girls over on that stack of straw."

As the girls tried on the gloves, Sam walked Mollie to the barn door. "Those two . . . I don't trust them." *And you shouldn't either, Mollie.*

"They're young, Sam."

Maybe in age, but not in the ways of the world. "Mollie, I wonder sometimes . . ."

"You wonder what?"

"I wonder if you understood the risks for yourself, bringing them into your house like you did."

She exhaled a laugh, flat and aching. "It's a little late for that now."

"Come and get them before lunch."

She looked back at the two girls, who were whispering together. "Maybe I should stay."

"It'll be good for them, Mollie. Hard work is good for the soul."

"I just . . . am concerned they might do something . . ."

With an amused smile, Sam gently pushed her over the threshold. "Go. I can tell you need a break. You look a little peaked. Just don't forget to come back for them. Around noon."

Hesitating, Mollie walked backward, as if she was hoping Sam might call her back.

"Go!" he said, laughing. He waved and watched until she was out of sight.

"Hey, cowboy. You sweet on her?"

He whipped around to find the two girls staring up at him. He cleared his throat. "Let's get to work."

"Can you show us how? We've never done this before."

How hard was it to scoop manure? Sam showed them how to fill the pitchfork and dump it in the wheelbarrow, then handed the pitchfork to one of the girls to have them try a few scoops before he left. They seemed shockingly inept. "Hold it with both hands. Grip it tight. No, like this." He took the pitchfork and scooped a few more piles. "There, you see? Easy." He straightened up.

No answer. He turned around. The girls were gone.

As much as Mollie appreciated Sam's willingness to hold the girls accountable for their behavior, she had a funny feeling as she left his barn. He was a horse trainer, unaccustomed to being around young girls. Especially girls who had a certain streak of . . . how would one describe it? Independence.

Sam had told her that she hadn't understood what the risks were in taking on these girls. She thought she knew, though she hadn't. She'd had no idea. Roberta Watts had called to check in the other day, and Mollie asked her about the girls' parents. "So they're Hollywood actors?" It seemed astonishing to Mollie that parents could leave their children in foster care just because their jobs required too much from them. The Plain People loved children dearly. She couldn't think of a single family that would make a decision like that.

"Is that what they told you?" Roberta Watts said. "I told you to start slow. To let those girls prove themselves. That's a lie, if I ever heard one."

What? They'd lied to Mollie again? Even after she talked to them about lying, about how wrong it was, how it displeased the Lord. "Then, what did happen to them?"

"When they were just little toddlers, their parents left them at a fire station during the night and took off. Firemen found them shivering on the stoop, holding dirty old rag dolls. They've been in foster care ever since. One home after another."

Mollie's heart dropped to her stomach. No wonder the girls had lied about their background. Such a terrible story. Sad.

"Honey, is the honeymoon period wearing out?"

"Hold on. This is the honeymoon period?" What did that bode for the future?

"Yup. Usually lasts a week or two. Usually, about then, the real children show up. I was hoping we'd get the group home fixed before it ended."

Mollie squeezed her eyes shut. *Oh no. Oh dear.*

"Honey, you sound tired."

Mollie cleared her throat. "I'm fine. Really. All is well." No, it wasn't. Each day brought new struggles with Tina and Alicia. They challenged her on every single thing, even small requests, like "Please pick up your clothes." Worse still, they often ignored her. Just last night, they sat at her dinner

table and told jokes that were so rude and off-color that
Mollie, embarrassed, finally left the room. They laughed and
laughed at that—enjoying the shock effect they had on her.
And their language. It could peel the paint right off the wall.

Sam was right. She had no idea what she had signed up
for. But she was right in telling him it was too late now. It
was. She was committed. Mollie Graber was no quitter. She
would trust the Lord to see her through this.

It was disappointing, though. She had hoped to enjoy her
foster daughters, not just tolerate them. Not just tick off
the days until the group home was repaired. She went out
of her way yesterday to scooter past it, just to see if it was
getting close to completion. Not a chance. She didn't even
see construction workers on the site.

After leaving Sam's barn this morning, she went to the
schoolhouse for a few hours, partly to stick close by. She tried
to grade papers but was restless, easily distracted. She kept
opening the front door to see if she could see anything. Like
. . . curls of smoke in the air, in case the girls set the barn on
fire. She tried to wait until noon, but she just couldn't wait
that long. Around eleven, she decided to head over to check
on the girls. A black cat met her in the barnyard, tail stiff
as a poker, and she paused to scratch its ears. She found the
girls in the barn in a different stall, shoveling away.

Sam stood in front of the stall door like a soldier standing
guard, arms crossed against his chest. His hat brim hid his eyes,
and his mouth was set hard. "Mollie, you're early. They still
have a few more stalls to clean. More than a few, to be honest."

She blew out a startled breath. She wasn't sure what to
expect, but it wasn't this. What was going on?

They glowered at him and threw down their pitchforks.

"Mollie! What kind of crazy person did you leave us with? Take us home. He's psycho!"

The brackets around Sam's mouth deepened ever so slightly, and the wrinkles near his eyes crinkled at the corners. He scraped a hand over his whisker-roughened jaw. "Pay them no mind. They're having fun." He closed the stall door and put a padlock on it, locking them in. "Three stalls down, girls. Seven to go. Let me know when you finish this one and I'll escort you to the next stall." He saw the look of horror on Mollie's face. Before she could say a word of objection, he took her elbow and steered her toward the back of the barn and into the tack room.

"Sam," she whispered, "you can't lock them in a horse stall!"

"Why not?"

"It doesn't seem right."

"It does if they vanish each time I turn my back on them."

"No! They didn't."

"Oh yes, they did. I found them in the haymow, trying to light cigarettes."

Mollie clenched her fists in frustration. It never dawned on her that the girls would skip out on their work. It should have, though. And smoking in a haymow! They had no common sense. None! *He's right. I'm too naïve.* She could see that Sam had little patience left for the girls. "I'm sorry for the distraction they've caused you this morning. You probably haven't been able to get any work done."

"Not much." He tipped his hat back. "Those two need a full-time minder."

So true. She let out a weary sigh. "Try to see things from their point of view. They haven't had the right kind of examples in their life."

"Well, they're getting one now in you."

"Me?" She felt her cheeks grow warm. She breathed out a long, slow sigh.

"You can't let them get away with things, Mollie. It's not good for them."

"Love can work miracles."

He considered her words a moment. "Sure, if it's coupled with discipline, and consequences, and good expectations."

"Sam—"

"Listen, Mollie. I didn't grow up with Luke Schrock as my brother without learning a few things about the way juvenile delinquents think."

"Juvenile delinquents? They're just young girls."

He let out a laugh. "They're strong girls who should be able to clean a horse stall in fifteen minutes. They've been working two hours on one stall." He set his hands on his hips. "I've been standing in front of the stall for the last hour, thinking about something. Compassion is a good quality to have, but not everyone has it. And if they don't, they can take advantage of those who do. I've seen it happen with my own mother. She's got a soft heart, like you do."

Mollie felt a little swirl of pleasure spiral through her: a soft heart.

He stared at her, his gaze open and unwavering. "You make it too easy for those two to take advantage of you. To hurt you."

Now she was the one struggling to fill the silence. This was the most personal conversation Sam had ever offered up, and in his message was a compliment for her. She thought so, anyway. He was looking so intently at her, just inches away, that she thought she might just melt. Up close like this, he was even more handsome than any man had a right to be. A cleft chin, those bright blue eyes drilling down on her with a thick fringe of lashes. Dark eyebrows, furrowed together in concern. He smelled of hay and coffee and the crisp morning air. Mollie felt the same feeling she'd get as a little girl when she'd hang upside down by her knees from a tree limb. Dizziness.

"MOUSE!"

High-pitched screams from the girls ricocheted through the barn rafters. Sam rolled his eyes and sighed. "I'll go handle the mouse. You get on home. Get some rest. You look worn out and I can sure see why."

Leaning against the doorjamb of the tack room, she watched him head down the aisle of the barn. That man . . . he was wonderful.

Halfway down the aisle, he turned in a half circle, still walking, and said, "I'll bring those two barbarians to your cottage in a few hours. After they're done."

Barbarians? Oh, that seemed too callous a word for Tina and Alicia. Two girls who had been dealt a difficult hand in life, whose basic needs had been met so inconsistently. Those girls, Mollie was convinced, longed for unconditional, unwavering love. Deep down, deep, deep, deep down, they had good hearts. She was banking on it.

One curse word after another shot out from the horse stall as Sam patiently, silently, unlocked the padlock. Mollie had never heard those particular words, but from the vehement sound of them, there was no doubt they were cussing words. Mortified, Mollie decided she would let Sam handle the situation in his quiet, firm way, and she hustled out the side door before the girls could find her.

TWELVE

Early Monday morning, Mollie walked to the school-house, morning frost crackling beneath her shoes, feeling pretty good about life. At the bottom of the school steps she stopped and took in a deep breath of crisp morning air, exhaling puffs of steam. Winter was just around the corner.

The girls had come home exhausted on Saturday afternoon and Mollie let them sleep late on Sunday morning. It was an off Sunday, so it turned out to be a nice, lazy day. In the afternoon, the girls took a long walk by themselves. Mollie had told them she trusted them to return in time for supper and they came through. A victory! Things were finally turning around. Love could make a difference. It could work miracles.

As she walked into the schoolhouse, she heard a strange scratching sound in the front of the room. She put her lunch and books on her desktop, hearing more odd scratching sounds. She tipped her head, listening carefully, and tracked the sound to her top desk drawer. Slowly, she pulled open the drawer. A dozen mice poured out of the drawer, climbed down to the floor, and darted around and around the schoolhouse.

Sam was filling the water trough in the pasture when he heard a bloodcurdling scream come out of the schoolhouse. He dropped the hose and bolted over the fence, crossed the road, and jumped up the steps of the schoolhouse.

Mollie stood on top of her desk, hands covering her face. "Mice! Everywhere!"

Oh wow. She wasn't kidding. Little gray mice scurried in a panic all around the schoolhouse. He found a big rock to keep the door wide open, grabbed a broom, and started shooing them out the door. It took a while to get them all outside. Mollie stayed on top of the school desk, pointing and screeching whenever another one scurried past, but it wasn't long before Sam was confident all mice had been evicted from the schoolhouse. Fairly confident.

He closed the door, set the broom to lean on the wall, and helped Mollie down. "I blame myself. I should have known those two would think up something awful like this."

"Oh Sam, we don't know that Tina and Alicia are behind this. Rudy Miller is always playing pranks."

He gave her a look. She sighed. She knew.

"I left a hose running. You going to be okay?"

She nodded. "Thank you for coming to my rescue. I hate mice. Spiders and mice, both."

A smile tugged at the corners of his mouth. "Don't ever tell those two girls that you're afraid of spiders. You'll find your bed full of them."

She shuddered at the thought, and then they both stood there as quiet spun out between them. Sam suddenly realized he hadn't released her hand after helping her down from the desk. He dropped her hand and grabbed his hat from her desk, all in one fell swoop, jammed it on his head, and headed toward the door.

While Izzy collected eggs in the henhouse, the chickens came out of their roosts, one by one, clucking in that deep throaty way. It was how they communicated that she was intruding in their chicken world and they were not happy about it. She liked hens. Not as much as sheep, but she did enjoy their personalities. Each one, so unique. She tried not to have favorites, though, or to name them, because then she couldn't bring herself to eat them for supper. Better not to know, that was her chicken dinner policy. She heard the screen door open and assumed it was Luke. But when she turned around, there was Fern's girl. She hadn't seen her since the afternoon when she got dizzy in the yarn shop.

"I'm feeling better." She shrugged, her hands jammed into her sweatpants' pockets.

Izzy handed her the basket of freshly laid eggs. "Does that happen to you very often? It came on kind of suddenly."

She studied a brown egg, still warm, in the basket. "Like I said, only when I don't get enough to eat."

That was hard to fathom, because this girl ate like a lumberjack. But Izzy didn't say that out loud. "Sometimes being hungry makes me feel that way too."

"Yeah?" Relieved, the girl's whole being lifted, like the sun came out from behind a cloud. In that instant, she seemed like a sweet young girl, not a sullen, silent reminder of herself.

Izzy felt a little guilty for having such unpleasant thoughts about the girl. "How old are you?"

"Fifteen." She looked up, pleased to be asked. "I guess you've been wondering about me."

Nope. Izzy gave the girl a vague smile and walked out of the henhouse. The girl trotted right on her heels.

"I have big plans. A lot of things are ahead of me."

"Is that right." Izzy didn't mean it as a question, but the girl took it as an invitation to talk.

"My dad always said I was pretty enough to be a model. Travel the world. Have a new car every year and a house in the Hamptons."

"Oh my. Those are big plans." It surprised her that this girl wanted to be a model, because she didn't seem at all interested in clothes or fashion or make-up. She didn't even comb her hair very often. Or wash it. Each day, she wore big baggy sweats and pulled her thick long dark hair into a severe ponytail.

"A man stopped me in a store one day and told me that I could be a plus-size supermodel. He gave me his card." She pulled a business card out of her sweatpants' pocket and handed it to Izzy. The edges were worn down, like the girl had handled it too much. "What do you think of that?"

Izzy read the card. "Modeling agent?"

"Yup. He said he could get me some good photographs for a . . . hmm . . . there's a word . . ."

"Portfolio."

"That's it! That's just the word he used. A portfolio. He said he'd take pictures of me in his studio for a portfolio and introduce me to all the right people."

"For a fee, I'll bet."

The girl's dark brows furrowed in a frown. She took the card out of Izzy's hand and jammed it back into her sweatpants pocket. "Everybody has to start somewhere."

Izzy really wasn't interested in hearing more. She knew where this was all headed. She took the basket of eggs from the girl, set it on the porch for Fern, and started toward the yarn shop.

The girl caught up and trailed behind Izzy. Too eager, too eager. This girl hadn't learned to mask her feelings well, not like she should. When the group home reopened, those girls would be returning to it. Izzy knew the drill. They shouldn't lose their guard, their street savvy, just because they'd experienced a little bit of time in an Amish home. Just because they got a taste of what they'd always longed for. For Izzy, those first couple of weeks at Windmill Farm were heaven on earth. Every morning, better than the last.

"I heard that you were once a foster kid."

Izzy stopped and pivoted. She met her eyes, puzzled. "Who told you that?"

"Roberta Watts. She said you ended up here after rehab and stayed. You drank the Amish Kool-Aid, she said." She flashed her a brief, nervous smile.

Izzy felt her cheeks grow warm. Roberta Watts should keep her opinions to herself, that's what. "I chose my life. This is the life I want."

Though the girl shot Izzy a questioning glance, the remark went unexplained. She crossed the yard, unlocked the door to the yarn shop, and went inside.

The girl followed close behind. "But didn't you ever think about being a supermodel?"

"No."

"You could have been, you know. You're tall enough. And pretty enough. Prettier than me." The girl's lightheartedness slipped away, replaced with a troubled look. "Do you think I'm pretty enough?"

Izzy studied her face, as if she was taking this conversation seriously, though she wasn't. Greasy hair escaped the ponytail and hung along the sides of her face. She smelled like she hadn't showered in days. She had broad cheekbones, a high forehead, a wide mouth with deep dimples in her cheeks when she smiled. "Yes. Definitely."

"So why didn't you try to be a supermodel?"

"I don't want people to look at me."

"No kidding? I sure do."

"So that's why you want to be a model?" Izzy wasn't interested but felt she should try to pretend, just to be polite.

"A supermodel," the girl corrected. "Plus-size. Not just any old catalog model. I want everyone to stop and look at me and say to themselves, 'Why, look at her! That's Cassidy.' That's how they'll know me. Just one name, like Bono or KimKardashian."

Izzy nearly laughed out loud, but clamped down on her lips to stifle it.

"I want everyone in the entire world to recognize my face, just like they know Tyra Banks's face. I have Tyra's fivehead."

"Five head? Don't you mean forehead?"

The girl laid her hand flat across her forehead. "Not a 'four-head.' A 'five-head.' Get it?"

"So do you want to be famous or do you want to be a model?"

"Both. Being a model will make me famous. It's the road God put me on, seeing as how he made me tall as a giraffe and pretty as can be. That's what my dad used to call me. Tall as a giraffe and pretty as can be. The world's next supermodel. Plus-size." A faraway look came into her eyes. "My dad has a way about him. We have lots of dreams."

"So he's gone."

"Yup. In jail." She shrugged, like it was no big deal. "The judge said he's gonna be there for a long time. That's how I ended up in the group home. I used to live with my dad."

Izzy didn't even have to ask if there was a mother in the picture. "So you must be a ward of the state."

"Nah, my mom's in jail too. Somewhere in upstate New York. She promised she'd come for me soon." She lifted her shoulders. "One day, when I'm a plus-size supermodel, my dad will sure be happy. We'll be rich, and he won't have to deal drugs anymore, you know, to make ends meet. No more jail."

Izzy nodded solemnly, noting the absence of self-pity in the girl's voice.

"Girls like us, like you and me, we don't have many options. I've been taller than all the boys in school for as long as I can remember. We gotta make do with what we got. Modeling is the only way to have the life I dream about."

"It's one way," Izzy said. "But it's not the only way." *Look at me*, she thought, but didn't say aloud because she didn't want this girl to know anything about her. But if she did, she would have said, *Just look at me. I'm living the life I've always dreamed of having. Pretty much.* "It's good to have dreams, Cassidy." The words felt strange on Izzy's lips. Comfort was foreign to her.

Cassidy beamed. "You said my name. It's the first time you said my name."

"I've said your name before. Plenty of times." Hadn't she? She must have. Of course she had. "Your dreams may change as you get older, but don't let anyone steal them from you. They're yours."

"I won't," Cassidy said, a distant look in her eyes, as though she was processing Izzy's words. "I can't let anything stop me from becoming a supermodel. Plus-size." She crossed over to the window to gaze at the sheep in the pen.

Izzy stared at Cassidy's reflection in the window for a long moment. The deep hunger in her eyes, the utter vulnerability she revealed, made something sink inside Izzy.

⌒

Mollie couldn't sleep. She gave up around three o'clock in the morning, tiptoed past the girls' bedroom—stopping at the doorjamb to make sure they were indeed there. Satisfied when she heard their snoring, she went to the little kitchen table and lit the oil lantern. It hissed and spit, but soon its buttery glow spread out over her open Bible. She wrapped a blanket over her lap and searched through her favorite Scriptures, hoping they would give her guidance and reassurance.

This experience of fostering was nothing like she had thought it would be. Last year, when everything changed for her, she promised the Lord that she would live brave, take risks, offer all she had for God's purposes.

Had she done something wrong? Had she misunderstood the gift of extended time God had given to her?

Because something wasn't working. This was too hard. Too, too hard. She couldn't get a good night's sleep because she feared what those girls might be up to. She couldn't relax during the day because she half expected the sheriff to arrive with news of some terrible mischief they'd done. She dreaded checking phone messages in the shanty, bracing herself for the school attendance office to tell her the girls had cut school again. She was exhausted, all the time.

It shouldn't be this hard. It didn't seem to be hard for Fern or Sadie or Alice or Mattie or Carrie or Birdy or Ruthie or the old Sisters. *It must be me,* Mollie thought. *I'm a terrible, terrible foster mother.*

Her eyes drooped and she leaned forward over her Bible, resting her head on her arms. Maybe she should give up. Tell Roberta that the girls needed to live elsewhere. The last thought that drifted through her mind was a prayer. One word. *Help.*

Cassidy stopped waiting for invitations from Izzy, probably because they didn't come. Instead, she just followed her everywhere, sunup to sundown, and talked nonstop. If it weren't for school, Izzy would never have a minute to herself. It drove her crazy at first, and she complained about the girl's shadowing quite vehemently to Luke. He listened patiently, and then his response silenced her. "Since when is it such a hardship to have a full-time admirer in your midst?"

Luke's blunt perspective changed the story for Izzy. She started to notice how Cassidy watched her with the sheep and then copied her ways with them. Gentle ways. As the girl proved herself with the sheep, Izzy found herself relaxing more around her. It was nice to have someone care for the woollies the way she cared for them, as if they were small children. Luke would help them with her when she needed help—shearing them in the spring, staying up nights with her during lambing season—but he didn't love them. Not like she loved them.

Sharing the yarn shop took more patience and tolerance for Izzy, especially when she walked in one day to find Cassidy at the spinning wheel. *My spinning wheel! The one Luke bought me as a wedding gift. No one but no one touches my spinning wheel.*

She was *this* close to snapping at Cassidy, but then she saw the look of complete joy on the girl's face as she held up a string of lumpy yarn. "I did it! I spun my first yarn out of wool! I've been watching you carefully and just had to try it. It doesn't look like yours, I know, but it does look a little like yarn, don't you think?"

Cassidy seemed so thoroughly pleased with herself that Izzy couldn't help but smile in return. "That's exactly how my first yarn turned out."

"Really? No kidding?" She ran her finger down the strand. "Do you think I'll ever be as good as you?"

Izzy shrugged. "Takes a lot of practice."

"I'll work hard. I'll keep at it. I want to try to get good at it. As good as you."

Annoyed, Izzy turned away. Who said Cassidy could keep working on the wheel? Who'd given her permission to try in the first place? To find the spare key at Fern's and enter the shop when it was locked up? No one.

There weren't many things that Izzy could call her own, but this yarn shop and that spinning wheel, they were hers. They gave her a sense of grounding, of belonging, and it was hard to share that feeling because it met a deep need. Not a want.

This yarn shop meant more to her than anyone could possibly understand. It filled a hole in her life, almost like there'd been dropped stitches in a sweater or blanket and someone—Fern and Amos and David, then Luke—took the time to unravel the yarn and go back to fix the dropped stitches. Her life was full of dropped stitches.

Correction. Had been full of dropped stitches. She was healing. Not fully healed, but on her way. What would her life have been like without Fern and Amos, David and Luke? She shuddered to think of it. They provided her stitches in time. That's how she came up with the name of her yarn store. Stitches in Time.

Almost as if Fern was right next to her, listening in to her thoughts, she could imagine what she would say to Izzy. "And who is going to fix the dropped stitches in Cassidy's life? If we don't help, then who?"

Izzy took a deep breath and spun around. "I'll get some more wool so you can try again. And this time, keep your hand clasped around the wool at a steady pressure. You'll end up with a more consistent yarn. It takes practice, but I'm sure you'll catch on."

"Really?" Excitement splashed across Cassidy's face. "Just watch, Izzy. I'll practice every single day. I'll make you proud of me. Watch and see. See if I don't make you proud."

Oh my soul. What kind of invitation does she think I gave her? It's just a piece of yarn, she wanted to tell Cassidy. Just a bit of fluff and wool.

But she knew it was more than that. She knew.

THIRTEEN

Izzy awakened to a pink sunrise creeping over the sill. A pink morning meant rain was coming. She peeked across her pillow at the alarm clock. Nearly seven o'clock. She put a hand on Luke's side of the bed. It was cold, untouched. After Sunday supper, he'd checked messages, listened to a call for some kind of deacon duty, and dashed off in the buggy.

Barefoot, she crept to the window. No sign of Luke's buggy. He hadn't been home all night. She closed her eyes, feeling an all-too-familiar sweep of sadness. Working on the baby project was becoming increasingly difficult. Luke was never home to work on the baby project.

He'd been a deacon for over a month and a half now. Izzy hardly saw him except at mealtimes, when he gulped down a meal and hurried back out to the fix-it shop or up to the orchards. He worked. And worked and worked. Sunup to sunrise, he never stopped. More evenings than not, he was called out for deacon business, and she'd be sound asleep by the time he returned.

Two nights ago was their fourteen-month anniversary, their monthiversary, a celebration Luke had started right from their first month of marriage. She had cooked his favorite meal, had it ready and waiting for him. But he didn't get home until it was cold because of some deacon work, and when he did, he didn't even remember it was their special night. He just wolfed down his supper, then complained about the work that was piling up for him in the fix-it shop.

When Izzy felt hurt or disappointed, rather than talk about it or address her feelings like a normal person, she went silent. She knew that about herself, didn't like it, but she couldn't seem to change once her upset settled in for a stay.

By the time Luke realized Izzy wasn't part of the conversation, she had flown past disappointment and was silently seething. Throughout the evening, he'd asked her if everything was all right or if he'd done something to upset her. She just shook her head. She felt if he loved her, he would've remembered. At bedtime, he tried once again to get her talking to him but finally gave up, too exhausted to keep trying. "Sometimes I think you'd just rather talk to your sheep than to me."

That remark just made her all the more mad. Hadn't she made his favorite dinner so they could enjoy the evening together? Hadn't she had a hope that the evening would end differently?

But did she tell him that the reason she was angry was because he'd forgotten their monthiversary? That ever since he became a deacon, she felt as if she was no longer a priority to him? Everybody else came first, his own wife came last. He was hardly home, and when he was home, he was exhausted. Did she tell him all those bottled-up feelings she'd been stuffing down?

No. She knew she should have, but she just couldn't seem

to put it into words. If a single word slipped out, she feared they would all burst out, all the ugliness inside her, exploding like a shaken-up bottle of soda pop. And then she would be acting just like Grace, her mother. Her missing mother. Instead, Izzy slept fitfully, got up extra early and set cold dry cereal out for Luke, and left their little broken-down house to go to the yarn shop.

Her refuge.

⌇

Luke had no idea what he'd done to make Izzy so mad at him. He'd asked her directly and she said if he loved her like he said he did, then he shouldn't have to ask. He tried to puzzle that out but couldn't make heads or tails of it. Lately, it seemed she was mad at him more often than she wasn't.

He could barely keep his eyes open throughout the day and went to bed early. He hoped he wouldn't be getting called out tonight, not like last night. He had stopped by the phone shanty to pick up messages when the phone rang. Martha Glick, the wife of Freeman Glick, was calling him for help. Him. Wonders never cease: she was calling Luke Schrock for help. And she was frantic too, yet insistent that he come alone. "Don't bring David or the other ministers. Please, Luke, I'm begging you. And hurry, please."

Luke dropped everything and took off, not even taking the time to tell Izzy he was heading out. He was astounded by what he encountered when he arrived at the Glicks' Big House. Freeman, one of the judgiest men in church, was riproaring drunk. He even took some swings at Luke when he tried to hold him back from tossing a chair out the window. Luke stayed there all night, until Freeman's drunken stupor wore off and he started crying like a baby, begging him not to tell David or anyone else, promising him it would never happen again.

Against Luke's better judgment, he agreed to keep Freeman's secret.

Those secrets, they were the worst part of deaconing for Luke. Martha, Freeman's wife, was just as adamant that Luke keep all this to himself. She was the opposite of Freeman in every way—meek to the point of mousy, with a high-pitched squeaky voice. He'd asked her if this had gone on before with Freeman. She said yes, that it started after the Quieting. That was years ago! He asked why she hadn't spoken up sooner or told others—because he was already learning that it was nearly always the women who instigated movement to improve things in the home, rarely the men—and she said, blinking her eyes rapidly the way she did, "But I don't want anyone to think poorly of him."

So she kept Freeman's reputation safely intact. And Freeman kept right on drinking.

Luke knew he should be trying to sleep, but this troubling situation kept circling through his mind. Cold moonlight lit the room, and he could feel the night breeze coming through the thin walls. He shifted to his side, wondering what could be done about Freeman, trying not to wake Izzy. He thought she was sound asleep, but then he heard her sigh deeply. "You up?"

"Another month has gone by, Luke."

This time, Luke knew what that meant. No baby. So that's what the last few days' tension had been about. He swallowed down a sigh and rolled over on the bed to face his wife. She was on her back, staring up at the ceiling. This was the way Izzy would talk to him about matters of the heart—in the dark, eyes averted. The sight of her, especially like this, with the moonlight limning her profile, took his breath away. Her beauty was still startling to him, almost shocking. He remembered the first time he'd ever laid eyes on her. They were both at the Mountain Vista rehab facility—he was on the way in and she was on the way out. They were in a group therapy session, and he was dumbstruck by her good looks. She had no memory of him. In a strange way, he admired that indifference from her. Girls had always been easy for Luke. He knew that. He had taken advantage of his appeal to girls, plenty of times. But Izzy? He held no magic for her. She was a girl who was hard to get. Even now, even married, he had to work for her.

She shifted in the bed to glance over at him, wondering why he hadn't responded, if he'd heard her.

He searched for the right words. So often, these were the moments he would gum it up and say something that only made things worse. Platitudes were out, he'd learned that much. Quoting the Bible shut the conversation down. Last time he'd done that, she accused him of trying to be a deacon to her and not a husband.

Okay, back to David's advice. Do the opposite. Ask her a question. "Honey, how does that make you feel?"

Wrong question.

"How do you *think* it makes me feel?" she asked, a tiny bit snappish. She rolled over to face the wall, her back to him.

How did he think she felt? He tried to put himself in her shoes. It took a while. Finally, he said, "Anxious. Scared. Empty."

She didn't respond for a long time, and then he noticed

her shoulders were trembling. She was crying. He pulled her against him, wrapped her in his arms. "Tell me what you're thinking."

It took her a while to speak. "Sometimes, I wonder if God might be punishing me."

"Whatever for?"

"For the way I lived. The things I did."

"Do you really think a loving God holds a girl responsible for doing what she needed to do to survive? To eat, to be safe?"

She shrugged, but he could tell he was getting through to her. She rolled over on her back. "Don't you ever feel that way?"

"I used to. But I think it's because I had things mixed up. The more I learned about God, the more I realized my thinking had to be corrected. Kind of like the way Sam works with a new horse to unlearn what it had learned on the racetrack. Then it's ready to move forward."

She groaned and rolled away again, turning from him. "Please don't go all deacony on me."

"Hold on . . . I'm not trying to sound deacony. You asked me a question and I'm giving you my honest response, so listen a minute. I think it all boils down to how a person views God. For a long time, I think I saw him like my dad— loving one minute, cold or distant in the next. I considered God to be the same way. Yeah, sure, he loved me, but he didn't really like me. God isn't fickle. His love is constant. It doesn't change, not the way people change. God's very nature is good, truly good." He let that settle in. "Does that make any sense?"

"Maybe."

"Once I started seeing God as good—always good, un-changing, everlasting, part-of-his-very-character kind of good—then I stopped thinking he was looking for ways to whack me on the head with the Bible. You know what I mean. 'You're not good enough! *Whack whack whack.* Try harder! *Whack whack whack.* And don't forget when you blew it here. *Whack whack.* And then there was *that* time! *Whack whack whack.*'"

She giggled, and her shoulders softened, and then she turned to face him. "You're not such a bad deacon."

"Improving each and every day. Easier to do when you start in the basement." He leaned in to give her a light kiss on her lips. "I love you, Izzy."

"I love you too."

He kissed her then, and she kissed him back, and soon they'd forgotten all about deaconry and infertility worries. Luke did, anyway. It felt good to patch things up.

⁓

Shivering on this chilly morning, Izzy dressed quickly, grabbed a thick sweater, and hurried outside to check on her sheep. Her breath puffed as she walked from the fix-it shop to the pen, so she put her hands in the sweater pockets and felt the index card she'd tucked away. She pulled it out and read the psalm she'd written out to try and memorize.

The Lord is my shepherd. The Lord is my shepherd.

Izzy repeated that line to herself over and over, commit-ting it to memory the way David had suggested, by matching each word to a finger.

The Lord is my shepherd, I shall not want.
The Lord is my shepherd, I shall not want.

What did that even mean? She climbed through the fence and walked among her sheep, calling to them. Their heads popped up from grazing at the sound of her voice, and they slowly started moving toward her. Soon she would be encircled by them, barely able to move. Tenderly, she watched her woollies, and thought of the things they wanted: safety, security, sustenance. They were such skittish things, near-sighted, easily frightened, utterly defenseless, thoroughly vulnerable.

The Lord is my shepherd. The Lord is my shepherd.

She thought of how she shepherded her woollies. Fussing over them like babies, counting them twice a day to make sure none was missing. If one had wandered off, she would drop everything to rescue it and bring it back to the fold.

Two twin lambs closed in on Izzy's legs and lay down on her shoes. Their pink noses were cold on her ankles, but their wool was warm. She bent down to stroke their heads, speaking to them in a soft voice, the way she'd done since they were born, so they would bond with her and know they belonged to her. Her voice was the one she wanted them to listen to.

The Lord is my shepherd, I shall not want.

If a sheep had everything it needed from God, if it wanted for nothing, and if the Bible said that people were like sheep and God was like a good shepherd—then what did that mean to her? Right here, right now? She wanted a baby so desperately and had a terrible dread that she would not ever be able to have a child. Did it mean that her desire was not a need? Not as important as food and shelter?

Or did it mean that God knew what she needed and when she needed it? And if that was so, then Luke's thoughts about having a baby were far closer to this psalm than her own.

Luke was always telling her that God would bring them the right baby at the right time.

Izzy was so sure the time should be now, just the way her sheep had thoughts of their own. She'd had enough experience with sheep now to know their thoughts were wrong 99 percent of the time, way off the mark. They would drink bad water if they could, eat poisonous plants, wander off away from the flock, and put themselves right smack into danger. She knew what was best for her woollies; they sure didn't.

The Lord is my shepherd, I shall not want.

That one line filled her emptiness, settling her day's anxiety, in a way she'd never experienced. The bleakness was gone, and life seemed full of promise. At least for today.

As she headed back to the fix-it shop, she thought she'd have an omelet ready for Luke, his favorite, rather than just another bowl of cold cereal.

$\mathcal{F}$OURTEEN

Each day, Mollie looked expectantly for signs that Tina and Alicia were settling in, getting accustomed to a new routine, signs of growing attached to her. Answers to her fervent prayers that love could bring about miracles.

So far, nothing.

The girls seemed to go out of their way to aggravate her and make her feel as if she was the guest visiting in their home. Just yesterday, Mollie scootered home after school, hoping to get to the cottage before the girls did so she could welcome them with a snack. She opened the door to find wisps of cigarette smoke curling through the small cottage. Turned out the girls had cut school midday and spent the afternoon puffing away in Mollie's kitchen. When Mollie tried to explain how wrong it was on so many levels, they looked at her with blank expressions on their faces, as if they were stone deaf and couldn't hear a word she said. Nothing seemed to break through their impenetrable shells. And cigarette smoke, Mollie discovered, lingered and lingered—in her clothes, in her bed pillow, in the air. Disgusting.

But today's stunt pushed her right over the edge. Mollie had woken to an empty house. She'd overslept after staying up late the night before, grading papers—a task she had planned to do yesterday afternoon but had to spend a few hours airing out the house from cigarette smoke and cleaning up ashes.

Tina and Alicia had left to catch the school bus—at least Mollie hoped they had—and she was gathering what she needed for the day, rushing because she was running behind schedule. She remembered her pills and went to the cupboard to take them, only to find the small amber-colored container was empty. Had she finished the bottle yesterday and forgotten? She blew out a puff of air. She'd need to stop in at the pharmacy this afternoon and get a refill. She paused for a moment, rubbing her eyes with her hands, as a sweep of exhaustion went through her. This wasn't the kind of fatigue that a good night's sleep could take care of. It was a bone-deep weariness.

Please, God, please no. Not again.

She dropped her hands. No time to worry. She needed to get to school before the scholars arrived, to start the wood-stove and get the room warmed up. She grabbed her bonnet, tied the strings under her chin, took her sweater off the wall peg, and put it on. She scootered down the road, faster and faster. She was so late! She was never, ever late for school. As she rounded the last bend, she saw the schoolhouse and a puff of smoke coming out of the chimney. Dropping her scooter in the yard, she darted up the steps and into the schoolhouse. And there was Sam! He was bent down by the woodstove, stoking the fire with kindling. She could see he had scraped yesterday's ashes into a pail.

"Oh Sam, thank you for starting the fire." The chill was already off the room.

He closed the door to the woodstove and straightened to his full height. "I was filling the water trough and noticed you hadn't come. Is everything okay?" He looked at her with concerned eyes.

Could he tell? "It's fine. Everything's fine. Just a busier than usual morning." That wasn't a lie, was it? She tipped her head. "How did you get into the schoolhouse? I didn't forget to lock it yesterday, did I?" In her haste to get home, it wouldn't have surprised her if she'd forgotten.

"It was locked." He thumbed toward a window. "There's one window that's easy to jimmy open." He grinned, and the room grew warmer still. "My brother Luke and I used to slip in and out through it when we were scholars."

Mollie tried to imagine him as a boy, following his brother Luke into all kinds of mischief. A smile spread across her face, and soon they both stood there, grinning at each other, until the sound of a car door slamming shut outside broke the moment of closeness.

The door opened. In walked the Stoney Ridge sheriff, with an odd look on his face. Sheepish.

"Oh no," Mollie groaned. "What have they done now?"

The sheriff took off his hat and gave Sam a nod. Everybody knew each other in Stoney Ridge. "I'm sorry, Mollie," and he did look genuinely sorry, "but those two girls came to the station early this morning to file a complaint against you. I have to investigate it."

"They did *what*?"

"They claim you're a drug addict. They said they've seen you take pills every day. They brought pills down to the station. I'm having the lab run a check on them now."

Her empty pill container. The girls. So they'd gotten into

it. She sank into a chair. "Those pills . . . they're a type of medication."

"I figured as much," the sheriff said. "But since the complaint was filed, I had to do a drug test on the pills. I'll let you know the results later today. Just wanted to give you a heads-up." He put his hat back on his head. "I'm sorry to say, but I need to let the social workers know. It's standard protocol."

Mollie nodded. "Do you happen to know where the girls are now?"

"I took them to school myself. Walked them right in." He went to the door. "I'll come by later."

As soon as the door shut behind the sheriff, Mollie could feel Sam's eyes on her, questioning her. "They're prescription drugs."

"That's not what I was wondering."

She glanced up.

"How much longer, Mollie, until you turn those two back over to the social worker?"

Her answer came reluctantly. "I need to see this through, Sam. All the way. It's hard to explain, but it's something between me and God." He looked at her with such concern, it almost made her cry. At the same time, she felt the tension drain from her. "Thank you for starting the fire in the stove. I appreciate it more than you can imagine."

The sound of boys running toward the schoolhouse signaled the start of the day, and Sam crossed the room. At the door, he turned to say, "I sure hope the day picks up from here."

She sure hoped so too.

Later that day, after the scholars had gone home, the sheriff returned to the schoolhouse. Roberta Watts drove up behind him, with Tina and Alicia in the back of her car. In they strode, the two girls dragging their feet behind them.

"Thyroid pills," the sheriff said, handing Mollie a baggie filled with white pills.

"Yes," she said. "I had my thyroid removed last year. These are replacement hormones. I need to take them daily to stay healthy." She glanced at the girls. They seemed unconcerned.

"Girls," Roberta said in a steely voice, "what do you have to say to Mollie?"

They exchanged a look. Tina spoke first. "How are we supposed to know? You never told us what the pills were for. We just figured you were a junkie."

Alicia nodded. "That's all we've ever seen, y' know."

"We gotta protect ourselves," Tina said.

Mollie hadn't thought of the situation from that angle.

Roberta Watts had a different perspective. "And you never thought to ask her? You just accuse her."

Roberta stared them down, until Alicia finally said, "I guess we could've asked first. Sorry." She sounded anything but.

"Mm-hmm." Roberta turned to Mollie. "You ready to say uncle on them two? I can find another home."

Tempting. Oh, so very tempting. Mollie considered it for a long moment. Long enough that Roberta took a step toward her. "I have separate homes in mind. I think it might be best to split those two up."

"NOOOOOO!" Tina and Alicia's big brown eyes went all round and innocent. "We'll be good. Don't make us go! Please, Mollie! We love living with you. You've been our favorite foster mother of all."

Mollie looked at them, surprised by their outburst. The

sincerity in their eyes. She'd have thought them to be living angels if she didn't know better. She felt herself weakening but tried to think this through objectively, despite being stared at by four pairs of eyes. Fostering wasn't about how she felt about the girls, this was about how she felt about God, about thanking him for what he'd done for her. She was offering her home and her time to God. And her heart. It's just that this offering had become a bit more sacrificial than she could've imagined. It downright hurt.

At last she let out a shaky laugh. "We'll keep things as they are," she said. "For now."

After Roberta gave the girls stern warnings to behave, and she and the sheriff left the schoolhouse, and Mollie was left alone with Tina and Alicia, she thought it was a very good thing no one could see the future. If she had, she would never have started the ball rolling on foster care.

During morning recess, as Mollie was out in the playground watching the children, Sam crossed the road to say hello. "I saw you from the barn. Thought I'd just come by to make sure you were doing okay."

"I'm fine, Sam. Thank you for asking."

"Well, I was a little concerned. After, you know, the hullabaloo with the sheriff."

Hullabaloo. That was a sweet word for something that was really quite awful. He meant after she was accused of being a drug addict by her foster daughters. It still astonished her that Tina and Alicia would go to such lengths to embarrass her.

"Mollie, I wonder if, maybe sometime . . ."

"You wonder what?"

Sam waited a moment, looking down at her, as if he had something to say. His face was caught in a sunbeam, lighting up those blue eyes—as blue as a summer sky. How could one man be so appealing? She felt her heart start to race.

"I thought that maybe—"

A child shrieked and Mollie's gaze suddenly snapped back to her scholars. Near the swings, a little girl was howling, stung by a bee. "I'd better see about getting some baking soda on that sting," she said.

Sam backed away, rubbing his hands on his thighs self-consciously. Mollie walked the wailing little girl over to the schoolhouse, mulling over what it was Sam was going to say. Disappointed, she wondered if she'd ever know.

FIFTEEN

It had become a regular afternoon routine, something Izzy could set a clock by. The school bus would drop Cassidy off in front of the group home at four o'clock, and she would head to Windmill Farm, straight to the yarn shop, walking through the door at fifteen minutes past four. On the dot.

Cassidy seemed hungry to learn from Izzy, whether it was spinning wool or knitting hats or cleaning up the shop. She watched everything with a keen eye, reminding Izzy of how she used to watch Fern and the other Amish women to see how things should be done. The difference between them, though, was that Cassidy was so obvious about the empty holes in her heart. Izzy had kept hers carefully hidden. Willingly or not, she found herself intrigued by the girl. There was something childlike about her, something not fully formed. She hadn't learned to protect herself the way most foster kids did. It amazed Izzy that Cassidy's heart remained so open to others.

On this gray afternoon, Izzy was spinning black fleece into yarn for Edith Lapp as Cassidy walked into the shop after school. The wool had been sheared from one black sheep, Daisy, whom Izzy adored. Concentrating carefully, Cassidy had been watching the tension in Izzy's fingers as she drew the fibers out of the roving, joining it piece by piece into the smooth, thin yarn that filled the bobbin. Twist, slide down, twist, slide down. "I can't get mine to look like yours."

"Think of how your yarn looked when you first started spinning, Cassidy. It takes quite a bit of practice to use both feet and hands at the same time. You've made huge improvements since then. Your roving doesn't break anymore."

"Yeah, I'm a little better at it." Cassidy seesawed her hand back and forth in the air. "Still ends up looking lumpy and bumpy and chunky." She picked up a fluff of roving from the basket. "Can I try?"

"As soon as I finish with this, I'll get you some practice fleece and set up a new bobbin in the flier. I need this black fleece for yarn for Edith. I only have that one basketful from Daisy."

"Why do you have just one black sheep?"

Izzy scoffed. "I wish I knew." She still wasn't sure how a black sheep ended up among her flock. Luke had tried to explain genetics to her but got overly detailed, a common occurrence, and she gave up trying to figure it out. All that mattered was that Daisy was the sweetest ewe in the flock, gentle with the lambs, and quick to come when called. But Daisy's sweet nature had nothing to do with why Edith Lapp wanted her black wool. She said Hank Lapp walked around the yard in the Christmas house slippers she made for him each year and she was done trying to make them white again. Black slippers were all he'd be getting this Christmas.

When Izzy emptied the basket of fleece, she switched the

bobbin out for Cassidy to practice. "I forgot something up in the fix-it shop."

She intended for the girl to stay and mind the shop in case anyone dropped by, but Cassidy took her words as an invitation. She followed Izzy like a puppy, right into the fix-it shop and into their little partially remodeled living quarters. Izzy saw her look around the rooms in amazement. She could take a guess at what was running through her head. How could anyone live like this? It looked so raw, unfinished with sharp edges. It didn't look at all like a home. "Luke's been awfully busy lately. He'll finish up those walls soon." One of these days.

Cassidy peered out the kitchen window. "So he's planning to expand it?"

"Yes, out the back. Plus a new kitchen and large living area. The other direction will be bedrooms. There will be a new front door, so the entrance isn't coming through the fix-it shop."

"It's going to be huge."

"Not compared to most homes. It's nothing, really."

"Nothing," Cassidy said in a wistful tone, ". . . and everything."

As they walked back to the Stitches in Time shop, Izzy saw Jenny's buggy drive up, so they met up with her at the hitching post. While Izzy tied the horse's reins to the post, she asked Cassidy to get Rosie out of the back seat. Jenny's new baby was due soon, and she had trouble with lifting Rosie.

To Izzy's surprise, Cassidy presented her palms, shaking her head, backing away. "Nah, I don't do kids. They don't like me and I don't like them. I'm just gonna head over to the yarn shop and practice on the wheel."

Izzy felt a little annoyed with Cassidy's remark. *Who doesn't "do" kids?* She thought it was weird. But then, she had to remember that Cassidy was only fifteen. At times she seemed older to Izzy, but then there were moments, like this one, when she seemed so young. She helped Jenny out of the buggy and then lifted Rosie up and out, holding her little warm body close to hers. "What brings you here on a day like today? It's going to rain soon."

Jenny held up a thin envelope. "I heard from Mama. I thought you'd want to read it."

The brief note Jenny had received from Grace Miller held just a couple of lines. She wrote she was missing Rosie and thinking a lot about the new baby and hoped Jenny's pregnancy was going well. No mention of where she was, why she had gone away, or when she'd be returning to Stoney Ridge. Nothing about Izzy other than a short postscript: *P.S. Tell your sister hello from me.* Izzy read the letter a couple of times and noticed there was no return address on the envelope, yet the postmark was stamped Lancaster. "Think she's nearby?"

Jenny shrugged. "I just can't imagine that Mama would be nearby and not try to see Rosie. You know how crazy she is about her. My guess is she gave the letter to someone to mail for her." A few drops of rain started, so she folded the letter back into the envelope. "I'd better get home."

"Thanks for bringing it by." Izzy helped Jenny and Rosie get settled back in the buggy, then waved to them as they went down the driveway. She appreciated her sister's thoughtfulness, but the letter only deepened her dismay over her mother. She should be immune to her mother's indifference by now, but it still hurt. There was no hope, things couldn't be put right. The past could neither be escaped nor undone. That familiar bleak mood came down hard and fast.

Over supper, she wanted to talk about her mother's disappearance with Luke, but he had to run off to another deacon crisis. Izzy had no idea where he'd gone or what he'd had to do, or even what time he'd gotten home.

In the morning, she could see he was drained and exhausted. His eyes were bloodshot, rimmed with dark blue circles of fatigue. "Do you want coffee? Or orange juice?"

When he didn't answer, Izzy set both down on the table and turned to head back into the little kitchen. She eyed the small torn-up room. The only progress Luke had made in the last month was to tear off more drywall, leaving the wooden slats showing like the bones of a skeleton.

Maybe it was just as well that they had no baby. This was no home yet. No place for a baby to grow up in.

Izzy busied herself with the pancake batter, whipping the wooden spoon through it. She stiffened when she felt Luke's hands settle on her shoulders. She hadn't realized he had followed her into the kitchen. "So aren't you even going to tell me where you've been all night?"

"I told you. Doing deacon work."

"And what would that be, Luke? Where were you?"

"I can't tell you, Izzy. You know that."

She shrugged his hands off her shoulders. "Forget about it, then," she snapped, impatient with him, upset with herself. Things would improve between them, closeness and intimacy would return, only to slip away again. One step forward, two steps back. This morning it felt like three steps back. Maybe four. She spooned a dollop of pancake batter onto the hot frying pan. She slammed the spoon back into the bowl so hard the batter splattered.

Luke had returned to sit at the table. "I'll probably be gone most of today." His voice carried right through the wooden slats, like he was still standing next to her.

She didn't even bother to ask why he'd be gone. As soon as the pancakes were done, she turned off the stove and set his plate in front of him.

He barely glanced up at her over the rim of his coffee cup. "Luke, I'm tired of this."

He looked up, eyebrows raised, genuine puzzlement on his face. "Tired of what?"

She knew he was trying to understand her and he wasn't even coming close. She herself couldn't grasp what it was inside her, this feeling of being unwanted, unneeded, that kept returning to her. "I'm going to the yarn shop. There's a class starting in about an hour and I've got some things to do to get ready." Silent as snow, she left the fix-it shop, closing the door behind her.

She stopped halfway down the hill, changing her mind, and went over to the sheep pen to check on her woollies. Watching them always cheered her up . . . almost always, but not this morning.

Surely, she thought, she should have learned her lesson from wanting too much from others. Still, the wanting kept stinging. The utter hopelessness of her longings hit her in a rush. Her shoulders slumped and her head bowed. She squeezed her eyes shut against the burn of tears, but they came anyway.

Her mother had left town without so much as a goodbye, her husband was too busy for her. And still no baby.

Come on, Izzy. Come on, she told herself. *Cut the self-pity. You've got a knitting class to teach.* She wiped the tears off her face with the backs of her hands and took in a deep breath.

The sheep were clustered together, lying contentedly, under the trampoline that Luke had brought in for them. They'd finally decided it wasn't a threat to them, and they were napping peacefully. Izzy did a quick head count. All there. There was no sight as satisfying to her as this one.

Her sheep were at peace, content. This didn't happen often. Hardly ever. A bunch of conditions had to be met for sheep to lie down in contentment. Their tummies had to be full, and they had to have no fear of hunger. At this moment, her woollies felt no fear. Normally, there was endless fretting among the flock, even on the best of days. And then there was often bullying among the flock, instigated by the bossy old ewes. They would approach a younger sheep with necks arched, heads lifted, and push the poor woollie away from where she'd been happily grazing. The butting order. The old ewe had no good reason at all for the bullying, just a need to be top sheep. Izzy saw it among her hens too. The pecking order.

But in this one, rare moment, there was no friction. No irritations. No enemies to fear. The last few frost-tinged nights had taken care of flies and pests. The shade of the trampoline created a refuge. Her sheep didn't need to fuss and fret because their needs had been met. They could lie down quietly because they had all the right conditions to rest. She took her index card out of her sweater pocket and read the next line of Psalm 23, trying to memorize it:

He maketh me lie down in green pastures.

A tingle went down her spine. That's exactly what she was seeing, right now. Exactly that.

The Lord is my shepherd, I shall not want. He maketh me lie down in green pastures.

The sheep could rest because they had a good shepherd. They had faith in their shepherd. Trust in their shepherd. Faith. Trust. Those two simple, overwhelming words. How many times had she heard David guide the church with this phrase: Faith is a devout trust in God, who does for us what we cannot do for ourselves.

She stilled. She kept looking to others—to Luke, to her mother, even to this baby who hadn't been conceived yet—to find her green pastures. And where had that gotten her? To continual disappointment. To putting pressure on Luke to fill that emptiness. Poor Luke. She saw it clearly now. Sheep weren't meant to rely on other sheep, only on their shepherd.

She felt as if she was discovering God again, for the first time. As if she had to keep going back to the basics. Back to picking up dropped stitches. *Oh my soul, I have so many dropped stitches!*

But then, maybe it was a good thing to never graduate beyond basic trust, to have a simple faith in God to provide, the same way her woollies depended on her. Her eyes grazed over her sweet woollies again, and she felt overcome with a rare, deep-down sense of settled peace.

The Lord is my shepherd, I shall not want. He maketh me lie down in green pastures.

That psalm. It was starting to change her from the inside out. The change was coming from the memorizing, the ruminating. She exhaled, releasing something invisible she

didn't even know she'd been holding on to, and turned to
head down to the Stitches in Time yarn shop.

~

From the fix-it shop, Luke watched Izzy as she leaned against
the fence to gaze at her sheep, then walked down toward the
yarn shop. He wondered what she was thinking. He could
never figure out what was on her mind, why she acted moody
the way she did sometimes. Should he go down to the yarn
shop and try to talk to her? But then he remembered she'd
said she had a knitting class to get ready for. He sat back down
at his lonely now-cold pancake breakfast, puzzling over what
she meant when she said she was tired of this. Tired of what?

His gaze took in the two-by-fours, the piece of plywood
that acted as a door between the fix-it shop and their little
living area. Maybe she was getting tired of the remodel. If
he were home today, he'd try to get something done on it,
just to show her that he was listening to her, even when he
had no clue what he was listening for.

But he wasn't going to be home today. David was picking
him up and they were spending the day at the hospital, visiting with Ezra Mast, a church member whose buggy had been
hit by a truck. Ezra had survived the crash but just barely,
and was listed in critical condition. David had warned Luke
that most of the day would be spent in the waiting room with
Ezra's family. Encouraging them, comforting them, bringing
them hope, waiting with them for updates. Luke was grateful that he was shadowing David on this ministry errand, on
most errands. His nature was such that he was not inclined
toward encouraging others, comforting them, or bringing
them hope. Or waiting. Especially that.

He tried not to dwell on the thought that was always circling around his head, like a flock of starlings: *Why in the world am I a deacon?*

Instead, he shifted his thoughts to the morning prayer of the old bishop: *"Lord, what do you want me to do today?"*

He heard the jingle of a horse harness and realized David was arriving at Windmill Farm. He gulped down the last bite of pancake, swallowed the last bit of coffee, and grabbed his hat to go meet the bishop. What did God want him to do on this day? He took in a deep breath, resigned. To spend it in the hospital's waiting room, like it or not.

But he did stop at the door and turn back, to grab a pen and paper and leave a note for Izzy.

Let's talk tonight. Love you.

Luke XO

Whatever was going on with Izzy, making her so tetchy, he needed to let her know she was on his mind today. It wasn't as obvious a sign as the bishop's buggy waiting outside for him, but Luke had that poking-the-bread-dough impression again from God. He was getting familiar with it.

Sixteen

Mollie wiped down the chalkboard with the eraser, trying to pump herself up to face the scholars as they arrived. Normally, she loved teaching. Loved the children, loved the rhythm of the school day, loved the challenge of filling scholars' minds with worthy topics.

Today, she wanted to quit, pack up, move home. Tell her parents that she gave up. Her mother would be thrilled. There was nothing she wanted more than to have Mollie at home, safely under her wing.

Tina and Alicia had promised Roberta Watts that they would be on their best behavior for Mollie. Their resolve lasted until breakfast the next morning. They told Mollie it was a teacher in-service day and they didn't have school. Unfortunately, Mollie believed them. It was another lie. The school called and left a message that they would need to inform the social workers of the girls' frequent absences. Since they'd been living with Mollie, they'd missed more school than they attended.

Mollie's arm slowed, and she leaned her forehead against the chalkboard. The coolness of the slate felt good. She was so tired lately. A terrifying thought kept emerging, though she tried to tamp it down. No, no, no. She was fine. Absolutely fine.

The door opened and Mollie startled, spun around, pasting on a bright artificial smile. "Aunt Fern! What are you doing here on this beautiful morning?" *Fake. I'm so fake. I want to burst out crying and instead I'm acting like I've just seen a rainbow.*

"Morning, Mollie." Fern walked into the classroom and leaned against Mollie's desk, facing her at the chalkboard. "Funny thing happened last night. I'm usually a champion sleeper, but I woke up in the middle of the night and couldn't sleep. The Lord was trying to get through to me. He's done that before, and I've lived long enough to know I need to pay attention."

Mollie set the eraser down.

"Your face came to mind. I thought of you, all alone with those two girls. Every other foster parent has someone, but not you."

"You're alone with Cassidy."

"Not really. I have Luke and Izzy nearby. Cassidy's easygoing too. But you . . . you're on your own. Those two girls . . . I've heard it's not all picnics and pillow fights."

"Roberta told you that?"

"Sam. He's worried about you." She folded her arms across her chest. "Honey, we're not meant to go it alone in this life."

Tears prickled Mollie's eyes. She looked down at the tip of her sneakers. "You haven't called Mom, have you? You haven't told her about fostering, have you?"

"No, no. This is your story to tell. But I thought you would have. You don't want to keep something like this from her."

"It was just supposed to be a week or two. I didn't expect it to go so long."

"Speaking of just that, Roberta Watts left a message yesterday that since the group home is taking longer to fix than anybody could have imagined, she thinks it would be good to have regular meetings with the foster mothers. Training sessions, she says." Fern's eyes lifted upward. "As if Amish women need lessons on how to be mothers." She let out a soft harrumph. "I called her back to tell her Amish women don't stop their day to talk, but we do talk while we work. So if she wants to come to our knitting class today, then we would welcome her. She wasn't too happy about that, but she agreed. I thought it would be good if you could join in. I think it would help you feel like you're not alone in this."

One tear slipped down Mollie's cheek, then another.

Fern noticed. With a single finger, she lifted Mollie's trembling chin. "Oh, honey, I'm sorry. I should've been keeping an eye on you. Sit down and tell me all about it." She sat down at Mollie's desk and patted a chair beside her.

Mollie shook her head so fast and hard that tears splashed down her dress. "I can't."

"Why not?"

"I . . ." She tried to take in a deep breath, but her throat hurt too much. She tried again. "I'm afraid you'll tell my parents."

"I won't." Fern splayed a hand across her heart. "It's a promise."

Mollie sank into the chair, and everything spilled out. All of it. The police visits in the middle of the night (twice), the girls' ditching school, the pills they found and took to the police station, even the stress they created between her and Sam, the worries she felt about her fatigue. Aunt Fern listened carefully, giving hmms and humms in all the right places. "Roberta Watts has said she's already got two homes in mind for Tina and Alicia. She thinks I'm in over my head, and that I should give the girls up." When Mollie ran out of troubles and tears, she leaned back in the chair and exhaled.

Fern moved her hand across the desk and gently rubbed the back of Mollie's. "Maybe you should do that. You can tell Roberta. She'll understand. We all understand. You have to take care of yourself."

"I need to see this through. I started this whole thing, Aunt Fern. I was the one who pushed and pushed Luke. And I'm the only one who's failing miserably. For heaven's sake, I have everybody giving me advice. I can't even go to the Bent N' Dent for a bag of walnuts without getting advice." She lifted her hands in the air. "Even Hank Lapp!"

"Der wu ken Kinner hot, kann sie es bescht uffziehe." *Those who have no children know best how to raise them.* Fern folded her arms against her thin chest. Then she asked Mollie to describe a typical day. "What do the girls do that upsets you? And how have you handled them?"

Typical? With Tina and Alicia? There was no such thing as typical. Mollie fanned out a few of the days for her aunt, who responded with an increasingly shocked look on her face. Aunt Fern . . . shocked. It boggled the mind. But then, so did Tina and Alicia.

"Mollie, are you afraid of them?"

"No! Of course not. I'm a schoolteacher." She shook her head tiredly and leaned her forehead on the heel of a hand. "Maybe I am. I think they know it too."

Fern drummed her fingers on the desktop, thinking for

a long moment. "If you think you've got the stamina and determination to hang in there for a little bit longer, I think I've got a solution."

Chin down, Mollie glanced up. "How much longer?"

"Roberta Watts said that the workers have finished getting all the moldy drywall out of the group home. They should be starting on the fix-up side soon. That shouldn't take as long."

Oh, thank God. The end is in sight. Mollie wiped her tears with the back of her hand and sniffed. "So what's your idea?"

"I think those two girls need a different way of being handled than the way you've been going about things."

"What do you mean? I've been treating them the way I was raised."

"Mollie, you are overly gifted in empathy. So is your mother. That's a good thing. Unless it's not."

"What does that mean?"

"It's not what those girls need most from you."

"So what do they need?"

"It's what worked for Luke and Jesse. Amos's children too. Living with his three daughters was no small thing." She clapped her hands on her knees. "Have you ever heard of Fern's Ten Rules for Wayward Teens? Luke named them."

Mollie tipped her head. "Rules?" She had plenty of expectations for the girls, they just paid her no mind.

"Only ten. But they're ironclad." Fern patted Mollie's shoulder. "I'll write them all down for you. Your job is to make sure they're obeyed."

"Aunt Fern, *that's* the problem. That's it right there! How do I do that?"

"Honey, have you ever asked those girls for anything?"

No. She guessed she hadn't. She'd felt so sorry for them that she'd given them whatever they'd asked.

"They should know they're part of the whole. That comes when they contribute to family life. They're needed. I think that's the core problem with these foster children. They've never felt needed or wanted. We can work on that. We can't fix everything, but we can fix that."

"What if it's too late?"

Fern smiled. "What if it's a stitch in time?"

Mollie let out a sigh. "You really think ten rules can fix my girls?"

"Only God can fix our brokenness. But my ten rules will help you live with them in harmony. Just look at Luke Schrock. Jesse Stoltzfus."

Okay, all right. There might be something to this. Sounds of scholars arriving in the schoolyard signaled the end of their conversation. Fern stood up. "I'll write down my ten rules and give them to you at the knitting class." Almost to the door, she turned back. "Honey, I'm going to make an appointment with Dok for you."

"No! I'm fine. Just a little worn out."

"Probably. But we'll let Dok decide that."

"Aunt Fern."

Fern turned around.

"Thank you for your concern, but I'm not a child. I can make my own doctor appointments."

Fern pursed her lips, then gave a quick nod. "Ten o'clock at the yarn shop. That's the class time."

She shook her head. "I can't leave the schoolhouse."

Fern knew that. "Birdy's coming to watch the children for

you, so you can attend." Then she swept out again, leaving Mollie feeling partly better, partly worse.

⁓

Birdy arrived at fifteen minutes before ten in the morning, a redheaded toddler on each hip, to take the scholars on a bird-watching expedition. She insisted Mollie borrow her buggy to drive to Windmill Farm. "It'll save you time," she said, gently pushing Mollie right out the door. "You get on over to that knitting class with the other foster mothers. It'll do you wonders."

Just what wonders did Birdy think Mollie was in need of? There was no time to ask, because she was suddenly in the buggy and the horse was on its way down the street, as if Birdy and Fern had whispered their plans to the animal.

She felt . . . what was the word? Managed. In the same way that her mother always managed her. Hadn't she come to Stoney Ridge to make her own decisions for a change, to have a little breathing room? She should just turn this buggy around and drive right back to the schoolhouse. Tell Birdy thank you very much but no thank you. You can forget those flapping birds in the sky and get on home now. That's exactly what she should do. But she couldn't make herself.

As she pulled the horse to a stop in front of the hitching post at the Stitches in Time yarn shop, she knew she needed to be here. Fern knew too. So did Birdy. So did everybody.

She was in over her head. Way over.

The knitting class was already in progress, but Fern had saved Mollie a seat and patted it. "Come on in, Mollie. Here's your needles and yarn."

Mollie slipped through the circle and sat down in between

Edith Lapp and Fern. In Edith's lap was a ball of black wool that fed a string of yarn to her needles like a spaghetti noodle. Her knitting needles were flying: *click, clack, click, clack.* Mollie had never seen anyone knit so fast. Why, she could practically see the black sock emerging. She leaned to her left to whisper to Fern. "I don't know how to knit."

Edith overheard. She poked her two needles into the ball of yarn and set the bundle on the ground by her feet. She took the needles and yarn out of Mollie's hands and said, "I'll cast on for you. Then I'll teach you the purl stitch. Easiest way to start."

"But what am I making?"

Click, clack, click, clack. Edith's hands were big, her knuckles red and swollen like cherry tomatoes, but she could make those needles dance. "A scarf."

A scarf? Mollie didn't really need a scarf.

Fern leaned forward. "Edith, you look after Mollie."

Edith didn't even look up. "I am."

Not again! Third time today that Mollie had been managed by an overly helpful woman. Even more frustrating was that she needed the help. She couldn't even figure out how to knit on her own.

A car pulled into the driveway. Izzy peered out the window and turned back to Fern. "She's here."

Fern went outside and returned with Roberta Watts. Goodness gracious, that woman scared Mollie. She peered around the circle of women, unsmiling. No one else seemed the least bit rattled, though. Needles kept right on clicking and clacking as the women murmured their hellos.

Roberta Watts settled herself into an empty chair and got right down to business. "Ladies, I'm here to do some training about foster parenting. Problems come with the territory."

Alice Smucker spoke right up. "Teddy and I couldn't be happier with Chloe. She fits like a glove into our family. She even likes Teddy's snakes. How about that?"

"That's good to hear, Alice," Fern said. Others murmured their approval.

"And I happen to know that the O'Henry girls at the Sisters' House are working out beautifully," Alice said, smiling. "God is just smiling down on us."

Mollie's heart sank.

Roberta folded her arms against her chest. "Well, that's good to hear. Mm-hmm. Let's keep it up." She launched into specific dos and don'ts of raising foster children, most of which she'd already gone over in the first meeting at Mattie's house: reminding the women they must not proselytize the children into the Amish faith, and all that went with that. They weren't to be forced to attend church on Sundays. They weren't to be expected to participate in family devotions or prayer.

Alice Smucker objected. "Worship is part of our life. It's like asking us not to breathe the air."

Roberta took Alice in, her eyes traveling up from her toes, landing on her prayer cap. "You can ask the girls to join in. You cannot insist they do. That's just the way it is. These children are under the supervision of the state of Pennsylvania. We play by their rules. Everybody clear on that? No turning these sweet little girls into Amish look-alikes."

Alice remained unflinching under her steady regard. Except for school, Chloe was already wearing the garb. "Children need guidance."

Roberta stared at Alice. "I am telling you the same thing I tell to all my foster families. Every"—she thumped the palms of her hands together for emphasis—"single"—*thump*—"one. Got that?" *Thump.* "Your job is to give these children a safe, stable, loving home for a period of time."

Alice grew huffy. Her shoulders went back and her chin jutted out. "It can be more than that. It can be a place where they learn they are a beloved child of God."

Roberta got a look on her face like she had *known* this was a bad idea, all along. "Now listen here. This happens all the time with religious groups. You Amish folks, you—"

A ringing sound came out of Roberta's large purse and all the needles stopped clacking, shocked. Roberta dove into her purse and emerged with her cell phone. She looked at it, frowned, then said, "Oh, for crying out loud. I've got to take this call."

Fern skillfully navigated Roberta out the door while she answered her phone, loudly, annoyed with Mavis Connor, who was calling about some crisis. She was so engrossed in the phone call that she seemed hardly aware she was being shuffled outside. The clacking of needles started up again. Moments later, Fern returned inside the shop. "Roberta had an emergency she had to tend to. She said she'll be back next week for more training."

Alice groaned. "Training?" She gave a smirk. "Sounds to me like the communists have taken over the government." She set her knitting down in her lap. "Chloe wants us to adopt her. She says she's happy in the home we've given her. She calls us her 'forever family.' I wonder what Roberta Watts would think of that?"

Mattie looked up from her knitting project. "Alice, keep

in mind what Roberta was inferring. You can't insist, but you can certainly ask. If Chloe wants to participate in our church, she is very welcome. And no one can stop any of us from praying for our foster children."

Fern gave a sideways glance at Mollie. "Is anyone having any trouble with their foster girls? Any concerns?"

Mollie kept her chin tucked, her eyes on Edith's click-clacking needles.

"Our girl has been challenging," Mattie said.

Mollie's head snapped up. "How so?"

Mattie looked across the room at Mollie. "Her name's Kerri. She hasn't had much structure in her life, so she sees structure as a straitjacket. She keeps asking when she can return to the group home."

That information actually made Mollie feel a little better. She looked down, watching her own fingers make a pleat in her apron. "Doesn't that bother you?"

"No," Mattie said. "I don't take it personally. We've done enough fostering of children to know that we're meant to be an example to these children, a good example, we hope. But the problems in their lives started long before we knew them. There's only so much we can do. We're in their life for a season."

"But . . . is that really enough?" Mollie blurted out. "Shouldn't we be trying to fix their problems? Be the family they've never had? Like Alice is thinking of doing . . . adopting Chloe. Becoming her forever family. Isn't God asking us to do more for these girls?"

"No," Izzy said in a firm voice. "No. He's not." Everyone stopped knitting to look up at her, even Edith Lapp. Up to now, Izzy had been keeping mum on the subject, walking around the circle to help the women with knitting projects. When she realized everyone was staring at her, she shrank back, shoulders drooping.

"Go on, Izzy," Fern said. "We need to hear what you have to say."

When Izzy remained silent, Mattie appealed. "Please, Izzy."

Izzy's face grew taut. When she spoke, her voice dropped barely above a whisper. "It's your example that these girls need. Stable homes, like you all have. Happy families. Loving families. That's enough. They don't need you to fix them. Besides that, you can't fix them anyway."

"But how?" Something broke inside of Mollie. "How can I be a good example to Tina and Alicia when they keep running off in the night to Las Vegas? When they ditch school and steal Sam's horse and buggy and smoke cigarettes in his barn and put mice in the schoolhouse?" Tears started, clogging her voice, making her feel all the more embarrassed. She covered her face with her hands. No one said a word as she sobbed. The only other sound in the room was Edith Lapp's knitting needles, still clacking away. It took a while for Mollie to pull herself together. She wiped her eyes with her apron and tried not to look at anyone.

"I think what Izzy is trying to say," Mattie said in a gentle voice, "is that fixing people is God's work, not ours. We're part of the story of healing for these young women. And it's helpful to remember that—to know that it's enough to be doing God's work. But if we layer it with our expectations, as well intended as they might be, we risk getting in the way. Does that sound about right, Izzy?"

Izzy nodded.

Now Mattie was talking directly to Mollie. "Alice's situation with Chloe is both wonderful and unique. It was God's doing to place Chloe in the Zooks' home, to Teddy and Alice, to a couple open to adoption."

Well, sure. Mollie would have adopted Chloe too, if she'd been placed with her. Everybody wanted Chloe. She was sweet, helpful, kind. Fit in like a glove. Mollie had *planned* to foster a girl just like Chloe—instead she ended up with Tina and Alicia.

Carrie picked up where Mattie left off. "All the other girls have a mother or father who want them home someday, and the state of Pennsylvania wants the families reunited. That's the goal. That's what always has to stay at the forefront. The best situation of all is to help a family reunite."

Mattie poked her needles into her ball of yarn. She looked like she was getting ready to leave. So soon? Mollie was just starting to feel some relief from the despair she'd woken up with this morning and couldn't shake off.

"There's a part of fostering that I'd like to do more with one day—helping those mothers learn how to be good mothers. I've heard about a program that visits women in jail to teach them parenting skills, so that they're better prepared for their children when they're released." Mattie rose to her feet. "This hour has gone too fast." She turned to Fern. "Same time, next week? This is a wonderful idea, Fern." She smiled at Mollie. "We're all in this together."

There. That was what Mollie needed to hear. Those words snapped any lingering hopelessness like a dry twig.

"Here," Edith Lapp said, handing Mollie her needles, yarn, and the first row of a scarf.

"But . . . I don't know what to do next."

Edith lifted a sparse eyebrow. "Sure you do. I saw you

watching me. You can figure it out." She heaved herself up out of her chair. In a strident, buck-up voice, she rose to her full height and said, "You can't go through life expecting others to spoon-feed you. Life is hard. You don't just throw in the towel when the road gets bumpy."

Mollie's jaw dropped open. Was that how she seemed to Edith? Weak and needy?

Oh my goodness. She was weak and needy, both. She wanted a foster child on her terms—smooth and easy. When reality kicked in, when she realized how difficult it would be to live with Tina and Alicia, she wanted out. Last night, she helped herself fall asleep by counting the hours until she thought the group home would be repaired.

On the way back to the schoolhouse, Mollie took out the list Fern had slipped in her hand as she said goodbye.

Fern's Ten Rules
Ask permission before you go somewhere.
Do what I ask the first time I ask.
If you make a mess, clean it up.
Treat other people's things with respect.
If you don't know, ask.
If you break it, fix it.
Say you're sorry and make amends.
No arguing.
Keep your promises.
Tell the truth.

Those ten rules pretty much covered the problems Mollie had had with Tina and Alicia. Every single one. Mollie read them over and over again, until she had them memorized. She steeled herself, mentally fortifying herself for the remaining weeks living with those two girls.

She passed a small pond in a farmer's field that looked like a study in stillness, so startlingly clear that she stopped the buggy to stare at it. Clouds reflected in the glassy surface like a mirror. She knew she should get back to the schoolhouse and relieve Birdy, yet she couldn't help herself. For this one moment, it seemed that all the earth, with all its creatures, was at peace.

He leadeth me beside still waters. He restoreth my soul.

A few Sundays ago, the bishop had asked the entire church to memorize Psalm 23. Mollie loved the assignment and had her scholars practice it each day. She'd tried to encourage Tina and Alicia to memorize it too, but they substituted words and made a mess of it and Mollie gave up. On them. But not for herself. The verses from Psalm 23 kept running through her mind. That's exactly how Mollie felt right now, as if her soul had been restored. She took in a deep breath of crisp autumn air. She could do this. She could see her fostering commitment through with Tina and Alicia.

As she drove the buggy down the road toward the schoolhouse, she came to a four-way stop and pulled back on the horse's reins. Right about then, she heard the squeal of a siren and saw the sheriff's squad car approach, revolving light flashing. As he crossed the intersection in front of her, Mollie noticed the small brown-haired heads of two oh-so-familiar girls in the back of the police car.

Oh no. Oh dear.

SEVENTEEN

Late in the afternoon, Sam returned to the barn after driving a chestnut gelding to town and back. It was this particular horse's first foray into traffic and he'd done fairly well. This athletic, graceful horse needed more conditioning to unexpected sounds; he startled when the sheriff's siren went off and danced on all fours. But he didn't bolt, and he was able to settle down once the car passed them. With a little more work, Sam thought this chestnut gelding would make a fine buggy horse. David Stoltzfus had already asked about him, for Birdy. Most women chose mares, but Birdy preferred geldings.

Sam liked knowing when someone had an eye on one of his horses. He liked the challenge of customizing a horse's training to suit its owner. Birdy, for example, wanted to get around town at a quick pace. This gelding moved at a clip. Earlier this week, Hank Lapp had put a deposit on a horse that Sam never thought he'd find an owner for—a stubborn black mare he'd purchased at an auction and quickly regretted. Unflappable, but also unmovable. That horse wouldn't budge unless she was in the mood. Hank said she reminded him of Edith.

He unhooked the chestnut gelding from the buggy traces and pulled him forward by the reins to take him to his stall.

As he turned, he noticed Tina and Alicia waiting for him, hanging on the paddock fence, patting the head of the saucy mare. "Does Mollie know you're here?"

Tina spoke up first. "Absolutely."

He didn't believe her. "I'm going to take this gelding to his stall. You two wait right here. Don't move. Don't touch anything."

"She's touching us! Your saucy mare came over to us and bumped us with her nose. We think she knows us."

He frowned. "She probably remembers that you two were the ones who set off those firecrackers at her when she first came to Stoney Ridge." He tried not to reveal how pleased he was by their shocked looks. "You two stay put. I'll be right back." He walked the gelding to his stall, closed it shut, then hurried back outside. He didn't want those two messing with his saucy mare. "So what do you want?"

The girls exchanged a look. Tina spoke first. "We want to learn to ride horses."

Sam shook his head hard, as if he wasn't hearing right. "You what?"

"We want to ride horses." Tina pointed to the saucy mare. "This one. She likes us."

"Nope." He shook his head from side to side. "Not happening. Not with my horses. Frankly, not with any horse."

"Why not?"

"You both can't be trusted."

"Oh! Not fair!"

"You had your chance. It took you six hours to clean out the stalls. And you stopped to smoke a cigarette in the hayloft. Do you have any idea what a fool thing that was?"

"It didn't even happen! We couldn't get the match lit."

Tina opened her hands wide. "Besides, that was before we knew how much we loved horses!"

"And when did you discover that?"

They looked at each other again. "When the saucy mare bumped us with her nose."

Oh brother. Sam wasn't about to budge. "These horses, they're not riding horses. I'm training them to become buggy horses for families. They're not for girls who suddenly think they love horses." He walked the sorrel bay past them into the barn and stopped in the center aisle. With a deft, practiced movement, he pulled the bridle off the horse's head and slipped the halter back on, buckling it and hooking it to the crossties. The girls followed behind, watching his every move. He dipped the bridle's bit in a bucket of water to clean it and took a rag to dry it off.

Finally Alicia dared to speak. "Could you at least teach us about horses? If we promise not to ride them?"

Turning his neck, Sam looked at them. They actually seemed earnest, but he was nobody's fool. "Look, there's a few farming families who have ponies you can ride."

"Would you ask them?" Alicia said. "If you ask, they'd say yes. If we ask, they'd say no."

"We'll clean out your stalls if you'll ask them," Tina said. She always had a plan. "Every single one. We want to learn all we can about horses." She made a big crisscross against her chest. "We really, really do, Sam. Cross our hearts."

"Starting from the ground up," Alicia added. "Even mucking stalls."

He finished wiping down the rest of the tack, thinking about their request. They had found his Achilles heel. This was how he had become Galen's apprentice as a boy—watching, learning, doing any small task that Galen would give him. Plus, the trip to town today had taken longer than expected and he was behind in the afternoon's routine chores. "Clean those five empty stalls out in the next hour and I'll think about it." It would never happen.

The girls looked at each other, eyes wide. "We're on it!"

He led the way to the barn, pointing out the wheelbarrow and the pitchforks hanging on the wall. "Leave them where you found them."

The girls pushed the wheelbarrow down to the first stall and got right to work. Sam hovered nearby, surprised that they weren't even talking or whispering. They were . . . working.

Forty-eight minutes later, they put the wheelbarrow back where they found it and set the pitchforks in it.

"All done," Tina announced with pride in her voice. "So will you ask your farmer friends if we can ride their ponies?"

"Not so fast." Sam inspected each stall. Shockingly tidy. Fresh hay scattered all around, spread to the corners. "Well done, girls."

"You'll ask?"

He looked them right in the eyes, hoping to see if they were truly sincere about their interest in horses, or if it was a passing fancy. Or worse, a means to mischief. They looked back at him, seemingly without guile. "I'll ask. No promises. For now, get on home so Mollie doesn't have to call the sheriff and ask how you spent the morning, up until the sheriff picked you up at noon and dropped you back at school."

They quivered slightly at that. Without another word, they turned to slink out of the barn. Through an open stall window, he overheard one of them say to the other, "How'd he know?"

⌒

The sun was setting when Tina and Alicia came bursting through the cottage door. Mollie didn't even waste her breath on a hello. She seized their arms and hauled them off to the bedroom so fast that their feet barely skimmed along the floor. She gripped them by the shoulders and gave them a little shake. "You are never again to leave school without first getting my permission."

The look the girls gave back to her was one of genuine surprise, as if they expected a desire to leave school to be permission enough.

"And where have you been for the rest of the afternoon?" She sniffed the air. "You smell like . . . horses." And worse.

Alicia gave a big smile. "Tina and me, we cleaned out Sam's horse stalls."

Mollie stared at them. "You did what? He let you?"

Tina nodded so fast her hair flopped forward. "And he's going to ask his farmer friends if we can ride their ponies." She pushed her hair behind her ears. "Mollie, on the way home, we had an idea. If you were to ask Sam to teach us how to train horses, he'd say yes. He can't say no to you."

"Did you even ask him if you could help clean his stalls?"

"We asked if we could ride his horses and he said no way," Alicia said. "Not a chance, he said." She crossed her arms. "You know, he's awfully fussy about his horses."

"No kidding." Tina rolled her eyes. "But then he said if we could clean out the stalls in one hour, then he'd think about asking his farmer friends if we could ride their ponies. So we did."

"Under one hour? Clean ten stalls? Impossible."

"We did it! Well, five stalls. It only took us forty-eight

minutes. He timed us. And on the way home we decided we want to be horse trainers."

Alicia clasped her hands together in a prayer. "Oh, Mollie, would you talk to him for us? He won't say no to you. He won't. He's crazy about you. We can tell by the way he looks at you."

"Please, Mollie?" Tina begged.

She stared at her foster daughters. After weeks of acting like tough cookies, bored with life, interested only in causing trouble for others, they looked as if they were facing a grand adventure. The first time, she realized, that they looked like little girls and not hardened teens. "I'll take it under consideration. But we're making some changes around here. I have a list of rules for you both to memorize. I'm going to test you on them after supper." She sniffed the air again. "First things first. You both need a shower. Now."

Cassidy had spun enough yarn to knit a scarf. Not a very wide one, but Izzy thought it could be long enough, and a nice keepsake. This morning Fern had said that the repairs on the group home were moving along, and the foster girls would be returning to it soon. Izzy felt an odd pang at that news. She'd grown fond of Cassidy and would miss her at Windmill Farm. She decided to teach her how to knit, using the lumpy yarn she'd spun herself. This afternoon was a good day for it—no classes were scheduled and no tour bus stops.

Izzy set up two chairs by the west window, where the afternoon sun streamed through. Normally, she started beginners out with medium-sized needles, numbered 7 or 8, but Cassidy was using her own heavy handspun yarn, full of clumps, so Izzy chose the largest size needle she had—a number 15. The bigger the needles, the looser the stitch, the faster the scarf would grow. While she waited for Cassidy, she cast on thirty stitches, held it up to see if that might be wide enough, then cast on ten more. She glanced out the window and saw Cassidy coming up the driveway, walking slowly, chin tucked down, as if it took effort to make the climb. It was a steep driveway, but still, she was dragging. Cassidy was a big, heavyset girl. Big when she arrived, even bigger now. Fern's good cooking was to blame.

Or was it more than a steep hill? Was Cassidy discouraged about something? Izzy remembered how slowly she used to climb back up the hill, much the same way as Cassidy looked now, after running down to the mailbox with hopes of finding a letter from her mother. One that never came.

She knocked on the window and waved. Cassidy instantly brightened, then picked up her step and hurried to the yarn shop. A moment later, she arrived, out of breath.

"Steep hill," Izzy said.

Cassidy nodded, still panting. Her eyes traveled to the skeins of chunky yarn waiting on one chair under the window. "That's my yarn."

"It's time I teach you how to knit."

"No kidding?" Cassidy's whole face lit up. "I spun enough yarn? Cool! I want to make a sweater just like that blue one over there." She pointed to the sweater Izzy had made for her mother, the one with the complicated cable stitching.

Whoa. "Let's start with a scarf." Izzy showed her how she had cast on for her, then she slowly knit the first row, carefully showing Cassidy how to move the needles at the same pace, and to not pull on the yarn to make uneven stitches. She handed the needles to Cassidy. "Your turn. I'll stay right here. I'm sure you can do this."

And she could. She was a quick learner. So quick that by the twelfth row, she dropped a stitch and didn't notice until she had knit another three rows. Cassidy held up the scarf and her eyes went wide. "Oh no! Look at the hole!"

Izzy had seen the stitch drop but didn't say anything until Cassidy noticed for herself. She wanted to teach her a lesson that Edith had once taught her, one she'd never forget. "You started going so fast that you lost focus."

"Sounds like something my dad used to tell me," Cassidy said.

"Let's go back and fix it."

Her brown eyes went wide. "But I've already stitched three rows! There must be some other way to fix it."

Izzy shook her head. "You can't leave a hole or it will unravel." Cassidy watched in dismay as Izzy pulled out stitch after stitch, row after row, to get back to that dropped stitch. Izzy finished undoing the stitches and showed her how to pick up the dropped stitch. "See? Not such a big deal."

She gave her a grin. "A stitch just in time."

Izzy smiled in return. "You can knit to this point and come back later. That's one of the best things about knitting. Stopping and starting again, whenever you have a few minutes to spare. But you should never stop in the middle of a row. Finish the row and put a stopper on your needles."

"Why do I have to finish a row?"

"Otherwise, the yarn will pull funny."

Cassidy held the scarf up to examine what she'd done. She scrunched up her face. "It already looks pretty funny."

"There's a beauty to handspun yarn, clumps and all. If you wanted a perfect scarf, you could buy the yarn. This will always be the first thing you knitted, from yarn you spun on the spinning wheel. From the very sheep you've helped me feed and care for. You should feel pleased about this scarf."

"My dad would wear this every day. Even in the summer." She grinned. "I made him a paper tie once and he wore it for a week, until it literally fell apart."

Izzy smiled in return. "You must miss your dad a lot."

"I sure do. Every day." Cassidy let out a sigh that said much. "What about your dad?"

"What about him?"

"Is he around?"

"My father . . . he's a complicated story."

"Oh, I get it. You don't want to talk about it. I've figured that much out about you. If you don't want to answer my questions, you fudge."

I fudge? Izzy didn't fudge. On the topic of her father, she avoided.

Then Cassidy brightened. "Did I tell you about my mom? She's gonna get released from jail soon. She promised she'd come get me."

Izzy couldn't even bring herself to ask why Cassidy believed that ridiculous wish to be true. The girl's hopes for her mother's return made Izzy's stomach twist in a knot. She almost wanted to shake Cassidy and say, "Stop wishing for something that isn't going to happen! Stop longing for someone who isn't even here. Move on and appreciate those who are." But those thoughts were the ones she needed to remember for herself.

❧

A few months had passed with Luke as a deacon, and most of the responsibilities were manageable, although time consuming. But the problem of Freeman Glick was keeping him up at night. At times because he couldn't sleep, so troubled over Freeman's weekly indulgence. Other times he couldn't sleep because he was called in by Freeman's wife to babysit him while he was on the bender. Try to get some food in him, some coffee. Come morning, contrite and sobered up, Freeman would beg Luke not to say anything to David. This would be the last time. Freeman promised to end his intemperance and his wife would back him up. Until the next time Freeman fell off the wagon and his wife would call Luke to come and help. Those two were wearing Luke to a frazzle.

He wanted to get David involved, yet he also wanted to keep his promise to Freeman. When Freeman wasn't drunk, which was actually most of the time, he was quite condescending to Luke, doubting his ability to be a good deacon, to keep it up, to not quit or bail. There was a part of Luke that wanted Freeman to have an opportunity to keep his word to stay sober. After all, he'd been in Freeman's shoes, plenty of times.

And then . . . there was a part of him that was just plain scared of Freeman. He was a bear of a man, huge and imposing. He was Birdy's oldest brother, which made him David's brother-in-law. It was no small thing to accuse Freeman Glick of a sin, to put him under the ban. Luke knew he shouldn't let Freeman intimidate him, but it was easier to think it than to do it.

Luke felt caught between a rock and a hard place. It was the deacon's job to handle these situations; without David here, he had no idea what to do. Yet he had obligated himself to not talk to David about it.

Finally, he decided to try to bring it up to David without offering any names or identifying details. He went to the Bent N' Dent and was grateful that Hank Lapp wasn't hanging around. He usually was here. The store was empty but for David, whom he found back in his office.

Luke didn't even start with a hello. "There's a situation brewing. Someone in the church who has a bad habit. He promises to quit this habit, but then he reneges on his promise."

David leaned back in his chair. "This fellow, he wants you to keep this quiet for now, I presume."

"Yes. Exactly. But I feel like I'm in over my head. It's like walking in the wilderness in the dark. I don't know which wrong step might take me right off the cliff." There. Now David would insist that he'd handle it. Luke waited. And waited. David had tucked his chin slightly, and it occurred to Luke he might be praying. Or sleeping?

After a very long pause, David lifted his chin and surprised him with his response. "Luke, you have to trust God to take you into the wilderness. Sheep have to learn to rely on their shepherd for the leading."

"Huh?"

"There's a verse in Psalm 23 that's been running through my mind today. *Lead us along paths of righteousness.* What do you suppose that meant to a shepherd boy?"

Luke took off his hat, scratched his hair. He had no idea, but he could tell David expected some kind of response. "Eg geht der Herd noh, wie en Schof." *To be mindful not to follow the herd like a sheep.*

"Maybe so." David tipped his head slightly from side to side. "But maybe King David was thinking of something even more simple. In Israel, where he cared for his flock, there's not lush grass pastures like in Stoney Ridge. The terrain in Israel is vast, rocky and dry. There are springs of water, but they're not easy to find. Sheep without a shepherd couldn't

227

last long in the wilderness. The thing is"—he leaned forward in his chair and pointed to Luke—"you don't know how skilled a shepherd is until you go into the tough terrain, the real wilderness. When you're on your own in a treacherous situation, you'll find that God can lead you to what you need." David smiled. "'Lead me along paths of righteousness.' That's what you're looking for, Luke."

Wrong. That was not the advice Luke was hoping David would give him. In fact, it only confused and perplexed him.

The bell on the store's front door jingled as a customer arrived. "Hello? Hello? Anybody here?" There was no mistaking the deep voice that bellowed through the empty store. Freeman Glick.

Luke bolted from his chair. "Is there a back door?"

"Yes, but it's broken. Permanently locked."

Oh boy. He shot a glance at the door to David's office and there stood Freeman, filling the doorway like a giant. Goliath-like.

"Luke Schrock," he said, as if identifying Luke to himself. His brother Levi stood right behind him, trying to see over Freeman's big shoulders. "What are you doing here?"

Wow, he was big. Bigger than the other night, even. "Just, uh, saying hello."

Freeman knew. He took a few steps into David's office, glaring at Luke the entire time with shaggy gray eyebrows knitted together. Luke tried to hold his ground but soon caved in. He gave a hurried goodbye and darted past Freeman and Levi to flee the room.

It had happened again. Each time Luke went out on a branch, sure enough, it broke, and so did he.

EIGHTEEN

A barn swallow fluttered through the rafters to disappear into its nest. Sam watched it for a while, wondering why it wasn't going south like most birds did. He wondered if birds ever regretted their decisions, like people did.

The barn door creaked open and he craned his neck around the stall door, curious as to who had come. He saw Mollie's head peek inside and he hurried to greet her. "Come on in," he said, holding the door open for her. "It's freezing this morning." The black bonnet brim set off her fine-boned fragility—the delicate jaw, chin, and nose; the mouth shaped like a leaf of sweetheart ivy. Around her face, tiny springing curls escaped her prayer cap. Her cheeks were pink with cold and he could see she was shivering.

Her blue eyes sought Sam's and he felt as if someone had just cranked the heat up in the barn. Those blue eyes, they were as soft and gentle as a summer sky.

"Sam, the girls have been bitten by the bug. The horse bug. They said that your saucy mare came to them and bumped her nose at them. I know this sounds funny, but I think it was the first time they'd felt a connection with something other than themselves."

"How so?"

"They have a way of pushing others away. I don't think they have any friends. Your horse . . . she sought them out. It sounds crazy . . ."

"Not so crazy." He understood what it was like to feel a connection with a horse; he felt it each time he held a horse's reins in his hands. It continued to fill him with awe to realize he was in control of this powerful animal, and with it came a sense of responsibility, of stewardship. Of privilege. "Carrie and Abel have a pony. I'll ask them if they'd let the girls ride it. I'm sure they'd say yes. I could even stay and supervise. Make sure there's no funny business going on."

"It's more than pony rides they want. They want to help you train them."

He could feel his mouth open in shock. "Oh no, Mollie," he sputtered. "No. Not a chance."

"Animals can teach children so much. About discipline, about self-control, about consistency. Hasn't horse training given you so much structure and guidance?"

She had him there. Still, it was an audacious and unreasonable request. To allow two girls who had proven themselves to him, numerous times, as mischief makers, to be near his beloved horses . . . on a *regular* basis. No way. He couldn't do it. "Mollie, you can't keep pretending those two girls are sweet as honey. They're an accident waiting to happen." His words were said in a gentle tone, but he could see that they hurt her.

She sighed. "Those words, those labels, that's all Tina and Alicia have ever heard, all their life. That they're trouble.

They're a nuisance. They're a bother. The words we hear as children are the ones we end up believing about ourselves. Imagine if we changed those words. Imagine if someone like you, someone they admired as much as they admire you, were to say to them, 'You're worth my time. Teaching you about horses, about something I love, would be a privilege.' Imagine that, Sam. Spirit-lifting words. Why, such words could change their entire perception about themselves. Words can do that. Time given to a child can do that. Their stories can be rewritten."

For a long moment, he could only stare at her, trying to absorb those words she'd spoken. "I'll give it some thought." He touched the brim of his hat. "I have to go now." And he pivoted on his boot heels and left her at the barn door.

Surprise held Mollie still a moment as she watched Sam go. He had a long-legged stride, and when he disappeared into the tack room, she let out a breath she hadn't realized she'd been holding.

She left the warmth of the barn to head home, wrapping her sweater tight around her middle and tucking her hands in the sleeves as she felt the shock of the brisk November air. She rubbed her throat, running her finger along her scar, wondering if she was coming down with a sore throat and cold. She hoped that's all it was. Oh, how she hoped so.

She'd said something wrong to Sam, something that had caused him to grow upset with her. He didn't move or make a sound, but she could feel the change in him. She had looked up, into his eyes. He was so tall, she had to raise her chin to see them. And he was so fine to look at that she wanted to smile at the sheer wonder of him. Whatever she'd said, it was like she'd slapped him with her words. She could sense him recoil and withdraw, could see his Adam's apple bob above his collar and his jaw pull rigid. In an instant, those beautiful eyes of his had gone from bright blue to stormy gray. What could she have said that caused such a strong reaction?

Halting uncertainly, she turned back.

Sam knew Mollie must feel puzzled by his abrupt departure. He practically shook as his breath rushed in and out of his throat. He had to get away from her, from what she had said to him.

He marched straight to the tack room and plopped down on a trunk. He dropped his head, holding it in his hands. His whole body shuddered hard, as if he were trying to throw off the mantle Mollie had tried to place on him.

The words we hear as children are the ones we end up believing about ourselves.

There it was. She struck an arrow at his heart, at the very target. The core of his insecurity, the reason he tried so hard to be invisible. He had such a yearning to have heard different words about himself. To have been seen as Sam Schrock, not as Dean Schrock's son, the man who hurt so many people. Or the brother of troublemaker Luke Schrock. *Those Schrocks* . . . It was spoken as if it were one word, *thoseSchrocks*, with contempt, with a jeer.

Imagine if Sam's own story could be rewritten, like Mollie said. He took a deep breath and leaned his back against the wall. Imagine if he had grown up with a different set of words, viewed as an individual, not lumped together as a worthless Schrock and written off. What if he'd heard affirming words like those Mollie spoke of him, the way he knew she viewed him, as a man with something to give to others. As a man who could help rewrite the story for others.

Again, his whole body shuddered. He closed his eyes, his lips moving in prayer. *Lord, let me be that man. Let me become the man you want me to be, throwing off those hobbling labels.*

He opened his eyes and blew out a breath. *Let me be the man who Mollie thinks I am.*

He took off his hat and raked a hand through his hair. He slapped his hat against his thigh as if he was knocking mud off it. Then he placed his hat on his head. First thing, he needed to go find Mollie and tell her he would help change those girls' stories. He stood up, and there she was.

"Sam, I'm sorry if I said something to offend you."

He shook his head. "You didn't. It's me." He took off his hat and held it against his stomach. "Mollie, when I was growing up . . ." He stopped, feeling that familiar knot in his throat.

Her eyes swept to his. "What about when you were growing up?"

She had a way about her that loosened his jaws, made him want to trust her with the secrets that hurt most. "When I was growing up," he started again, "my father had an investment business. He did the best he could. He liked helping people. But he made some mistakes, big mistakes, and lost a lot of money for people. That's how we ended up living at The Inn at Eagle Hill. It was my grandmother's home. We couldn't afford to live anywhere else. For a long time, Luke and I were known as the sons of Dean Schrock, and—" He glanced away, reluctant to complete the thought after all.

"And what?" she encouraged.

"And not in a good way." He studied the tips of his boots, remembering. "Then, my brother Luke broke out from under that cloud and created his own identity. So then I was known as the brother of Luke Schrock."

"And not in a good way."

One corner of his mouth lifted. "Luke's come a long way."

"I think I understand what you're saying, Sam."

Did she? How could she? He hardly understood himself.

"About the girls . . . this morning they told me they want a new foster mom."

"What? Oh, Mollie, I'm sorry."

"Don't be! I was pleased. They told me I say no too much. Me?! Can you believe it?" Mollie's whole face lit in a smile, and he couldn't help but smile back. "These girls live under a cloud. The same way you did. I don't want them to end up there."

"So what is it you think I could do for these two girls?" *So they don't end up under a cloud?*

She took a deep breath. "I was hoping you might allow the girls to come help you after school, maybe just for an hour." Before he could object, she added, "I'll come too. I'll be here the whole time. An extra pair of eyes on them. I won't let them out of my sight."

"Mollie . . ."

"Would you be willing to give it a try? Just once? See if they can prove to you that their interest is sincere? If you're willing, I'd like to use time with the horses as a reward for good behavior." She scrunched her face. "I don't have much else to hold over them, but the horses . . . that might be just what I need. If you'd be willing to give it a try."

He looked at her. Looked at her and smiled, for how did a man say no to those big blue eyes? "I suppose I can give it a try."

"Oh Sam, I appreciate it more than you can imagine."

But he could imagine, because she was nearly radiant with thanks. For a while, neither of them moved. They smiled at each other and a moment of blatant attraction fluttered between them. Sam bent over and took her face in his hands, his thumbs lightly tracing the bones in her cheeks. "Mollie, I . . ." He took a deep breath and started again, like the way he'd been practicing these last few days. "Mollie, I have some real fond feelings for you. And I wondered how you'd feel about courting. Us, I mean. You and me."

Mollie looked at him, stunned silent.

The next morning, Mollie found a bouquet of wildflowers sitting by the front door of the schoolhouse in an empty peanut butter jar. The last of the flowers for the year. A note was attached:

To Mollie. Would you like to go on a picnic with me at Blue Lake Pond this Sunday afternoon? Weather's supposed to be real nice.

Love, Sam

Oh my. Oh dear. Yesterday, he threw her for a loop when he asked to court her. She knew she should've said something in return, but her mind went blank, and before she could put a string of words into a sentence, a horse started kicking his stall and Sam dashed into the barn. When he returned, he seemed preoccupied, as if the moment had not happened.

She read his note over again, and those last words twice. *Love, Sam.*

Mollie squeezed her eyes shut. A panic gripped her chest so tightly that she had to sit down on the porch steps, afraid she might fall down.

Yes, she'd like to go on a picnic with Sam Schrock. She'd like it very much. But no, she wouldn't go. She couldn't do that to him. It just wouldn't be fair.

NINETEEN

Sam laid down strict rules for Tina and Alicia around his horses. They were to obey him without question. One mistake and they would be sent home. "Got it?" he asked. "One mistake, one ignored request, one forgotten chore"—he pointed his thumb toward the road—"just one, and you're out."

Alicia nodded vigorously.

"We totally got this, Sam," Tina said.

"Last thing," Sam said. "One hour. At the end of one hour, you need to head on home. No hanging around."

They both gave him their biggest smiles. So bright he could light the barn with them. Hmm, he wondered how this was going to work.

He told them to sit on a fence post and watch as he exercised a horse. Around and around and around the paddock, over and over. It was the least exciting thing he could think to do, apart from mucking out stalls. He wanted to bore them out of this imagined fascination they had for horses. Fifteen minutes, twenty, tops. And they'd be heading off down the road, off to chase another passing interest.

Unexpectedly, the opposite happened. They grew enchanted. As he curried the horse after the exercise session, they peppered him with questions. Intelligent questions, which surprised Sam, as he hadn't considered the girls to be particularly brainy.

"Why'd you keep turning the direction that the horse was going?" Tina asked.

"The horse has to learn the signals for left or right, so that when it's out in traffic, pulling a buggy, it'll know which way to go."

"Why did you keep stopping and starting so much?"

"Think of how often a car has to stop in traffic. A horse has to be able to come to a complete stop, then start again."

As soon as he finished answering Tina's questions, Alicia piped up with her own questions. "What words do you whisper to horses?"

"What do you mean?"

"You speak to them in words we can't understand."

"They're Penn Dutch words. A dialect of German. That's our people's first language."

Alicia seemed to think that answer over briefly, then posed a surprising question. "How can one person know so much?"

"From years and years of watching my stepfather as he worked with the horses."

Alicia looked thoughtful for a moment. "I meant . . . about everything."

Her comment threw him for a loop, and he didn't know how to respond, so he didn't even try. Instead, he let the girls lead the horse to its stall and fill its bucket with water. He showed Alicia where he kept the oats in the tack room and had her fill an empty coffee can half full. "A treat for his

238

good work today." He let her spill the oats into the horse's feed bucket.

Tina remained glued to the stall door, adoring eyes fixed on the gelding. "Can we give him a carrot?"

"Please, Sam?" Alicia asked.

Gone was the mischief shining in their eyes. Why not? Sam showed the girls how to keep their palm open so the horse could mouth the carrot with its lips.

"Can we come back tomorrow?" Tina asked.

There'd been no cigarettes, nothing had been set on fire, no mice caught, there was no need to lock the girls in a horse stall to keep them out of trouble until Mollie arrived. All in all, a shockingly successful afternoon. "Tomorrow. Same time. Just for one hour."

He watched them run down the driveway—no, not running. They were loping, like horses. Like little girls. The sight of them made him smile, especially when he recalled how they looked when he had first met them: droopy shoulders, hands jammed in jeans' pockets, chins dropped low. And their eyes—they were constantly rolling upward in disgust. He wished Mollie were here to see those cantering girls, but Tina said she wasn't feeling well this afternoon.

He walked out to the pasture to bring in a mare, and his mind was filled with memories. Lately, unbidden memories kept floating through his mind and he wasn't sure why. Maybe because he was about the same age as Tina and Alicia when Galen had taken time to show him how to care for horses. He had fallen hard for them, and he wondered if Tina and Alicia were headed down the same path. It surprised him to even think such a thought, as not much more than an hour ago, he would've written them off. Time would tell for

Tina's and Alicia's interest in horses to fade away or grow steadfast, just as time had done for him as a boy.

Galen had been tough on Sam, tougher than he needed to be. Sam wasn't Luke, but everyone thought he was. They looked alike, they talked and walked alike. But their similarities were only skin deep. Sam remembered a time when he and Luke were small boys, and their grandmother had given them both coloring books and a new package of crayons. Luke, for some strange reason, didn't color the figures but everything outside of the picture. Colored outside the lines. Carefully and intentionally, Sam colored inside the lines. A perfect metaphor for the two brothers.

When Galen finally gave Sam the opportunity to apprentice as a horse trainer, he took it very seriously. He wanted to prove to Galen that he could measure up, and in doing so, he proved a lot to himself too.

And he felt protective over those horses in a powerful way. If he allowed himself to love them, he feared it would overwhelm him. The one time he had loved a horse, it *had* overwhelmed him. That horse was the reason why he wouldn't name the horses he trained. He referred to them, even in his mind, as the chestnut, or the sorrel, or the bay. No distinctive names. They weren't pets. They were working animals. They were meant for someone else to love.

That thinking allowed him a sense of detachment, so that when it came time to sell a trained horse to a buyer, he could let the horse go. Open palms. Detachment had worked well for Sam, a good strategy for coping with life. But then he met Mollie Graber.

On Friday morning, before school started, Mollie scootered to Sam's place. She knocked on the front door but there was no answer, so she went to the barn, the next most likely place to find him. The large sliding doors were open, and as she walked inside, the barn held a mixture of sweet and pungent smells, hay and horses and manure. Familiar smells.

Sam was in the center aisle with a horse held in crossties. He had the horse's left rear hoof up on his thigh, and he was scraping caked dirt and dung out of it with a hoof pick. He straightened as soon as he saw her. She hadn't seen him since the day he'd asked if he could court her. She hadn't thanked him for the flowers or responded to his note.

She came around to the mare's right side and petted the soft nose. "Sam, I'm grateful to you for what you're doing for Tina and Alicia. They talk about horses all the time. Morning, noon, and night. I took them to the library last evening and got library cards for them. They checked out books about horses. Not story books, but nonfiction books. *How to Care for Your Horse,* that was one title."

He had yet to take his eyes off her. He didn't say anything, but she could tell he was listening.

"For the first time, they have something to look forward to each day. They feel like they're helping you, though I'm sure they're creating more work than help. I think it's the first time they're thinking about something bigger than themselves."

The creases around his mouth deepened for a moment. "They do seem to be having themselves a time."

"They do," she said. "It's been four days now without a single call from school. Four days in which they haven't ditched school, they haven't even disappeared during gym class. I don't think they've smoked a single cigarette this entire week! I think I would've known by the smell of their clothes. It's been a very peaceful week with Tina and Alicia. And I thank you for it. For all you've done for them. For us."

"I'm glad for you, Mollie. For the girls too. They haven't caused any trouble for me, just the opposite. They're good helpers."

"The wildflowers you left me . . . they were the prettiest flowers I've ever seen. That was very thoughtful of you, Sam. And I haven't had a chance to respond to your invitation about a picnic at Blue Lake Pond this Sunday. It's a lovely invitation. Any girl in Stoney Ridge would be over the moon to receive such an invitation from you. Thrilled."

He reddened to the tips of his ears. Silence spun out between them, and Mollie caught a look on Sam's face that said it was bracing for disappointment. He bent down to finish cleaning the last hoof, then tossed the hoof pick back into the box. She watched him exchange the hoof pick for a curry brush and begin to run it over the mare's neck and withers. She watched his hands move over the horse's glossy mahogany hide. Those hands of his, so strong but so gentle too. That was the thing she was most attracted to in Sam. He was both strong and gentle. A rare combination in a man.

She breathed in. "Sam, I've been giving a lot of thought about us, these last few days. About courting."

His look of apprehension grew, and he bent his chin down to hide it, but she still noticed how his fingers tightened on the curry brush. Clenched.

She drew out the words with the slow easing of a pent-up breath. "And I think it's better to end it now."

He snapped erect and their eyes met. In his she saw uncertainty and hurt, but then his gaze fell away from hers, and he went back to currying his horse. "Whatever you think is best," he said, a strange roughness in his voice.

She reached across the horse's withers, to touch one of the smile lines that edged his mouth, although he wasn't smiling.

He shook his head, stepping back, moving away from her touch. Out of her reach.

TWENTY

Late on Friday afternoon, Jesse Stoltzfus came by the fix-it shop at Windmill Farm. "Jenny's asking for you," he said to Izzy. "Labor started midmorning, but it's going slow."

Izzy was thrilled to be asked for. She grabbed her sweater and blew out the lantern, then stopped short by the door. This time, it was she who left a note tacked up for Luke, in a place where he'd see it.

> *At Jenny's. Baby's on its way. I won't be home until the baby arrives.*
>
> XO Izzy
>
> *P.S. Leftovers for dinner in the fridge.*

Jenny had wanted a home birth this time around, with a midwife in attendance. The midwife arrived late in the day, but warned them it looked like a long night ahead. After getting Rosie to bed, Izzy told Jesse to sleep while he could. She and the midwife took turns walking Jenny around and around the little house through the wee hours. Nearing dawn, the midwife delivered Jenny's baby girl. Ten miniature fingers and toes, a tiny rosebud mouth. Soft, pink baby skin. Hair as fine as cobwebs. So fragile, so perfect.

Izzy would never forget those miraculous moments of the baby's first experience in the outside world. Her little face, so pinched and mad it was almost comical. Red and squawking, full of complaints. And then, placed in her mother's arms, her crying stopped immediately. She opened her eyes to peer at her mother for the first time. Izzy felt her heart swell with love so unexpected it made her eyes sting. Followed by a desperate longing to have a baby of her own.

When the sun was fully up, Birdy and Fern arrived to meet the new baby and watch Rosie and offer any needed help. Jenny asked Izzy if she'd give Chris a call, to let their brother know the baby had come.

"You go. Fresh horses are here to help," Fern told Izzy as she gathered her sweater and gloves to go outside. "Make the call to Chris and then get home to sleep."

A warm bed sounded pretty good to Izzy. In the phone shanty, she sat on the little stool and noticed that the message light was blinking. She found a pen and paper to write down the message and pressed the blinking button. As soon as she heard the familiar voice on the recording, she stilled.

"Jenny-girl, hi there, it's Mama. I'm, uh . . . just checking in to see how you're doing. I had a dream last night about your baby. A little blonde girl, looking just like you and me, that's what I dreamed. Funny, huh? Well, I just wanted you to know I'm thinking about you. Give Rosie a big hug and kiss from me. And, um . . . tell your sister hey for me. I'll call again soon. Love ya."

Izzy shrank on the stool as if she'd been kicked in the stomach. She closed her eyes for a moment, as a sweep of

exhaustion hit her. She was tired from being up all night . . .
and then this. *"Tell your sister hey for me."* Her mother's
indifference stung. But it didn't hurt quite as much as it had
in the past. She was okay.

Basic trust. That was her dropped stitch. She had to keep
going back to that dropped stitch and repair it. Make it whole.

On the way home, she ruminated. *The Lord is my shepherd,
I shall not want.* Over and over and over. *I shall not want.*

When Luke saw Izzy after returning from Jenny's, he was
afraid something had gone wrong with the baby.

"The baby's fine. Jenny's fine. Everything's fine." Izzy
walked straight through the fix-it shop and into their bedroom to flop on the bed.

Luke knew, because he could see through the walls.

He put down the broken buggy lantern he'd been working
on and walked right through the two-by-fours to check on
her. "Can I get you something? Are you hungry?"

"No, thanks."

He sat on the bed and rubbed her back in circles. "Feeling okay?"

"I'm fine. Just tired. Was up all night, walking around the
house with Jenny."

"Walking?"

"That's what the midwife said to do. Every time Jenny
sat down or lay down, the labor stalled out. Walking kept
it going."

Luke tried to puzzle that one out and couldn't. He'd seen
plenty of farm animals give birth, but he'd never seen one
walk its way through labor. "David is coming by soon. We

shouldn't be too long." He wasn't really sure when he'd return, though. David was vague about this errand.

"Why don't you just say what it is?" she asked. "Deacon duty."

He'd learned by now that she had a certain tone in her voice when it came to his deacon duty. The best way to soften her was to be soft himself, so rather than point out that she didn't sound like she was supporting his deaconing (like he'd done once before, and that didn't end well), he changed the subject. "You came back earlier than I thought. I'd figured you'd be gone for a couple of days." Really, he had no idea how long it took a baby to get born.

She'd been turned away from him, but she craned around to look at him. "Fern and Birdy arrived, so I went home. I stopped to call Chris, to let him know the baby was born. There was a phone message from my mother. To Jenny. She'd had a dream about Jenny's baby. Said she even knew what the baby would look like. Just like her and Jenny." She lifted her head slightly. "Funny thing is . . . she was right. The baby does look like them. Not like me."

"Man, oh, man. Grace sure is crazy about babies. Seems like she's trying to make up to Jenny for being a lousy mother by being an overly attentive grandmother."

She rolled on her side away from him. What had he said that was so wrong? After all, it was true.

"Izzy . . ."

"I think I hear David's buggy coming up the drive. You'd better go." Her voice was muffled under her arm, but nothing was wrong with her hearing. The jingling sound of David's buggy grew louder.

"I'll be back by supper."

"It's okay, Luke. Just come back when you can."

She didn't sound upset with him, not like he'd expected, and that worried him more than a frown. This quietness, it was hard for him to understand.

As Luke climbed into the buggy, David glanced at him. "Everything all right?"

"Sure. Fine. Everything's just fine." No, not at all.

David didn't say much for the rest of the ride. He seemed just as preoccupied as Luke. As they arrived at a farmhouse, David turned to Luke and said, "Today, listen and learn."

He didn't need to tell Luke that. It was exactly what Luke tried to do whenever he was on an "errand" with David. Today's errand turned out to be a dramatic confrontation with a man in their church who had been making phone calls to an indecent source. His wife had turned him in. The man denied it at first, defiant and furious, but then his wife pulled out their phone bill and placed it on the table, right in front of David and Luke. Hard evidence. At that point, the man broke down and cried, begging for forgiveness. The entire scene was very upsetting to Luke. This man, he was held in high regard. And his wife Luke had never thought much of—she seemed like the timid type who wouldn't say boo to a goose. It turned out, he should have had the opposite view. The wife had the strength to force a needed change.

Another example why Luke shouldn't be a deacon. He had no sense of discernment. "What's next for him?"

"I want to give him the opportunity to come to me, to ask to bend at the knee in church."

Public confession of a sin. Luke was well acquainted with bending at the knee. He'd done it many times. "If he doesn't?"

"Then he'll be placed under the ban. But my hope and

prayer is that he will seek repentance and restoration. I've found that it's most effective when it comes from within a person, not when it's imposed on them by church leaders."

There. That was exactly why Luke didn't want to push Freeman Glick. That was the answer he was looking to hear.

David pulled the horse to a stop at a red light. "So, being a deacon, how's it affecting your marriage?"

Luke felt his collar tighten up. He cleared his throat. "It has its ups and downs." More downs than ups.

"It's quite an adjustment. Takes a toll." The light turned green and David made a clucking sound to get the horse going.

"Not for you and Birdy."

David glanced at him, surprised, and let out a laugh. "Of course it did. Especially during our first year, when I became bishop. I'll be honest with you, most of our misunderstandings could've been easily avoided."

"How so?"

"I tried to keep Birdy sheltered and protected from all the bishop work I had to do so that I wasn't dragging her down with the church's problems. That was a big mistake."

"Whoa. Hold on, David. Just hold on a minute. I thought this church work had to be top secret."

"It has to be held in the greatest respect. We're involved in people's private lives, and we're trying to bring God's goodness to them. Sometimes that involves some rather unpleasant encounters, like today."

"No kidding." Luke felt weighed down with sadness after leaving that couple's farmhouse. It gave him a sick feeling to confront a man with his sin, especially when you knew you were just as much of a sinner in your own way.

David flicked the reins to get the horse to pick up its pace.

"God didn't intend for man to do this work alone. Birdy wants to help me with it, either by talking things through or praying over them. She's an utterly trustworthy partner, just like I imagine Izzy to be. Am I right?"

"Izzy?" Luke scoffed. "She's a sphinx. Fort Knox. You know that as well as I do." He looked at David, astounded. "So you're saying I can discuss deaconing with Izzy?"

"Of course, Luke. I'm sorry I didn't make that clear to you. I thought it would be obvious. Use your judgment, because there may be some situations she's better off not knowing. But don't let the deacon work interfere with your marriage. I know it did at first for me and Birdy. She felt very left out, very distant from me, and yet my schedule had an enormous impact on family life. I can hardly bear to think of all the missed opportunities I had to make her feel like a true partner to me. Once we worked that out, our marriage took off."

Luke lifted his hand in the air, like a plane taking off. "Smooth sailing from there."

Again, David laughed. "No, I wouldn't call it smooth sailing. Not with eight children. But it definitely helped us feel more satisfied with our marriage. And I'm very grateful for Birdy's input. The way she thinks, the insights she has. She sees things I miss. I think I learn more from her than just about anybody else. That's what a good marriage is meant to do. Sand down our rough edges."

"David, you just contradicted yourself. Good marriages don't have rough edges."

"Oh, but they do. And they should. That's exactly what I'm trying to get at, Luke. Thinking that a good marriage isn't made, that it just *is*, well, that thinking can get you into a lot of trouble. It's like a farmer who expects the sun to shine every day. But that's not the way of life. Rain comes, and it has a purpose too."

"I'm not sure what you mean."

"Most young couples go into marriage with the expectation that it will be sunshine and roses, every day. All smooth sailing. You love each other, you want to be together. And then reality sets in. You have a misunderstanding, or an argument. Suddenly, married life isn't so wonderful." He lifted his hands, palms up. "It's not unusual for couples to think they've made a mistake."

Luke felt a bead of perspiration on his forehead. It was like David could read his mind. That's exactly what he'd been thinking lately—not that he shouldn't have married Izzy, but that they married too soon. If they had waited, had more life experiences and maturity and time to develop better patterns of communication, then it would have made their marriage less bumpy. More smooth sailing. And he wouldn't have become the deacon either. You had to be married to be a deacon. Just think! He could've dodged that bullet.

Somehow, David once again seemed to have a sense of what was running through Luke's mind. "The mistake isn't that a couple in love shouldn't have married."

"Then what's the mistake?"

"Assuming that marriage wouldn't be difficult. God designed it to be a refining tool. To grow our characters. All marriages have their challenges. Every single one. But it's how we allow God to use our marriage to make us more Christlike, then those challenges become opportunities. That's the difference between a marriage of ups and downs . . . or an excellent marriage."

This wasn't the way Luke had viewed his marriage. He perceived each problem that he and Izzy faced as insurmountable. Another hurdle, another disappointment. He'd had enough counseling to know that he had serious shortcomings with awareness, thoughtfulness, and empathy. Izzy's upbringing—or lack thereof—brought all kinds of problems with it: reluctance to trust, to be forthcoming, to be intimate. They loved each other, but they didn't seem to be able to make much progress with their weaknesses. He'd assumed that he and Izzy would always have a more difficult marriage than others did. It was just their burden to bear.

It never dawned on him that the friction they felt in daily life was normal, that it could be a tool. Sandpaper to smooth out those rough edges.

How many lessons were there in life? He had no idea. Luke chewed on that line of thinking for the rest of the ride home, feeling cheered up after the afternoon's grim errand.

They drove past the schoolhouse. Luke saw Mollie Graber out in front of the schoolhouse and waved. She was picking up her scooter and didn't look up. Then she let it drop.

He craned his neck to look at her. She leaned back against the schoolhouse as if she suddenly had no more strength to stand. He squinted, wondering if they should stop and see if she was all right. Before he could say anything, she had pushed herself from the wall and picked up her scooter.

See? What did he know about women? Not much.

As Mollie scootered home, she felt exhausted from a long school day. She had so much to do before she could climb into bed tonight, but that was all she could think of doing, as if her bed was calling to her. She needed to mend a tear in Tina's jean jacket, help Alicia with her math homework, grade papers, make supper, clean up, make lunches for tomorrow . . . the list seemed endless. *Listen to you, Mollie Graber. For shame,* she tsked, scolding herself. *Just two weeks ago, you would've been wondering what trouble Tina and Alicia had gotten themselves into today, and whether the sheriff would be making a visit. You should be grateful that all you've got on your mind today is chores.*

Mollie opened up the door to her cottage and her eyes fell right on the small sofa that Aunt Fern had handed down to her. Tina and Alicia were over at Sam's barn and weren't expected home for another hour. Maybe she could just catch a little nap. She untied the strings beneath her chin and set the bonnet on the wall hook. Without even taking her shoes off, she climbed on the couch, pulled the heavy knitted afghan over her, and closed her eyes, overwhelmed by a weariness that went bone deep.

It was nearly dark. Sam was crossing the yard to the house and heard a terrible banshee scream coming from the road. He stopped, squinted, and saw Tina running toward him at a full gallop, arms spinning like a windmill. "She's dead! Mollie's dead!"

TWENTY-ONE

S am paced the waiting room of the emergency room, waiting for Fern Lapp to return from checking on Mollie. He was having a hard time. Hospitals made him anxious; they reminded him of his father's death, when life had spiraled completely out of control. Sam was a young boy when his father died, but the effect on his family was like they'd all been involved in a horrific car wreck. Like each family member had suffered injuries from the impact. Sam remembered feeling as if his childhood had come to a screeching halt. After that, life grew somber.

Right now, it felt deadly serious.

Tears floated in front of his eyes. He tried to curb his anxiety with rational thoughts: Mollie wasn't dead, she'd only fainted.

Then irrational thoughts would invade his mind: being unconscious was bad too.

Rational: The ambulance driver said she had a strong pulse, a steady heartbeat.

Irrational: Sam had held Mollie's hand as they waited for the ambulance to come. Her hand felt so small and fragile in his, and he couldn't bear it.

Rational: She had regained consciousness.

Irrational: But she had looked pasty white. And she was so weak.

Rational: She was young. She might have caught a virus from the scholars.

Irrational: Viruses can kill you.

Fern walked through the swinging doors before he could counter his last irrational thought with a rational one. He bolted toward her. "How is she?"

"She's doing better," Fern said. "They're giving her an IV to get some liquids in her. She's run-down, is all."

Oh no. No, no. He knew there was more to Mollie's fainting than being run-down. He'd seen how tired she'd become these last few weeks. He hadn't forgotten that she needed to take some kind of prescription pills each day. Something was going on with her. "Fern, I have a right to know what's wrong with Mollie."

Her sparse eyebrows lifted. "How so?"

"Because . . . I care for her. And she cares for me."

Fern openly regarded him. "She said that?"

"Not exactly. In fact, she told me she wanted to end us before we began. I've been giving that a lot of thought. I don't think she told me that because she doesn't care about me. I think it's because she's afraid of something. Is this it? Is something wrong with her? Fern, I need to know the truth."

She looked at him, shoulders stiff, then dropped them. She thumbed toward the chairs. "Better sit down for this."

"I can't." Too antsy.

But Fern sat, smoothed out her apron over her dark green dress. "When Mollie was eighteen, she had a sore throat that just wouldn't quit. The doctor did a bunch of tests and finally determined it was thyroid cancer."

He made a raw, gasping sound, as if the breath had backed up in his lungs, hot and thick.

"She went through surgery and treatment. It took quite a toll on her. It left a mark."

"Her voice," he whispered, stunned. How he loved her husky voice.

"That, yes, and the scar on her neck. She's worried the cancer has come back."

Sam's head rocked back a little, as if he'd just been slapped hard, and in a way, he was. *Oh, God, please no.* The room dipped; he had to sit down. "Why hasn't she told me? Why didn't she tell me that she'd had cancer at all?"

"She didn't want anyone to know."

"Why not?"

"Her mother, my brother's wife, she's a born worrier. Worst worrier I've ever known. I think my sister-in-law had made Mollie feel so sheltered that the poor girl couldn't really live, all she could do was not die. She had to get away, have a fresh start somewhere. So when the school job opened up, I invited her to come out, stay with me at Windmill. She agreed to come but she wanted to find a place to rent on her own. To have a say-so, to make her own decisions."

Sam rubbed his face with his hands. "Like fostering children."

"Yes. Just like that." Fern shifted in the chair. "Speaking of Tina and Alicia, I should make a phone call. I left them with Luke and Izzy and Cassidy. They'll need to stay the night at Windmill Farm."

He put out his hand to stop her from getting up. "I'll head home. I'll let Luke know."

Fern looked at him, perplexed. "Don't you want to go in and see Mollie?"

Sam stood and shook his head, backing up. "I . . . can't. I just can't. Tell her I'm sorry." And he hurried out the swinging doors, taking in great gulps of air. He was suddenly a small boy again, hearing the news that his father had just died. At that moment, he remembered wishing he'd been born an animal. No feelings. No disappointments. No broken hearts. He thought that if he lost Mollie, if he lost any more, he would never be able to bear it.

Sam lifted his eyes to the black night sky and shook his fist. "Why?" he shouted. "Why do you keep doing this to me?"

Then he fled.

Mollie lay in the hospital bed, longing to fall asleep, but her mind had trouble settling down. Finally, she closed her eyes and repeated Psalm 23 to herself, slowing over the verse "Yea, though I walk through the valley of the shadow of death, I will fear no evil."

So here she was again. Another trip through the valley of the shadow of death. She'd been here before. Most people only went through it once, but it was familiar terrain to her. *I will fear no evil, for thou art with me.*

Thou art with me. Thou art with me. Thou art with me.

Even here. Even in a hospital bed, waiting for tests in the morning. Facing another unknown future. *Even here, thou art with me.*

She thought of Sam, of the worry in his eyes as he sat

next to her in the ambulance. He had a peculiar look on his face, almost like fear, although it was hard to say. She'd never known him to be afraid of anything.

Poor Sam. He tried hard to be tough and strong, invincible, yet he was so soft inside. She wished she could share the peace that she felt. Sam didn't understand simple faith, he told her once. It takes more work.

He was wrong. The only work it took was surrendering.

A sense of quiet contentment stole over Mollie. Her eyelids felt heavier and heavier, and soon she nodded off.

The next day was bitter cold, the leaden skies threatened rain or possibly even snow that evening. All afternoon, Sam exercised each horse, around and around in a circle, until the horses were covered with sweat and so was he.

Around four o'clock, Luke drove up the driveway and hitched his horse to the post. He walked over to the corral and leaned his arms against the top rail. "Looks like you're trying to wear those poor ponies out."

"They need it," Sam said. "They need to be in good shape."

"Sam, stop for a minute. Let's talk."

He couldn't. He couldn't make himself stop. He kept turning the horse around and around in a large circle, snapping the whip behind it to keep it going. Suddenly Luke grabbed the long exercise line and the whip from him. "Whoa, whoa," he said to the horse in a gentle tone. He walked up to the mare and stroked her neck. He took out a handkerchief and wiped the froth dripping from her mouth. "You did well, you can rest now." He unhooked the lead line from the horse's harness and let her roam free in the corral.

Sam stood there, arms dropped.

"I heard about Mollie. I came to take you to the hospital."

Sam turned his head toward the mare as she made her way to the water trough. "I can't go back. I won't."

"Why not?"

Because he couldn't face it. Because he was in unbearable pain. Because he had let himself love a girl and look what had happened.

"Sam, you don't know what Mollie is facing. It might not be a recurrence of cancer."

"But it might. She hasn't been well lately. Not well at all. I could see how tired she looked, but I assumed taking care of Tina and Alicia was wearing her out. I had no idea she'd had cancer."

"She never told you?"

"No."

"Why do you think she didn't?"

He shrugged his shoulders.

"Seems to me that Mollie is all about living strong. Fern said she came here because she didn't want to be living under a shadow of cancer anymore."

"She should have told me."

"Maybe so. But what would that have done? Knowing you, you'd run for the hills. Instead, you've gone and fallen in love with her."

Sam didn't even try to deny that he loved Mollie. Out of him burst a fury. "And look what it got me." He pointed in the general direction of the hospital. "She might be dying."

"Look what it *got* you?" Luke seemed perplexed, incredulous. "Sam, are you telling me that Mollie hasn't brought you happiness? And fun? And laughter? That she hasn't pushed you out of your protected life so you're finally living again?" He shook his head, disgusted. "You're like a turtle."

"What?"

"You're a turtle. You are! You've always been that way. You pull back in your shell at the slightest sign of emotion." He pointed to the house. "You live alone in this big empty house. You take care of Galen's horses all by yourself. Man, you don't even have a horse you call your own. This isn't living, Sam."

Sam stared at him. "Why do you think that is?"

"I don't know."

"Because of you, Luke! You turned this entire community against the Schrocks." Sam saw him swallow hard, and he felt bad saying it, but it was the truth. "Why do you think Mom and Galen moved to Kentucky? Because they couldn't live here anymore." The shocked look on his brother's face only fueled his upset. How could Luke be so obtuse as to not know that? "And then you killed that sorrel." His voice choked up. "The best horse there'd ever been. Or ever will be." The rush of pain brought with it the memory of what had happened, and the hurt from this, from remembering. He took a breath, inhaling deeply, frustrated to the point of tears. He turned around and walked to the fence, pressing his hands on the railing with his head hung low.

After a long moment, Luke walked over to him, stood beside him. After a long pause, he said quietly, "Brother, I didn't know how I hurt you. I should have. I should have been looking out for you. I've had to ask forgiveness from a lot of people, and I've done just that. But now I see that I should have started with you."

Sam shook his head. "You don't have to ask for it. You've

always had it." He wiped his eyes with his shirtsleeve. "It's not you I'm mad at. It's this whole situation. Every time I care about something, or someone, it gets taken away. I don't know why God is always beating down on me."

"I've felt that way too. Especially after Dad died. But I've learned something these last few years. The Lord disciplines those whom he loves."

"So you're saying I've done something to deserve this? That loving Mollie was wrong?"

"No, no." Luke took off his black felt hat and scratched his head. "Memorizing Psalm 23 this fall, there's a verse that keeps hitting me in a new way. The one about God's rod and staff bringing comfort. I think I've realized that when I have felt God's hardness, it's ended up in my best interest. Like, maybe he's saving me from myself." He plopped his hat back on his head. "Mollie's given you a lot, Sam. I've never seen you as happy as you've been since she moved here last summer. Are you going to toss all that out the window so you can avoid pain? If you don't feel the pain, you can't feel the happiness either. Trust me on that." He pushed off from the railing. "I'm heading over to the hospital. You coming?"

Sam watched him stride toward the gate. Could he go? Could he handle what he might discover there? No. No, he couldn't. But he couldn't deny that Luke was right. Mollie had brought him laughter, and happiness, and joy. She made him feel as if he was important. Was he going to forgo that, all that, just to avoid heartache? Was that the kind of man he was? Maybe so. But he didn't want to be that kind of man. "Hold on. I need to get these horses fed. It'll take me a little while. Then I'll go."

Smoothly, as if he'd been expecting such a response, Luke pivoted around on his boot heels. "I'll help."

When Sam walked into the barn, leading the mare to her stall, he was astonished to discover that Tina and Alicia were already feeding hay to the horses. Water buckets were full. Stalls were cleaned. Tina held up three fingers. "Three fingers' width of hay for each one. An extra handful of oats for the saucy mare."

Sam nodded. "Nice work, girls."

Alicia tipped her head toward the barn door. "Ruthie, next door, she said we could stay at the Inn at Eagle Hill tonight. As long as we needed to, she said. We can take care of the horses for you in the morning, in case you stay at the hospital for a long time."

Tina handed Sam some cards. "We made these for Mollie. Tell her that we're sorry she's not feeling well and that we want her to come back home soon. That we miss her."

"That we love her," Alicia added.

With one last surge of strength, Sam said, "I'll tell her." Then he left the barn quickly and went to sit in Luke's buggy, tears streaming down his face.

When Mollie woke, she saw Sam sitting in a chair by the window. She blinked a few times, not sure if it was really him. "Sam?"

He rose to his feet.

"I wasn't sure you'd come," she said.

"I wasn't either."

"I'm glad you did," she added.

"Hope you don't mind. I came to see how you're doing."

"I'm . . . I'm fine." She tried to smile, but she could feel it coming out all wrong, like a grimace. "Fern told you about the cancer, didn't she?" He knew. She could see it in his eyes. He was looking at her in a different way, as if she were made of spun sugar. As if she might shatter.

He raised his hand to stroke her cheek, but then he let it fall without touching her. "Mollie, why didn't you tell me?" His voice was deep with caring.

She lifted her head and drew her shoulders up. "I suppose I should have told you right away, but I didn't realize that I . . . that you . . . felt the way I did . . . and then I wanted to pretend everything would be all right." She smoothed out a wrinkle in the thin hospital blanket. "And then I didn't know how to tell you. Especially after . . ." Involuntarily, she touched her heart. Realizing what she'd done, she dropped her hand. Too late—she was already blushing.

"After I asked if I could court you."

"Yes. You surprised me, Sam. I didn't expect it and I didn't handle it well." Her glance wandered nervously before flicking back to him.

"Mollie, do you know yet if the cancer is back?"

Oh my. Gone was the shy, awkwardly reserved Sam Schrock, so reluctant to share what was on his mind that it took Mollie a steady priming of the pump to get him to talk. In front of her was a bold man who wanted answers. She had a pretty good idea why he was asking too. She fiddled with the corner of her bedsheet. "They did some tests today. And one is scheduled for the morning. It'll take a while to find out the results." She looked up to find his face filled with pain and longing, and wondered if it was just a matter of time before he found a way to leave. Not just leave the hospital room, but leave their budding romance too. "I don't blame you for not wanting to stick around, Sam. I really don't. I have a solitary journey ahead of me, and I'm at peace with that because I'm not truly alone. God is with me, every step." She tilted her head back on the pillow and gave him a gentle smile. "It's okay to go."

Sam went utterly still, and Mollie thought he was going to tell her goodbye. That he wished her well, all the best, but that he couldn't handle the uncertainty of her illness. She braced herself for it, held herself ready for the rejection. She could feel patches of sweat on her forehead and cheeks. The room had grown so hot. But, strangely, her hands were cold. She wrapped them in the bed sheet.

But then his face softened and a tenderness came into his eyes. He sat on the bed, leaned into her, tilting his head, and his mouth came down onto hers. His lips were warm. He kissed her with such sweetness it was almost unbearable. She closed her eyes and trembled. He touched her nowhere else, just his lips pressing against hers.

He pulled back from her. "I think . . . ," he said, fumbling for the words a moment, the way he struggled when he had something important to say. Then he found them. "I think of how swiftly time passes, and I don't want to waste a single minute without you."

He put his hands on either side of her face and kissed her again, strong and sturdy. It was a new kind of kiss. It was grown-up and decisive. She knew without thinking how to kiss him back the same way.

TWENTY-TWO

Sleep was impossible for Luke that night. He didn't even bother to try. He sat in the fix-it shop, tinkering with a broken dish of Fern's that needed glue. A simple fix, if there was such a thing.

He'd just come from another one of Freeman Glick's drunken benders. The worst one of all. By the time Luke had arrived, broken furniture littered the room. His wife was trying to get him to bed, and he hauled off and punched her, right in front of Luke. It was the final straw, even for Freeman. When he realized he'd hurt his wife, he dropped to his knees and started to wail.

First off, Luke had made sure Freeman's wife wasn't seriously injured, got an ice pack for her cheek, and sent her to bed. Then he sat across from Freeman and waited for his crying jag to run out of steam. "Freeman, you've got to get help. This drinking has gone on long enough. You can't stop. Look, I want you to go to the Mountain Vista rehab facility. It's where I went to get help. They have counselors who speak Penn Dutch, they work with our faith, they'll help you get on top of this. You're not able to stop drinking without help."

Freeman glanced up, refocused his eyes. Something seemed to be stirring in him. Had Luke made a small breakthrough?

"You'll go then?" he asked hopefully.

"No. But I'll stop the drinking."

Recalling the scene, Luke let out a sigh. He tried to shake it off and focus his attention on fixing Fern's broken dish. Amos had given her this dish, and she loved it. Fixing it for her felt like one thing—the only thing—Luke could do right lately.

"What's wrong?"

He turned to see Izzy at the door, wrapped in her bathrobe. "Did the light wake you?"

"Yes. No. I can't sleep unless you're next to me."

He opened his arms and she leaned into him. "Freeman Glick. He's a drunk."

She jerked her head up. "Freeman Glick? That stern, proud, humorless man?"

"The very one. Starts drinking Sunday afternoon and goes off on a bender. Once he starts drinking, he can't quit. I've been staying there until I'm sure he's asleep. In the morning, he cries like a baby. Promises to stay sober."

"So that's where you've been on nights when you don't come home?"

"Yup."

"What does David say?"

"He doesn't know. I've hinted that I have a problem that's too big for me to handle, and he's only encouraged me to depend on God's guidance."

"Why don't you tell David about it?"

"Freeman and his wife have begged me not to tell."

"I'm surprised you're telling me."

"David corrected me on that. He says I'm missing God's

gift if I don't share my burdens with you. To listen to your advice." He brushed her hair out of her eyes. "I'm sorry I've kept things from you. It's not because I don't trust you. I've just been trying to be the best deacon I know how to be. And the truth is that I don't know how to be one."

"I know you're trying." She smiled. "But I hate these secrets. I hate having you keep things from me."

"Me too."

She snuggled against him. "Luke, you've got to get Freeman into rehab."

"I've suggested it, but he won't listen to me. He says I'm young and inexperienced and shouldn't be the deacon, anyway. No one should be the deacon with just one vote, he says." Luke wiggled his eyebrows. "And he says so many times."

That lone vote. It felt like a jab to Luke's solar plexus, a hit to the jugular. It shamed and embarrassed him. Freeman knew that.

A weird, weird thought popped into Luke's head. *Thou preparest a table before me in the presence of mine enemies. Thou anointest my head with oil.*

Was Freeman an enemy?

No. Not Freeman. He was annoying, but he wasn't an enemy. He was just a messy, sinful man. Luke's insecurities— those were the enemies. God had a task for him to do and those insecurities kept tripping him up, stopping him from doing what he knew he should do.

"You're the deacon, Luke. If you say Freeman has to go, he has to go. Period." Izzy tipped her head back. "And you and I both know, he has to go. He can't do this on his own. He needs help."

"He'll be furious with me. It's risking a lot, Izzy. For him to go to rehab, to admit he's an alcoholic? Think of what that will mean for him. He's a proud man."

"Think of what it means if he doesn't get help."

An image of Freeman's wife with her sad, bruised face floated through his mind. "Okay. Tomorrow. I'll get him there."

"You'll need David's help. No one can say no to a bishop."

Luke scrunched up his face. "But Freeman's begged me not to tell."

"Oh, Luke, Luke, Luke." She shook her head. "This is David we're talking about. He already knows."

Izzy was spot on. The next morning, when Luke finally told David what had been going on with Freeman Glick and what Luke felt needed to happen, the bishop nodded his head. "This problem has been going on a very long time. Years."

"Years? Years! Then . . . why didn't Amos do something about it?"

"I think he wanted to believe Freeman's promises to stay sober."

Luke understood that. He tipped his head. "If you knew about it for that long, why didn't you do something about it?"

David's lips lifted at the corners. "But I did."

Huh? Oh. *Oh!*

"I'll make a call to Mountain Vista and get things set up for him."

"Actually, I already did."

David's eyebrows lifted. "Good work, Luke."

Luke hesitated. "David, would you come along? Freeman doesn't much care for me." If Freeman had started up his drinking again, he wasn't sure he could manhandle him into the buggy. "Plus, it's hard to say no to a bishop."

"Absolutely, but"—David's grin spread—"tell that to my children. They say no to me plenty of times."

On the drive over, David had prepped Luke about what kind of reaction to expect. "Brace yourself, Luke. I've had run-ins with Freeman many times, over many issues. He is a force to be reckoned with."

Oh boy. Was *that* ever the understatement of the year.

When they arrived at the Big House, Freeman held himself gingerly, especially his head, as if he feared it might fall off if he moved too abruptly. Luke recognized that look: a whopper of a hangover.

Luke explained that he had told David about Freeman's excessive drinking and that he no longer believed he could control it, and he had come to take him to Mountain Vista rehabilitation facility to get the help he needed.

Freeman disagreed with Luke's assessment rather strenuously. In fact, the roof fairly shook as he accused Luke of being the worst deacon Stoney Ridge ever had, the worst deacon the world had seen, quite possibly the worst deacon in all of history, backing him against the wall, emphasizing his slurring words with jabs of his finger to his chest.

David stepped in close. "Freeman—"

"Get y'r hands off me," he shouted, backing away, almost falling down. Then he had some sharp words for David as bishop.

This intervention wasn't going well.

But then Freeman's wife came downstairs holding a packed suitcase in her hand. "Freeman Glick," she said, nearly choking over his name, "you go with them to that place, or I go."

"You what?" Freeman growled, stumbling a little as he tried to take a few steps toward her to face her squarely, his eyebrows drawn down into a fierce scowl.

Her mouth was pursed tightly while her eyes blinked rapidly in fright. Silence settled, growing oppressive, like the quiet that blanketed the sky right before a storm hit. She stiffened her shoulders and hefted her bag. "I mean it this time," she said, her voice trembling with fury. "You go or I go."

Luke saw Freeman swallow hard, twice, and his legs swayed like a tree in a summer breeze. Then his arms fell to his sides, and something collapsed inside him. He sank down in a chair and leaned his elbows on his knees. Tears started running down his cheekbones and into his beard. "I'll go," he sobbed. "I'll go."

Luke would never forget that moment, when a man came to the end of himself. It was dramatic, solemn, what he considered to be a holy moment, because it was only then that God's redemptive work could begin.

A few hours later, Luke and David settled Freeman Glick into a room at the Mountain Vista rehab facility. Freeman had turned from a lion into a kitten, cooperating with the nurse who checked him in.

Luke left Freeman and David for a few minutes to go get some fresh air. This place, it brought up a lot of difficult memories for him. Not so long ago, he'd been in and out of the facility for the better part of a year. He walked past his old room and suddenly pivoted to stand in the doorjamb. Whoa. Hold it a minute. Whoa, whoa, whoa. "Grace?" He took a few steps into the room. "Grace Miller?" *So this is where you've been hiding.*

His mother-in-law looked up from a book she was read-ing, startled by his voice, then frowned. "You."

Luke smiled at her, but she didn't smile back. She always frowned when she saw Luke. Always, always, always.

"What are *you* doing here?"

"I'm checking someone in from my church." He walked into the room and stood at ease, across from her. "So, what are you doing here?"

"I'm delivering cookies and flowers to the patients." She rolled her eyes. "What do you think?"

"Let's see. The last time I saw you, you had promised Izzy you were coming to the one-year anniversary of her yarn shop."

She sighed. "Something came up."

"So you blew off going to your daughter's party?"

"No," she said firmly. "No, I was planning to go."

He sat in a chair, waiting patiently for her to continue.

She ran a finger along the corner of her book, avoiding his eyes. "Social things, they make me nervous. Very uncom-fortable. Especially around you Amish." She looked over at him with an accusation in her eyes. "I know what you're all thinking about me."

"What are we all thinking?"

She stared at him as if expecting him to supply the words. "There goes Grace Mitchell Miller. Sinner. Loser. Drunk." She shrugged her shoulders. "The one who caused them all so much trouble."

"No one I know would think that." That's where Grace didn't understand the Amish. Yes, she had caused unnecessary heartache to the church, a great deal of it, but she was trying to make amends in her own slow start-and-stop-and-start-again way. And she'd also brought three children to Stoney Ridge—Izzy, Jenny, and Chris—all three much loved. He straightened his legs, crossed one ankle over the other. "So that's why you didn't come to Izzy's party?"

"That's why I didn't *want* to come. The reason I didn't come is because . . . I slipped."

"You fell?"

Grace smirked. "Off the wagon. Big time. I couldn't handle the pressure."

"You were afraid of us? Of facing the Amish?"

At the word *afraid* her eyebrows puckered. "Of facing Izzy among the Amish." She closed her book. "So I checked myself back in here."

Luke knew she was telling the truth. It was something to do with her voice, or with her voice and her face combined, or perhaps with her eyes. He couldn't pinpoint what it was that gave her away, not exactly, but he could tell she was being truthful. "You never bothered to explain any of this to your daughters."

"I let Jenny know I'd be gone for a while."

"Why didn't you let Izzy know? Why Jenny and not Izzy?"

Grace rose and went to the window, staring outside at something. She crossed her arms, gripping her elbows. In that moment, Luke saw Izzy in her. Same way of holding her shoulders so stiff and straight, same way of clasping her elbows, arms crossed against her middle. The sight startled Luke, the same way he felt when he caught unexpected glimpses of Jenny and Izzy's similarities. You'd never know they were all related, yet suddenly you knew it without a doubt. They were all a part of each other, and always would be.

Grace swiveled around, almost as if she knew he was studying her. "Jenny's always been easier for me. She doesn't ask anything of me. Izzy wants something from me. More than I can give her. She always has, even as a baby. Even as a little girl."

"Why do you think that's so?"

Grace shrugged. "She's her father's daughter, I suppose. Looks like him, acts like him."

Oh, now *that* was a subject Luke was eager to explore, but he knew not to touch it. Not now. Someday, though. Izzy never ever spoke of him and shut the conversation down fast if Luke brought him up. He was a mystery, that missing father. "For the last two months, Izzy's assumed you did what you've always done."

"What's that?"

"Left her to fend for herself."

"She's not alone. She's got Jenny. She's got"—she waved her hand in a circle—"all you Amish people."

"She has us, it's true. But it's a funny thing about parenting. She'll always only have one mother. No one can replace you, Grace." As much as he wished for it.

To his surprise, Grace's face mellowed from its sharp angles, and her eyes grew soft and shiny. "It's too late for that."

Luke walked toward her to grab her hands, squeezing them until she looked him in the eyes. "It's not. It's not, Grace. It's never too late. Alle wege führret haem." *All roads lead home.*

She squinted and frowned. "What's that jibberish mean?"

"It means . . ." He hesitated, because this was hard to say, and even harder to mean with sincerity. But this autumn he had come to discover that feelings followed intention. Outlook determined outcome. "It means there's always a place for you in our home. In our hearts."

A smile flickered in her eyes and then was gone. Yet for Luke it was enough. He felt himself smile in return. This was what it meant to be a deacon, he thought. Care and concern for the well-being of individuals, whether he wanted to give it or not. Whether they wanted it or not.

TWENTY-THREE

There were plenty of reasons that Izzy admired Fern— how she had cared for Amos so tenderly, right to his very last breath. Then, after he passed, unlike a lot of widows Izzy had observed, Fern got on with living. But watching how Fern handled Cassidy might've topped the list.

That girl wore a big baggy sweatshirt and sweatpants every single day, no matter the weather. And she didn't comb her hair, or shower often enough. Izzy was surprised that Fern didn't object, but she didn't seem to mind. Once Izzy hinted that maybe someone (Fern!) should suggest a new outfit to Cassidy. Fern shook her head. "Lamps don't talk, they shine." That was Fern's way. She never tried to change Cassidy.

To be honest, Izzy thought she would've seen more transformation in Cassidy, outside and inside, over the two months she'd been at Windmill Farm. When Izzy had come to live with Fern and Amos, she'd soaked up everything she could— cooking, housekeeping, hospitality, quilting, knitting. She dressed like them, talked like them, tried to learn the language as quickly as she could. She studied the Amish the way a scientist studied his subjects.

Izzy read the *Budget* each week, front to back, so she could try to understand what the Amish valued, how they spent their days and weeks and months. The first thing she noticed, besides how much they loved to talk about the weather, was that stillborn babies had obituaries. The second thing she noticed was that handicapped people were called "special children," no matter what age they were or what disability they had. The value placed on human life was dear. It was a complete flip-flop from the world Izzy had come from. She never wanted to go back.

She would've thought Cassidy would have the same feelings about being here, a desperate desire to stay put and never leave, like she'd had. She could see that the girl enjoyed farm life, caring for animals, and the yarn shop. She talked all the time about what a nice place this farm would be for children to be raised, so much so that Izzy wondered if that was Cassidy's roundabout way to ask why she and Luke didn't have any children. Well, she could just keep on wondering; that was nobody's business but Izzy and Luke's. More hers than Luke's. He seemed not at all concerned about it.

The only real change Izzy noticed in Cassidy was how plump she was getting from Fern's good cooking. That girl loved to eat. Loved it. Izzy couldn't blame Cassidy one bit for eating all she could, while she could. Home-cooked food meant more to foster children than anyone could understand. It meant someone had shopped and cooked and prepared nourishing meals. It meant someone had been thinking about you. Izzy understood all the feelings that swirled around a home-cooked meal. Dropped stitches, trying to get fixed. When she watched Cassidy chow down, all she could think was, *Eat up! Eat all you can. Eat your fill. That way, maybe you won't miss it so much when you're gone.*

Because the day was soon approaching when the group home would be ready for the foster girls to return to. This morning, Luke said Roberta had called to say the group home was ready for final inspections by the county. If all inspections passed, the home would be reopened on Monday morning. The girls should get packed up, Roberta said. They couldn't stay with the Amish even if they wanted to, because it had been an emergency situation. "I bent the rules," she told Luke, "thinking it would only be a week or two. Didn't know it would end up being longer than two months! I gotta get those girls back in the group home before the state of Pennsylvania comes snooping around."

Mattie and Sol's foster daughter would stay with them because they'd already been licensed to be a foster family. Alice and Teddy Zook had already started the process to adopt their foster daughter, Chloe, so she would be allowed to stay with them. But the other girls had to go back. The Amish families could start the process of getting officially approved to foster, but it would take time. And, most likely, they wouldn't be fostering these particular girls. Roberta had warned everyone about the tricky balance of attachment— love these children, but let them go too.

As soon as Fern heard that the group home was getting reopened, she decided to throw an impromptu goodbye party on Saturday for all the foster girls, even though they weren't going far. The group home was right next door to the Sisters' House, not far from Windmill Farm. The foster parents talked about wanting to keep up the relationships, to visit the girls frequently and include them in activities, even after the girls were reunited with their families.

Izzy wondered about how those intentions would play out, at least for most of the girls. Once they were back into their routine, she knew it wouldn't be easy to stay connected. Even if the actual distance between them wasn't much, the differences between the two cultures were vast.

Frankly, Izzy doubted she would ever see Cassidy again. Cassidy wouldn't be going back to the group home but straight into her mother's custody, Roberta had told Luke. Apparently she'd been in jail in upstate New York for a misdemeanor and was recently released. She was coming for Cassidy.

Izzy wondered about the relationship between Cassidy and her mother, if it was like her own relationship with Grace. Be careful, she wanted to warn Cassidy. Don't expect too much from your mother. Izzy knew all about mothers and daughters, about jail and foster care.

She wanted to do something special for Cassidy and finally decided to give her the sweater she had knit for her own mother. Cassidy had seen it in the yarn shop and oohed and aahed over it many times. She, unlike Grace, would appreciate all that went into the making of that sweater, starting with the fleece sheared from the woollies, carded and spun into yarn, then carefully knitted. She rewrapped it in a box and tied it with a pink ribbon.

On Saturday afternoon, just before the guests were due to arrive for the goodbye party, she gave Cassidy the gift. "To keep you warm," Izzy said. "An early Christmas gift." What she wanted to say but couldn't bring herself to put into words, was, *To remember me. To never forget that I care about you. Someone cares, Cassidy.*

When Cassidy opened the box and lifted the sweater, she held it up, amazed. "That sweater? The one I love?"

Izzy nodded, then looked away, hands held behind her back.

Cassidy's voice was choked with tears. "Thank you, Izzy. I'll take it with me wherever I go." And she folded up the sweater and tucked it back in the box, then rubbed her eyes with the back of her sweatshirt sleeve. "When I first came here, you told me that you'd chosen your life here. When you said that, I thought you'd made a big mistake. You could be a supermodel. But now . . . it seems like maybe this kind of life, among the Amish, on a farm, well, maybe it's the way a kid's life should be lived. Like, if a kid had a choice, you know?"

Izzy knew. *Oh my soul, I know.*

After the party, after the goodbyes and promises to keep in touch, Fern and Izzy washed up the remaining dirty dishes.

"Sam Schrock told me that today was a joyous hullaba-loo," Fern said. "Now there's a phrase to remember. And even more noteworthy is that silent Sam said so."

It had been a wonderful send-off. And now the house seemed too quiet, even to Izzy's ears. Roberta had taken Cassidy along with her to the agency's office to be reunited with her mother. The house seemed too empty.

As Fern waited for the sink water to get hot, she said, "This reminds me of Amos's last few months, when you and Luke were here around the clock." She poured some green liquid soap into the sink and watched the bubbles form.

Quietly, Izzy said, "There's not a day that goes by when I don't think of Amos, of all he taught me. About sheep." About life. "I miss him each and every day."

"Me too." Fern's eyes grew shiny as she reached out to

cover Izzy's hand with hers. "I don't know if I have ever properly thanked you for helping me during that time—thanked you enough, that is."

Izzy looked down at the hand that held hers and was startled by it. This was an old woman's hand, webbed with wrinkles, dotted with brown spots, rivered with veins. She looked up into Fern's face, so beloved and familiar. "You don't have to thank me. I'm the one who should thank you. You took me in and gave me a home. You taught me everything. You showed me how to be . . . myself."

"You were always yourself," Fern said. "Right from the word go, you were yourself."

Izzy shook her head. "No, Fern, you helped me become who I was meant to be, all along. So it's me who should be thanking you."

"Well then," Fern said matter-of-factly, "we're both thanking each another." And she picked up a dish to swish in the soapy water. Back to business.

⌒

Late that night, lying in bed, Luke listened to Izzy's steady breathing. "Are you asleep?"

She rolled over on her side to face him. "No. I'm still thinking about the party."

"That sweater you gave Cassidy. I didn't know you were going to give it to her. I remember you made it for your mother. That pattern, she had once said she liked. I remember something about wooden buttons too."

"My mother loved those wooden buttons."

"I thought you were saving the sweater for Grace. When she comes back someday."

"Better for it to be used."

"Cassidy understood how special it was. Did you see her face when she opened it? I bet she'll keep it for the rest of her life. To remember you by."

She glanced at him. "But she put it away. She didn't even try it on."

"Maybe she was worried it was too small for her, that it wouldn't fit her. She's kinda . . . substantial."

"Maybe. She does loves Fern's cooking. Did." She sighed and rolled back again to face the wall. "I worry about her."

"And to think you didn't want to bother with her."

"I know, I know. You were right."

Luke coughed. "Excuse me? My hearing must be going. I thought you said . . . I was right about something."

She covered her head with her pillow.

"There's something I need to tell you."

Curious, she lifted her head from under the pillow to look at him.

"Izzy, the other day . . . I saw your mother."

"She's back?" She sat up in bed. "Where? When? Why didn't you tell me?"

"I've been waiting for the right moment. I thought I should wait until after the party today, and then I saw the sweater you gave Cassidy. Made me think I should've told you sooner. But I have been meaning to tell you. Turns out, Grace never really left the area. She's over at Mountain Vista. A few months ago, she relapsed. She knew she needed more help."

"She checked herself in?"

"Yup." He watched her for a while, wondering what was going through her mind. "It's a step in the right direction. She's making some changes."

"But she didn't want us to know. Not Jenny. Not me."

"No. I think she's embarrassed."

"If you talked to her, then she knows I know she's there. We don't keep secrets, right?"

"She knows. I'm sure she's expecting you and Jenny to visit soon."

She plopped back on the bed. "Drop everything and run after her."

He laughed. "That's your mother. Always ready to receive."

She stared up at the ceiling. "It feels better, somehow, to know where she is, and why. I don't feel quite so . . . mad at her. Actually, I haven't felt so mad at her for a while now."

He'd noticed, but he had just thought she'd forgotten about Grace. That was dumb, he realized now. You don't forget about your missing mother. He lifted an arm to pull her close to him, and she snuggled against him. "Honey, you know what we haven't done to help the baby project along?"

She gave him a gentle kick. "You're never around to help the baby project along."

"Besides that. We haven't really prayed about it. We've done everything but pray." He put his arm around her and said a prayer aloud, something they hadn't done before, as it wasn't done much in their church, but it just felt right. He asked God to bless them with a baby, in his timing, in his will.

And then they got to work on the baby project.

TWENTY-FOUR

The first night Mollie was back in her cottage felt strangely quiet. No Tina, no Alicia. They had gone back to the group home when it reopened, while Mollie was still in the hospital. Sam said they planned to keep up with horse training each afternoon, though she wondered if they would, if they'd even be permitted to. She hoped so. Those horses, they were reaching the hearts of the girls. Maybe people can change, she thought. Experiences can make a very big difference, especially if you're a child.

She walked around the cottage, happy to be home. It felt enormous to her after two months of sharing it with Tina and Alicia. To her surprise, she missed them. Not everything about them, she thought, but many things. Most things, she realized. They'd been so sweet to her in the hospital—coming with Fern or Sam each day to visit.

And when she found out that the cancer had returned, that she would need more treatment, which meant more radiation and all its awful effects, they were unwavering cheerleaders. "You can beat it, Mollie!" they told her, and then, "So you can adopt us!"

She hoped they were right about her prognosis. She hadn't been surprised when the doctor told her the cancer was back. She had sensed it, had recognized all the familiar signs of illness. In a way, the Lord had been preparing her for this, fortifying her. The doctor said that her cancer recurrence had been caught quickly, and that was a good sign. And Sam remained unfazed by her diagnosis. On the way home from the hospital today he'd told her that he decided to keep the saucy mare for himself. "I'm gonna call her Saucy," he said, eyes smiling so that the corners crinkled. She loved his eyes best. In a way she couldn't put to words, Mollie knew that was his subtle way of letting her know that he was sticking by her, come what may. Something important had been settled within him. Resolved.

But if she did beat the cancer like she thought she would, well . . . adopting Tina and Alicia, *that* would take some serious thought. *Serious* thinking. And even more serious prayer.

But she was going to be fine, no matter what.

Surely goodness and mercy shall follow me all the days of my life, and I shall dwell in the house of the Lord forever.

Mollie Graber would be just fine.

Luke handed Fern the dish he had glued back together in the fix-it shop. "It's not perfect, but I think it'll hold up for you."

"You can hardly see the crack," Fern said, holding it up to the light. "Just like new."

Not really, but it was nice of her to say so. Luke sat down in the kitchen chair. It was his chair, the one that was always there for him. How many times had he slunk into this chair over the last few years, needing to talk, or get advice, or just feel like he belonged somewhere. Dozens of times. Maybe hundreds. "Roberta Watts has been calling me to see if I've lit a fire under Amish families to start the licensing process. During Christmas, of all times, she asks me this." He leaned his elbows on the table and cupped his cheeks with his hands. "Fern, I promised Amos that I would empty out the foster care system in all of Lancaster County. Seriously, what was I thinking? How am I going to do that? It keeps filling up again. Roberta said three more girls moved into the group home this week."

Fern set down the dish and pulled out a chair. "Amos had a lot of big ideas, Luke. More ideas than action." She clasped her hands together. "It was you coming to live here, that's when things started to happen around here. The new farm stand, the yarn shop, the fix-it shop. Goodness, even getting that red windmill fixed."

All that, Luke knew. The farm looked run-down when he first arrived there. Amos had a hard time getting anything done but taking care of his orchards. Those trees, they were his top priority. His only priority. "Still, a promise is a promise."

"Yes, it is. And you've been making good on that promise. My father had a saying: Don't let your branches go out farther than your roots go deep. When that happens, you topple."

Like many things Fern said, that stumped Luke. "Um, can you explain that?"

"A big thing like that, emptying out the foster care system in our county, it can't happen overnight. It happens little by little, as hearts open up. Look at these last few months in Stoney Ridge. The girls in the group home needed help, and our church stepped up. Alice and Teddy are adopting their foster girl. Relationships have continued between some of the girls and their foster families, even after they've left us. That's important. And Roberta Watts has us on speed-dial for emergencies, she said. Whatever *that* means. You've gotten the ball rolling, Luke. That process is every bit as important as the final goal."

"How so?"

"Because you've gotten everyone involved. It's not just between you and Amos anymore. Even Edith Lapp had a good word for you."

His ears pricked up.

"She said our church had never been more knit together. She thinks fostering has had a lot to do with that. It's pulled people together for a common cause."

Knit together. Unified. Luke pondered that thought for a long while. "Fern, who do you think was the one person who voted me in to the lot to be deacon?"

Her sparse eyebrows lifted in an arch. "Are you still chewing on that?"

"I just want to know. I want to know if it was a joke or for real. It wasn't Edith, was it?" He scrunched up his face. "Couldn't have been Edith."

"No, not Edith." Fern sighed. "Luke, you've asked almost everyone, haven't you?"

"I have. No one seems to know."

"Would it really matter if it was a joke or if it was for real? After all, being deacon means being the deacon."

It was a hard thing to explain why he felt so bothered by that lone vote. Izzy rolled her eyes whenever he brought the topic up. She was tired of him talking about it. "In a strange way, I think it would make a difference to me. If it was done for a joke, I hope I've proved the person wrong."

"And if it was done for real?"

That side of the equation was very unlikely. Luke hadn't even given it much thought, if at all. Only who might have played a prank on him. "I hope I've made him . . . or her . . . glad of the vote."

"It wasn't done as a joke." A soft pity filled Fern's eyes, stinging Luke's tender pride. "Luke, who haven't you asked? Think about that."

And so he did, all the way back to the fix-it shop, hearing his boots crunch on the frost-covered grass. Just as he reached the door, he realized there was one person he'd never thought to ask. Just one.

Oh. Oh! Oh, of course. Of course.

David.

Izzy sat in a chair in the reception area of Mountain Vista rehab, waiting for her mother to finish a group therapy session. The name of this place was ironic because there was no mountain and no vista. It was set in a wooded property on the farthest corner of town. But then again, Izzy realized just now, maybe the name was a metaphor. Maybe patients felt as if they were climbing a steep mountain, hoping to reach the top and see something new on the other side. That's how she had felt, anyway.

She looked down at her nails—bitten-down stumps—and curled her fingers into a fist. This was a difficult visit for her to make, a hard place for her to be. She wondered if this was how Luke might feel on some of his deacon duties. Like she'd rather be anywhere but here.

"Izzy?"

Izzy's head jerked up to see her mother looking at her from a doorway, a surprised look on her face. Their gaze met, briefly, then Grace's eyes flicked away. She was never good at eye contact . . . but neither was Izzy. She glanced at her mother again and realized she looked good. Really good. That strained, tired look was gone. She'd gained some weight, and her hair was pulled back in a barrette. The comparison to how Grace looked before she went missing was notable. It made Izzy realize that her mother had not been doing well, not for some time, and that she had done the right thing to check in to the facility when she did.

"Hello." Izzy rose to her feet and took a few steps toward Grace. "I came because . . ."

"Luke told you I was here. I figured he would. He doesn't seem like the type to keep secrets from his wife."

Oh, you'd be surprised. Izzy held out some banana bread, wrapped in foil. "Still warm. I thought you might like something home baked."

Grace took it and held it against her middle. "How are those needy beasts of yours?"

"The sheep? They're fine. They enjoy winter. No pests to bother them." And then she ran out of things to say. Her mind went blank, a complete void.

"Do you want to come see my room?"

Izzy nodded calmly, as if to say, "Yeah, sure. I'm cool with all of this." But inside she was not remotely cool. She followed Grace down the long aisle and into her small room. She closed the door behind her and then she was left alone with her mother, in a still, strange silence. Why hadn't she brought Jenny with her? She should have.

Grace motioned to an empty chair, and sat on her bed, facing Izzy. "So tell me about Jenny's baby. She's due about now, isn't she?"

"Yes." Phew! Something to talk about. "A little girl. Wispy blonde hair. She looks like Jenny. Like you."

Her mother clapped her hands together at that, pleased. "I knew it. I just knew she'd have a baby girl. I can't wait to see her. Think Jenny will come visit, now that the cat's out of the bag that I'm here? Maybe she'll bring Rosie."

"I'm sure she'll come soon. I haven't told her you're here. Luke just told me, just last night. I . . ." She paused. "I wish you would've told us." When she saw her mother wince, she quickly added, "We would've understood."

Grace got up and strode to the window, appearing lost in thought. "Understood?" she said at last. "How can somebody understand that their mother's nothing but a drunk?"

"Not a drunk. She's a woman who is facing her addictions, head-on. That's what we would have understood. I'm proud of you, Mama. For being here."

There was silence. Grace turned around. She seemed flummoxed, embarrassed, and her eyes darted around nervously. "I'm paying for it myself this time. Not having your people pay for my mistakes. Not anymore."

That was the first time Izzy had ever heard her mother own up to making mistakes. Usually she made excuses. First time. Maybe there was some hope for them, she thought. Maybe there's always a chance. "I knitted you a sweater. Blue and white, with a cable pattern. Just like one you had shown me in a magazine."

Grace's eyes lit up. "The one with wooden buttons? Did you bring it?"

"I didn't think you were coming back, so I gave it to someone who needed it."

Grace nodded with obvious disappointment, and then they lapsed into an awkward silence again.

"Maybe I could make you another one. Just like it. Actually, even better. I've learned some new stitches. I thought that . . . maybe . . . it could be your Christmas present."

Grace looked up in surprise. "You'd do that for me?"

Izzy reached for her mother's hand. It was made of bird bones, so fragile. It suddenly dawned on her that her mother was not a strong person, that she never had been. Izzy had wanted her to be strong, had been angry with her most of her life because she wasn't strong. Her mother's weaknesses had wreaked havoc in her life, and Jenny's and Chris's. As she gazed at their hands joined together, she realized that she was the strong one. She was sturdy, despite everything. Maybe even because of everything. And her mother was trying to get stronger. That counted for a great deal. Tears quivered in her eyes and her throat felt tight and achey. "Of course. Of course I would."

"With wooden buttons?"

Izzy let out a half cough, half laugh. She felt relief spread over her face and something like freedom in her heart. They were going to be okay, she and her mother. "Yes. With wooden buttons."

A little smile broke over Grace's face. "You know, I think I'd like that."

The first snowstorm of the year had blown through last night, covering Stoney Ridge with a soft blanket of white. Not enough snow to make life difficult, but enough to slow and quiet the world down, to remind them that Christmas was coming. Taking his time, Luke stomped a path through the snow to the phone shanty to pick up messages, pausing now and then to appreciate the muffled silence. Now and then a winter bird, high in the branches, broke the quiet with a song. This time of year, it was the best of all.

In the phone shanty, he pulled off his gloves and pressed the blinking button. Only one message was waiting for him, but it was a significant one. He hurried back up the hill to the fix-it shop.

Izzy was drying breakfast dishes in the tiny makeshift kitchen, wearing a big coat and gloves as she worked. "Fire's gone out in the woodstove," she said as he came in the door. She put a dish on the wooden plank that doubled as her counter.

It was cold in here. He could even see his breath. "I'll get it warmed up."

"Don't put more than one log in. I'm spending the morning in Fern's kitchen. Jenny's coming over with the babies. We're going to make some Christmas cookies to take to the group home this afternoon." She gave him a look. "You don't even have to ask. We plan to make some to take out to Mountain Vista too."

Luke tried to hide his grin. He was so proud of Izzy. Two times she'd gone to visit her mother at the facility, once alone, one time with him, when he'd gone to visit Freeman. They weren't easy visits for her, but she kept trying. She had never given up on her mother. Impressive.

"Listen to this message." In the gruffest, toughest voice he could imitate, he said, "I'm coming by Windmill Farm at nine o'clock sharp."

Izzy stilled. "Roberta Watts?"

"The very one."

"Think she's got news about Cassidy?"

"What kind of news?"

"I don't know. Like, maybe her mother never showed up. Or maybe she showed up and left her again, like Grace did to Jenny once. Maybe Cassidy doesn't want to stay in the group home."

He gave her a smug look and pointed a finger at her. "You miss her. You do. You miss Cassidy."

"I worry about her. That's different from missing her."

"Well, Roberta gave no hint of why she was coming. Only that she was coming. Nine o'clock. Notice there is no question. No wondering if we might be available. She's coming. And we'd better be here." He bent down by the woodstove and opened the small door.

"Do you think she has another foster care emergency?"

Still squatting, he stirred the coals with a poker, then added one oak log on top. That would warm up the room fast. "Probably."

"Well, that's one more reason you'd better get this house done."

He spun to face her so fast that he fell right on his backside. "You'd be willing to foster?"

She shrugged, then her eyes smiled in amusement. "Maybe."

Now, that was a twist Luke hadn't expected. He couldn't stop grinning as he finished up the morning chores in the barn. This very day, he decided, he would get back to work

292

on the remodel. Maybe he'd even ask Teddy Zook for help to speed it up.

A few minutes before nine o'clock, Roberta's big Buick drove up the driveway and stopped in front of the fix-it shop. Luke and Izzy went out to meet her. When they brought her inside, she gazed around with shocked eyes. "*This* is where you live?"

"There's two rooms in the back."

"Mm-hmm. I can see that."

And so she could. All the way through into their little bedroom.

"I'm finishing a remodel."

"Mm-hmm." She walked around the framing and peered into the makeshift kitchen. "Mm-hmm."

Izzy snorted at the double murmur. Luke looked around, surprised by Roberta's disapproval. Seeing it with her eyes, it did seem unlivable. Last summer, he'd had so many plans to improve the place, to finish drywalling the walls, to paint them, to put doors on cabinets. And then there was his big idea to add on square footage. He'd gotten as far as putting stakes in the ground last August. Snow covered those stakes. He wasn't even sure he could find them anymore. Man, oh, man, what had happened to the last six months? Die Zeit hot Fliggel. *Time flew.*

Roberta went to the door and looked up at the big house. "Fern Lapp around?"

"Yes. She's up in the main house."

Roberta clasped her hands together. "Let's go there and get warmed up." She sailed out the door and marched toward the house, Luke and Izzy tramping behind, following her footsteps through the snow.

Fern opened the door and welcomed Roberta in. "I saw you drive up," she said. "Coffee's almost ready."

They sat around the kitchen table as Fern filled four mugs with coffee. Something important was about to happen, something good, Luke could sense it. As he sat looking at the steaming black coffee, he thought again of the profound moments he'd had around this very table. So many convicting conversations, so many loving exchanges. He'd fallen in love with Izzy here, day by day, when he came up to the house for meals. Why, it was here that Amos had asked him to empty out the foster care system. Just a plain, simple table, but it provided a stable place for important moments.

Roberta poured three teaspoons of sugar into her coffee, stirred, added one more, then took a sip, satisfied. She set down her cup but kept her hands around it. "There aren't many things that surprise me in life, but this one sure did." She took another sip of coffee, dragging out the suspense they all felt. Her face grew serious. "Did y'all know Cassidy was pregnant?"

TWENTY-FIVE

Izzy's hands flew to cup her cheeks. "Oh my soul." She was bowled over, completely astonished. "Are you sure?"

"Oh yeah, I'm sure," Roberta said. "No doubt about it."

Izzy glanced at Luke, who was stunned silent, and that didn't happen very often. He lifted his hands in the air. "I had no idea. None."

They both turned to Fern. Even she seemed gobsmacked. Fern! When was Fern Lapp ever surprised?

Roberta took a sip of coffee. "Cassidy told me she has a dream. She told me she can't let nothing interfere with her dream. She said that's what Izzy told her." She pointed a thick finger at Izzy. "You told her that?"

Izzy's mouth went dry, her palms damp. "Not exactly. I mean, I didn't think we were talking about a baby." She tried to remember what she had said to Cassidy. "I told her that dreams were good things to have. I told her to not let anyone take away her dreams, but I meant her mother. I didn't mean . . . I didn't know . . ." Her hands clasped her cheeks. "She's only fifteen years old."

"Mm-hmm. A baby having a baby." Roberta took a long

295

sip of coffee, then another. "She doesn't want to keep this baby. Her mother doesn't either. She doesn't want another mouth to feed, she told me." She mm-hmmed to herself. "As if that woman bothered to feed anyone but herself."

A baby! Oh, Cassidy. A baby. Izzy rubbed her face. How in the world had she not realized something like *that*? How did she miss the signs? But then even Fern, with her studied eyes, living with Cassidy for months, even she had missed them.

Izzy shook her head. "I'll talk to her. I'll talk to them both. I'll help them understand."

"Too late for that. Cassidy's gone. She took off to New York City this morning. Something about an agent for models. She had a business card. Said it's her ticket to become a supermodel."

"No!" It came out of Izzy so loud that Roberta spilled her coffee. "We have to stop her! That agent—it's nothing but a racket. A scam! She'll end up on the streets. Or worse."

"Mm-hmm. I know, I know. But at least her mother's gone with her. At least she has someone with her. Not much more we can do about it."

We can pray, Izzy thought. *We can pray for Cassidy, each and every day.*

Roberta leaned back on the chair until it creaked. "So the reason I'm here is because Cassidy wants the two of you to adopt her baby. She says this baby should have a good life, a real family. Isn't that something, at least?" She made a clucking sound. "Only a child herself, but she had enough sense to make a plan for her little one. I'm guessing her mama helped her, because they signed all the right papers for a private adoption. All legal-like. Just waiting for your signatures."

Luke reached over to squeeze her hand, but Izzy felt as if

Roberta were speaking underwater, or in another language. She could hear what Roberta was saying, but she couldn't quite untangle what it meant. "Cassidy . . . she wants . . . *what*?"

"She wants you to adopt her baby. Said she thinks that you, Izzy, would be a real good mama to her baby. Said the way you care for your sheep, that's the kind of mama she wants for her baby. Said something about how you've taught her all about dropped stitches. Said she hopes you'll be her stitch in time. Said you'd know what that means."

Roberta paused, as if waiting for her to explain what that meant, but Izzy couldn't speak without getting choked up. She knew exactly what Cassidy meant.

"She didn't say anything about you, Luke Schrock." Roberta rocked back in the chair. "But, then, she didn't say anything bad about you, neither. I take that as a good thing." She sipped her coffee. "So then, what do you two say? Ready to go get that baby?"

"Hold on," Luke said, his face blanching. "Are you telling us that the baby has already been born? Cassidy just left here before Thanksgiving."

An ear-to-ear grin covered Roberta Watts's face, a rare sight. "Born yesterday morning. Strong and healthy. Big too. Almost nine pounds, six ounces. Twenty-two inches long. Gonna be a tall drink of water, the doctor said." She took another sip of coffee. "So, what do y'all think?"

Izzy's heart went wild. She had no idea what to think—she felt struck by lightning. She stammered in a choked voice, "L-Luke? What do we think?" She saw his face change, from confusion to clarity.

"What do we think?" He looked at Izzy and then he smiled,

a confident, reassuring smile. "Honey, if you're willing, I'm willing."

Luke seemed so sure. Roberta seemed so sure. Panic was rising inside her as she looked at their faces. "We should talk about this." Slow down. This was going too fast. Izzy's heart was pounding like a drum. "Take time to think it over."

"Y'all have ten minutes," Roberta said. "I have a busy day and I don't like the looks of that sky."

Izzy's legs were shaking so bad she didn't think she could stand up. "Couldn't we call you tomorrow?"

"That baby girl needs a mother." Roberta lifted her eyebrows to look at Luke. "And a father." She turned to Fern with a smile. "And a grandma who makes good coffee."

Softly, Izzy said, "A girl?" She'd dreamed of having a little girl of her own.

Roberta leaned forward and slapped her palms on the table. "So, is that a yes or a no? If it's a no, I need to start the process for that little precious child. Forgo all the benefits and smooth sailing of a private adoption and make that sweet little darlin' a pitiful ward of the state of Pennsylvania." She shuddered. "Sure do hope they can find somebody with a heart can adopt her." She tsked-tsked a few times. "Poor little baby. And she's a beauty too. Big dimples, just like Cassidy's. I told you about them big dimples, didn't I?"

Luke reached over and squeezed Izzy's hand. "We have a heart, Roberta. Big ones. We'll take her."

Oh no, oh no, oh no! one side of Izzy protested, while the other side wanted to shout oh yes, oh yes, oh yes! "Wait a minute, Luke. Hold your horses." She looked to Fern, who had yet to say a word. She'd been watching them this entire time, her eyes narrow and thoughtful. "What do you think?"

"I think . . . ," Fern said in her matter-of-fact way, "that there was a reason God brought Cassidy, of all the girls in the group home, to Windmill Farm. I think God doesn't make mistakes."

Okay, okay. So Fern credited this adoption with God's orchestration. Izzy's crazily beating heart eased with that reminder. But still, something nettled her, held her back. Her fingers curled around Luke's hand, squeezing hard. Her voice dropped to a whisper. "What if Cassidy changes her mind? In a few months, or a few years? What do we do then?" How awful that would be, to love an adopted child with wholehearted abandon, only to have to give her up. She couldn't handle that. A massive heartache.

"This is a legal adoption," Roberta said. "Chances are, that could never happen."

But there was still something else. "What if we have a baby of our own?" She could not, would not ever stop hoping for that.

"Then we have two babies." Luke looked her firmly in the eye. "We're not living our life based on what-ifs. We trust the Lord with our future."

Tears started building in Izzy's eyes and she blinked fast to hold them back. *Don't start,* she told herself. *Once you start, you won't stop.* "You've gone and gotten all deacony."

Roberta pushed herself up out of the chair. "So I'll take that as a yes." She glanced at Fern. "And, Grandma, I think that little family needs to move out of that see-through ice-box and come on up to this big warm house."

Fern nodded, looking pleased. "I think so too. Plenty of room."

"Good. Because that baby is ready to be released from the

hospital at noon today. I'll drive y'all over. We can stop at a Wal-Mart along the way and pick up a car seat and diapers."

"Now?" Izzy's heart started pounding again. "Today? This very day?" *Dear God*, she thought. *Dear God, how can this be happening?*

"Today, this very day," Roberta parroted. "Cassidy's signed all the necessary paperwork. So did her mother. Them two have moved on to those big dreams." She picked up her purse. "I'm thinking this baby should be named Roberta. Thinking y'all can call her Lil' Bertie, so the two of us don't get confused."

"Not a chance," Luke said kindly but firmly.

Roberta rose, folded her arms across her ample bosom, and looked down at them from on high. "You two waiting for the creek to rise?"

He gave Izzy's hand a reassuring squeeze. "You ready to be a mom? Ready to go meet our daughter?"

Oh my soul. She took in a deep breath, trying to hold back tears, but they came anyway. One after the other, like a dam that finally broke. So many thoughts were swooping through her head: *Cassidy thinks I'll make a good mother for her baby. Imagine that! Me! Chosen to be a mother.*

And Luke! The love she felt for him in that moment was eclipsed only by admiration. He had made a decision that would change their life from that day forward. No hesitation. Total commitment. All in. No fear of what-ifs. They woke up this morning as a couple and they would go to bed tonight as a family.

Oh my soul. My cup runneth over. She realized she was holding her breath. "I'm ready. Let's go."

My cup runneth over. Over and over and over.

Fern Lapp's Baked Apple Cider Doughnuts

Ingredients:

1 ½	cups apple cider
2	cups all-purpose flour
¾	teaspoon baking powder
1	teaspoon baking soda
1	teaspoon ground cinnamon
1	teaspoon apple pie spice*
¼	teaspoon salt
1	stick unsalted butter, melted
2	large eggs, room temperature
½	cup packed brown sugar
½	cup granulated sugar
½	cup buttermilk
1	teaspoon pure vanilla extract

Topping

1	cup granulated sugar
1	teaspoon ground cinnamon
1	teaspoon apple pie spice
1	stick unsalted butter, melted

*Apple Pie Spice (store in a sealed jar):

4	teaspoons ground cinnamon
2	teaspoons nutmeg
1	teaspoon cardamom

Directions:

Reduce the apple cider: Stirring occasionally, simmer the apple cider over low heat until you're left with ½ cup. Set aside to cool for 10 minutes. This step makes a big difference in the taste.

Preheat oven to 350°F. Spray doughnut pan with nonstick spray. Set aside.

In a large bowl, whisk together the flour, baking powder, baking soda, cinnamon, apple pie, and salt. Set aside.

In another bowl, whisk together the cider, buttermilk, and vanilla. Set aside.

In the bowl of a stand mixer, using the paddle attachment, combine butter, brown and white sugars. Mix on high, 3–4 minutes, until light and fluffy. Scrape down the bottom and sides of bowl. Add eggs, one at a time, mixing well between each addition. Add one-third of the flour mixture, and one-half of the cider mixture. Alternate between the two until the batter is just combined. Remove the bowl, fold the batter a few times with a rubber spatula to make sure the ingredients are smooth and combined. Batter will be slightly thick.

Spoon the batter into greased doughnut cups, filling about halfway. Bake for 15–20 minutes or until the edges and tops are lightly browned. To test, poke your finger into the top of a doughnut. If it bounces back, they're done.

Turn the doughnuts out into a wire rack. Immediately brush with melted butter, then dip generously in the cinnamon sugar topping.

Doughnuts are best served immediately. Leftovers keep well covered tightly at room temperature for up to 2 days. But there's a pretty good chance there won't be any leftovers.

Note: If you don't have a doughnut pan, you can make muffins or mini-muffins out of these. Don't overfill the cup, though.

Source: Fern was inspired to try this recipe by *Sally's Baking Addiction.*

Read on for chapter 1 from book 3 in

THE Deacon's Family
series

ONE

Growing up is hard on a man. If he'd done well for himself, coming home again should be one of his finest days. The kind of a day that kept him buoyed up with hopeful visions to survive his lowest moments: A mother peering out the kitchen window, eager for the first sign of her returning son. A sweet aromatic cinnamon cake baking in the oven. A loyal dog, muzzle now gray, sitting by the mail box.

Unfortunately for Jimmy Fisher, he hadn't done terribly well for himself since he'd left Stoney Ridge. Years ago, he'd left home to chase some big dreams but those had fizzled out like smoke up a chimney. As for a mother waiting anxiously for her son's return—Edith Fisher Lapp wasn't the type to hover or to wait. And she never did let Jimmy have a dog.

Jimmy stopped at the bottom step of the Bent N' Dent store, stalling. He recognized the beat-up buggy and tired old horse in the parking lot as belonging to Hank Lapp. That meant that Hank would be inside and, to be honest, he was not the person Jimmy wanted to see first upon returning to town. Closer to the last. He was still baffled that his mother

305

had married Hank. Of all the men on earth, she chose wild haired, wild eyed Hank Lapp.

Jimmy pivoted on his heels, wondering if he should just turn tail and flee. If he had a dollar to spare in his pocket, he would do just that. Sadly, he didn't. And he was hungry, too. He hadn't eaten since yesterday morning, when he came across an orchard filled with withered, wormy apples. He rubbed his stomach, still regretting that indulgence.

A buggy driven by a stunning white horse pulled into the parking lot. Intrigued by the horse's unique facial features, he walked over to it. Horses had always captivated Jimmy. They were the theme of his life, the very reason he had left Stoney Ridge in the first place. He'd been lured to Colorado to work on a ranch with the promise that he'd receive a few colts or fillies to start his own stable. So sure was he that he had landed on a gold mine that he'd even put a temporary long-term hold on his romance with girlfriend Bethany Schrock.

Sadly, Bethany got tired of waiting. She up and married a fellow whom she said could actually make up his mind. Jimmy was disappointed, but not completely heartbroken. That came later, when the ranch went belly up, the horses were sold off, and his only option to receive back pay was to sue the rancher, but he couldn't do that. He had plenty of character flaws, more than most men, but he was true to his church's teachings. The rancher knew it, too. Alas. So here he was, back and broke.

He ran a hand down the slightly concaved nose of the buggy horse and the horse jerked its head away. Jumpy. This was not a horse typical of the Thoroughbreds or Standardbreds that pulled Amish buggies.

"Prince don't like you."

Jimmy looked over the horse's head to find a solemn boy peering up at him. He was just a small boy, with a mop of curly hair under his black hat, but he stood with spread legs, stuck his fists on his hips, and jutted out his chin. You'd have thought he was David the Shepherd Boy facing down Goliath the Giant.

"Joey, honey, it's all right. He's just saying hello to our fine horse."

Jimmy turned. A young woman stood by the buggy door. Under the brim of her black bonnet were violet eyes—not just blue but truly violet. Pansy purple. The woman wasn't smiling at Jimmy but at the horse, with genuine admiration. For the briefest of seconds, Jimmy felt a spark of interest in a female, something he hadn't felt for a long time. But then he realized she was the boy's mother. *Lord-a-mercy!* The spark fizzled like someone had doused him with a bucket of water. He swallowed down a gulp and lifted his eyebrows in a greeting. "If I'm not mistaken, this horse is Arabian."

Her face registered surprise. "You're not mistaken. How'd you know that?"

"I've been out in Colorado, working on a ranch. Mustangs, Arabians. Hard working horses." He cocked his head. "So you use an Arabian—" he glanced underneath the horse's girth—"*stallion* as a buggy horse?" This little gal had guts.

Dark brows flared over indignant violet eyes. "Whoever wrote the rule that there's only one kind of horse to use for buggies?" She turned away to run a hand down the horse's neck, straightening his mane. Calmer now, she added, "If there's a job for a horse, there's a horse for a job. And I happen to think that nearly every job can be done by an Arabian."

Jimmy was more than a little flabbergasted. It wasn't every day you found someone who understood horses, especially not a female someone. "Interesting notion, to expand what's used for the buggy. The Arabian and the Thoroughbred are both efficient movers. They share that daisy cutter action, keeping their feet low to the ground." He could keep going on, as he considered himself something of an expert on horses, but he didn't want to show off.

She tipped her head up to study him for a long moment. "Any chance you're looking for work?"

He felt a little dizzy from those twinkling eyes of hers. Positively bedazzled. Or maybe he was just hungry.

Lord-a-mercy. Jimmy Fisher, what is wrong with you?! He was getting all jelly-kneed over somebody else's woman, and a stranger to boot. She waited for him to respond, but before he could gather thoughts into words, the door opened to the Bent N' Dent and out walked Hank Lapp.

"SYLVIE SCHROCK KING! THAT BOY IS NOT AVAILABLE!" Hank roared at them from the top of the Bent N' Dent stairs.

Jimmy sighed. "That's Hank Lapp."

"Everybody knows Hank," the little boy said.

The woman, Sylvie, gave the little boy's hand a tug. "Let's get our shopping done." She gave Jimmy a courteous nod and turned to head to the store.

Hank held the door open for her, then came down the steps, arms flung wide to embrace Jimmy in a bear hug. Hank squeezed him so tight that he practically jolted some of Jimmy's molars loose. "Hank, let me go," Jimmy gasped.

Hank released him but slapped him on the back. "YOUR MOTHER IS GOING TO BE TICKLED PINK THAT YOU CAME HOME FOR HER BIRTHDAY."

Oh boy. Jimmy had completely forgotten his mother's birthday.

"SON, YOU OWE ME A THANK YOU. I JUST SAVED YOU FROM THE CLUTCHES OF A WIDOW LADY. YOU KNOW WHAT THEY SAY ABOUT WIDOW LADIES. AL-WAYS ON THE HUNT FOR A NEW HUSBAND." Hank tried to lower his voice to a whisper and it came out in a regular speaking voice. "Jake King. Remember him?"

"Jake the Junkman?"

"THAT'S HIM. Always trying to HOBBLE things together to make a living."

"So Jake finally got married." Jimmy shook his head. He remembered Jake, a neighbor, as a strange guy. He was al-ways heading off to tag sales or auctions, lugging home odds and ends. And old. Why, he must have been forty or fifty years old. Or older. Everyone considered him on the shelf and there to stay, a lifelong bachelor. It was hard to see a match with Jake the Junkman and the twinkly violet-eyed beauty.

"She's the one who got him tangled up in that horse breed-ing business. NO ONE WANTS THOSE FUNNY NOSED HORSES."

"They're Arabians, and they're probably the best horse anyone could ever have."

"WHAT?" Hank stroked his wiry beard, if you could call it a beard. More like whiskers. "YOU DON'T SAY."

"Maybe she's got some good reasons for the decisions she's making."

Hank looked all around, before leaning close to Jimmy

to shout, "SOME SAY SHE MIGHT BE THE REASON JAKE DIDN'T LAST LONG." He wagged a bony finger in Jimmy's face and lowered his voice to a roar. "Some say she brings BAD luck wherever she goes."

"You've got to be kidding. Hank, even you don't believe nonsense like that."

"OF COURSE NOT. BUT . . . SHE'S A SCHROCK, YOU KNOW."

"Why would that matter?"

"DON'T YOU KNOW ABOUT THOSE SCHROCKS?" He slapped his knees. "OF COURSE NOT! You've been off playing cowboys and Indians."

Jimmy frowned at him. Ranch work could hardly be described as playing cowboys. It was backbreaking work; long, hard days in the saddle. There were times he thought he'd always walk like he was holding a barrel between his knees.

"I'll fill you in later on the SCHROCK SAGA. Sylvia is a cousin to LUKE SCHROCK. AND YOU KNOW ALL ABOUT LUKE SCHROCK."

"Hank, is it possible for you to not talk so loud?"

"I'M NOT TALKING LOUD. I'M JUST TALKING." But then he did drop it a tidge. "And then there are some that say Sylvie might be a LITTLE BIT . . ." He whistled a note up and down, while whirling his finger around his ear like a clock. "As for me, I just figure some folks are down on their luck. Permanent-like."

"No such thing as luck, good or bad." To be honest, Jimmy had wondered now and then if he might be prone to bad luck. Things never seemed to end up the way he'd planned. "Besides, that's no way to talk about old Jake. Or his widow."

"I'm only repeating what folks are KNOWN TO WHIS-

PER." Hank shrugged his thin shoulders. "MOSTLY YOUR MOTHER. She's had some run-ins with Sylvie."

Jimmy rolled his eyes. His mother was legendary for her disapproval. "How did Jake die?"

"ROPING A DEER."

"He did what?"

"Jake figured it would be easier to just CATCH IT that-aways."

"So what happened?"

"A sharp hoof to the head." Hank thumped his forehead. "Deer reared up and KICKED him. A trapped deer can be a savage beast. Did you know that?"

"The deer attacked him?"

"Yup. A severe blow to the head, Dok said."

"Huh. That's sad."

"MAYBE YOU SHOULD MARRY HER." He gave Jimmy a sharp jab with his bony elbow. "Nice piece of property she's got from Jake. You like those funny nosed horses. And that boy o' hers needs a daddy."

No way. No way! Change the subject, quick. Jimmy squeezed his eyes shut. Why had it ever seemed like a good idea to return to Stoney Ridge? His stomach rumbled and he remembered why. Hungry and broke, in that order.

The door to the store opened and out came Sylvie Schrock King, now with a bulky package added under an arm. Jimmy walked over to help her but she shook her head and said crisply, "I can manage just fine, thank you."

She swept right on past the two men, which only proved to Jimmy that Hank was dead wrong about women—widow or single or anything in between. She wasn't husband hunting; she paid him no mind.

After getting her boy settled into the buggy, she untied the horse's reins and turned to face Hank. Her voice became sharper. "Neighbors shouldn't go telling tall tales on each other. That's written in the Good Book." She shifted her gaze to Jimmy. "And just so you know, I am not on the hunt for a new husband. Consider the job offer withdrawn." And then she winked at him.

Jimmy's eyebrows shot up. "Did you see *that*?"

"SEE WHAT?"

"Ah, nothing." He must've imagined it.

"IS it really in the GOOD BOOK for neighbors to not tell tales? I never heard it."

"I don't know. Probably. Sounds like it."

Sylvie's horse stepped backward gingerly, as if on tip toe, then gracefully shifted forward into a smooth trot. Lord-a-mercy, that stallion was a fine specimen. Jimmy watched the horse, enchanted. "You know, I wouldn't mind being around that."

"Son, if you want to marry her, then go right ahead. BUT DON'T SAY I DIDN'T WARN YOU."

Jimmy felt a stitch in his stomach—those bad apples were catching up with him. "I was talking about the horse, Hank. I wouldn't mind working with horses like that." He rubbed his sore stomach. "And I sure do need a job. Why'd you have to go and ruin it for me?"

"RUIN IT? Not hardly." He untied his old weary looking horse's reins. "Hop into my chariot and I'll take you home."

The bad apples poked at Jimmy again, higher up, and he winced.

Hank was already backing up the buggy and waving for Jimmy to jump in. As he climbed in the passenger side of

Hank's beat up buggy, Jimmy thought he might know how that roped deer felt. The noose felt tight around his throat, and he could feel a panic rise up. The closer the buggy got to home, to his mother, the tighter it felt.

Naturally, Hank didn't notice Jimmy's discomfort. All the way home, he nattered nonstop, catching Jimmy up on news and gossip, as if he'd been gone weeks and not years. As they passed the property that belonged to Jake the Junkman, Jimmy saw Sylvie Schrock King at the mailbox. The buggy rolled past, and Sylvie looked over at the last minute. Her violet eyes caught with Jimmy's and she winked at him, as if they shared a private joke. This time, there was no mistaking it. Jimmy knew all about winks and what they meant.

Hank, who generally noticed nothing, noticed *that*. "HA! I TOLD YOU SO! BOY, SHE'S ALREADY SET HER SIGHTS ON YOU. SHE'S GOT THE FISH ON THE LINE. NOW SHE JUST HAS TO REEL HIM IN."

Jimmy's stomach did a slow, sickening turn.

⌒

Sylvie Schrock King was a pretty good judge of people. She knew who to offer a job to and who to send packing, and that was why she spent the rest of the afternoon regretting how she'd snapped at that poor pathetic homeless man who was patting her sweet Prince at the Bent N' Dent. It shocked her that he recognized an Arabian horse, shocked and intrigued her. It seemed like he knew a lot about horses. When she pushed a little more, he sounded both supremely confident and totally vague. That she understood as a way to keep people at arm's length. She wished she hadn't been so quick to withdraw her job offer from the homeless man. She might not see him again and she sure needed help around this place.

It was all because of that loudmouthed Hank Lapp. Whenever Hank or Edith Lapp were involved, mostly Edith, Sylvie's hackles rose and she felt like she had to ready herself for battle. Sharing a creek as a boundary line with Edith Lapp had created all kinds of headaches, especially after the heavy storms they'd had this last year, and Hank didn't help. He made a mess of everything.

She checked on her napping boy and went outside to fill Prince's water bucket. As she made her way down the grass path to the paddock, that familiar swirl of anxiety began and she tried to fight it down. She thought of all the endless chores that needed to be done around Rising Star Farm, and she still hadn't had any success with Prince as a stud for buggy horses—and then she remembered that it was the horse's name which rankled Edith Lapp most of all. She had accused Sylvie of being prideful, despite how many times she explained it was the name the stallion came with, and you just didn't change a horse's name. That was how things were done in the horse world, Sylvie had told Edith.

"This isn't a horse world," Edith had crisply replied in her stony-faced way. "This is an Amish world."

Well, to Sylvie's way of thinking, the two didn't have to cancel each other out. Besides, Bishop David Stoltzfus didn't mind the name of her horse. Sylvie's cousin, Luke, was a deacon. If the bishop and the deacon didn't object, why did Edith Lapp think she was judge and jury of Stoney Ridge? Who wrote that rule for her?

Sylvie had pointed out to Edith some might consider the

name of the property to be a smidgen prideful: Rising Star Farm. She was well acquainted with the history of the farm, and that Edith's grandfather, the original owner, had been the one to name it.

"That's entirely different," Edith huffed.

"How so?"

Edith's sparse brows came together in a V. "It just is." She had pivoted and stormed home.

Up from his nap, Joey called out to her from the porch and she waved to him, then turned off the water spigot and pushed the bucket under the bottom rail. By the time she finished, Joey had joined her. "Mem, the crabby lady from across the creek is waiting for you on the porch."

Sylvie dried her hands on her apron and went out to greet Edith Lapp, feeling cornered. What now? Edith's visits were never social calls. She had yet to have a conversation with Edith that ended well.

As they walked up the path to the house, Edith looked Joey over from head to toe as if seeing him for the first time. She clicked her tongue in mock reproof. "He must take after his daddy, because he sure doesn't look like you."

Stung, Sylvie smoothed Joey's flame of hair where it tufted on top. "He takes after himself, that's who." She bent down to talk to him. "Go on down to the barn. Prince told me he's been wanting a carrot for his afternoon snack."

Edith sniffed. "Horses don't talk. You shouldn't fill the boy's mind with silly tales."

"Prince talks," Joey said, his chin jutted out. "But he just talks to Mem."

Sylvie gave Joey a gentle push toward the barn before he could say anything more to annoy Edith.

"I've come to make you an offer on Rising Star Farm."

"It's my farm now and it's where we plan to stay. Me and Joey. Jake left it to us."

"Oh?" Her sparse eyebrows lifted. "Is that in Jake's last will and testament? I'd like to see it."

Sylvie hesitated just a moment too long. She had no idea about Jake's will, if there even was one, and Edith read her thoughts in her hesitation.

"You certainly can't run this place all by yourself," Edith continued, sweeping the yard with a disapproving glance. "I'll pay you this amount for it. Cash." She handed Sylvie a piece of paper. "It's more than fair." She grinned and it was so unnatural-looking on her dour face that it gave Sylvie the shivers.

Sylvie's eyes flickered to the amount on the paper, then she took a second look. "Fair? Edith, this property must be worth a lot more than that."

"No, it isn't. Not in the condition it's in." The odd grin slipped off Edith's face and the frown returned. "Besides, I've had to look at this junkyard for years now. Seems like I should be getting a discount. Plus it's my birthday today. That should count for an extra discount." She crossed her arms over her ample chest. "This property belonged to my grandfather. Used to be the prettiest farm in Stoney Ridge. Now look at it. Years of neglect have taken a toll. And then in you come with your idea of breeding horses." With a grimace she added, "You'll only ruin this land."

"Ruin it?"

"You heard me. It's high time that piece of property returns to family instead of going to an outsider."

"Outsider?!" Sylvie slapped her palm against her chest.

"Outsider? You make me sound…like I'm English. Hardly that!"

"That church you came from is just about as far from Old Order Amish as the English." Edith clapped her palms together. "I'm making you a very fair offer. Very fair." She wagged a finger at Sylvie. "If you're smart, you'll take it. A bird in the hand is better than two in the bush."

Sylvie was so angry her knees shook. She tried to keep her voice as calm as she could. "Edith, thank you for your offer. I'll give it some serious consideration." *Just long enough to toss it in the trash.*

Edith didn't look at all happy to be dismissed, but she did take her leave. Sylvie felt her eye twitch wildly as she watched her make her way home. *That woman!* She'd been a thorn in Sylvie's side since the day she married Jake. Sometimes, she could almost feel Edith Lapp's disapproving eyes on her from wherever she happened to be on the farm. She quickly learned to take care to avoid her, even to the point of standing at the doorway and watching, waiting until she saw Edith's buggy's dust trail disappear before she went out to the garden. The fewer interactions with Edith Lapp, the better.

Calm down, Sylvie, she told herself. *God doesn't give you more than you can handle.* She didn't know exactly where that phrase was in the Bible, but she'd heard it repeated so often that she was sure it was true. It didn't always feel true, though. She squeezed her eyes closed, to shut out the sight of all the work to be done around the farm—stalls to muck out, horses to exercise, animals to feed—and she felt a weariness clear to her bones. She hated the feeling of helplessness that was always lurking nearby, a feeling that had been with her long, long before Jake had died. Overwhelmed by all that needed to be done, she closed her eyes and squeezed her hands together.

Just thinking about Edith's request to take a look at Jake's last will and testament made her chew on her fingernails, already bitten down to the quick. His last will and testament? Where in the world would Jake have kept something like that? She had no idea. He was the most disorganized man in the world.

She saw Joey wander from the barn, up the path, and over to the creek to pick up sticks and throw them in. She sat on the porch steps, watching him. The sticks landed in the water with a satisfying plunk, only to have the rushing current bring the sticks back to him. He couldn't understand why the same stick kept returning to him.

That was exactly how Sylvie felt. As hard as she tried for a fresh start, the same thing kept coming back to her.

Must everyone think the worst of her, of Joey?

Discussion Questions

1. "When I pray," said the old bishop, "things happen." Have you experienced that saying to be true? Or not?

2. How much of a person's character would you say is shaped by their childhood?

3. When Izzy shows Cassidy how to knit, she lets her drop a stitch, purposefully, to teach her a lesson. "It happens when you go too fast," Izzy told her. "You lose focus." How does that apply to more than knitting?

4. Another lesson from the dropped stitch: Cassidy had to unravel three rows to go back and pick up the stitch. "You can't leave a hole or it will unravel," Izzy told her. What are your thoughts about the "dropped stitches" metaphor in this story? What do they represent? Can or should "dropped stitches" be picked up?

5. Did it bother you that Izzy refused to host a foster child

despite having been raised in the foster care system? How did Cassidy win her over?

6. "Lamps don't talk, they shine," Fern said. How did that frame of mind unroll in the way Fern treated others?

7. Fern gave Luke some advice about emptying out the foster care system in Lancaster County. "Don't let your branches go out farther than your roots go deep. When that happens, you topple." She was talking about sustainability. Have you seen situations in your church or community, or even your family, when the branches were out farther than the roots went deep? What were the results?

8. Knowing the truth about Mollie's health, look back through the book. Did you see what was ahead?

9. What do you think happens to Mollie after the book ends?

10. What does Sam find appealing about Mollie? And why did he feel comfortable opening up to her?

11. Throughout his first few months of being a deacon, Luke learned quite a few life lessons. One big discovery: Feelings follow intention. Outlook determines outcome. How did you see that perspective play out in Luke's story? How and when have you experienced it?

12. Naively, Luke agreed to keep Freeman Glick's secret

and learned a painful lesson: Keeping secrets never goes well. What kind of effect did that secret have on others? What about on Luke and Izzy's relationship?

13. When Izzy visited her mother, she realized something for the first time: "It suddenly dawned on her that her mother was not a strong person, that she never had been. Izzy had wanted her to be strong, had been angry with her most of her life because she wasn't strong." Who is the person in your life whom you want something from that he or she is just not able to provide? What can you do to accept his or her weaknesses or limitations?

14. Luke was determined to find out who cast the lone vote that made him deacon. Were you surprised when you found out who it was?

15. Is there a person in your life who sees you in a way that you can't see for yourself? What kind of impact has that person had on you?

16. Izzy wanted a baby so desperately. What happened when she finally relinquished that dream? Has something similar ever happened to you? Is it just a coincidence?

17. "'Lord, what do you want me to do?'" the old bishop told the church leaders. "That's a dangerous prayer. But it's more dangerous not to ask." How did that wisdom change Luke? How could it change you?

A Brief History of Foster Care

It might surprise you that the Old Testament of the Bible has some of the earliest known documentations about foster care. Caring for dependent children, often referred to as fatherless, was not only a duty for the Israelites but a reflection of God's character (Pss. 10:14; 72:4, 13–14; 82:3–4; Prov. 31:20; Isa. 1:17; Hosea 14:3). In the New Testament, records from the early Christian church revealed that needy children boarded with "worthy widows." The church collected and distributed aid to those widows to provide for them and their foster children (James 1:27).

Fast forward through the centuries to England in 1562. The English Poor Law led to the development and eventual regulation of family foster care. Those laws allowed the placement of poor children into indentured service until they came of age, and began the practice of placing children into homes. Indentured service, for all its shortcomings—and there were many—was better for children than the poorhouse.

In 1853, Charles Loring Brace, a minister in New York

City who founded the Children's Aid Society, began the foster care movement as it exists today in the United States. Concerned about the large number of immigrant children sleeping in the streets—over 30,000!—he advertised for families around the country who would be willing to provide free homes for these children. This was the start of the Orphan Train Movement.

Brace's efforts led to social agencies and state governments getting involved in foster home placements. Three states led the movement: Massachusetts paid families who took care of children too young to be indentured. Pennsylvania passed the first licensing law in 1885. South Dakota began providing subsidies to the Children's Home Society in 1893.

The early 1900s marked a dramatic shift in the approach to foster care. For the first time, the individual needs of children were considered when placements were made. Social agencies began to supervise foster parents, records were kept, and the federal government began supporting state inspections of family foster homes. Perhaps most significantly, services were provided to biological parents to enable the child to return home, safe and sound, and become a healthy family. Permanently.

Acknowledgments

Stoney Ridge keeps expanding! During the writing of this new series, I had to go back and check galleys of previous manuscripts, to make sure I used correct names and circumstances of previous characters. They drift on and off screen, and most don't have the set of lungs that Hank Lapp does, a man who is hard to forget.

Thank you to Lindsey Ross, who took the time to read this manuscript late at night, after she and her husband settled their five children into bed. Somehow, she squeezed this manuscript in between huge life events: newly married, raising a "blended and blessed" family of five children, working, and studying for her master's degree program. You're amazing, Linz! I couldn't pass this manuscript into Andrea Doering's hands without your encouragement and valuable insights.

And then there's Andrea Doering, now editorial director of Revell, who finds the dropped stitches in my manuscripts. I always look forward to your revisions because they help make each story the best it can be.

A thank-you to the Revell team: marketing duo Michele

Misiak and Hannah Brinks, publicist Karen Steele, and so many others who help promote, market, and move a book from the warehouse and into readers' hands. Barb Barnes, project editor extraordinaire, deserves a big shout-out. Barb, you give so much time and attention to each manuscript. Every line! I've learned a great deal from you.

Joyce Hart, of the Hartline Literary Agency, has been a faithful support. Besides being a wonderfully dedicated agent, her book club reads each of my books! I'm so touched by that.

A thank-you to A. J. Salch for her equine advice . . . answering texts late at night for me. And to Kathy Jenke, for being such an encourager as you read a first draft. I grabbed it back from Andrea to add in a few of your insights. There are times when I write a scene and think to myself, *Kathy will like this!*

My heartfelt gratitude goes to my readers. Much of my time is spent in a cramped laundry room, with two big dogs for company. When I receive emails from readers, they lift my spirits more than you can possibly imagine. It tells me that the stories are connecting with you! What could be better?

Finally, a thank-you to the true Artist, the Almighty God, who gives each one of us a voice to use for his work. My prayer is to always keep that in mind.

Author Note

Have you ever felt the tug to become a foster parent? On any given day, there are nearly 438,000 children in foster care in the United States. Most states have a critical need for more foster parents, and the number of children placed in foster care increases yearly.

There are plenty of assumptions about having foster children, but most are incorrect. The media has a tendency to focus on the negative, but from all the research I conducted to write this book, for every bad news story, there were two good ones. Good stories just don't make the news.

Below are some of the most common assumptions about foster care, with corrected information that is applicable across the United States (but keep in mind that each state has their own requirements).

Myth: Kids in foster care are bad or troubled.
Truth: Children in foster care are good kids taken out of a troubled situation. They need a caring foster parent who

is patient and understanding. When given the opportunity, most of these children begin to thrive.

Myth: To be a foster parent, you need to be married and own a home and be a college graduate.

Truth: You don't need to be married or own a home or even be a college graduate. That means if you're single or renting, you can be a foster parent.

Myth: I can't afford to be a foster parent.

Truth: There are monthly reimbursement rates for children in foster care based on the level of care you provide. Medical and dental care is paid through state Medicaid programs.

Myth: Most kids in foster care are teenagers.

Truth: The average age of a child entering foster care is seven years old.

Myth: Most kids are in foster care because their parents have abused drugs.

Truth: Now, this one is not a myth. It's true. There are fifteen categories that can be responsible for a child's removal from a home. Drug abuse by a parent has had the largest percentage increase.

Myth: Fostering could require a commitment until the child turns eighteen.

Truth: Generally, children remain in state care for less than two years. Only 6 percent spend five or more years in foster care.

Myth: It's too hard to give a child up to his biological family.

Truth: Most children are in foster care for a short time, returning to their biological families. Reuniting a child to his family is the ideal situation. Foster families provide a safe haven for a child. Healthy grieving is to be expected, but it's for the right reasons.

Myth: You can't adopt foster children.

Truth: In 2016, more than 65,000 children—whose mothers' and fathers' parental rights were legally terminated—were waiting to be adopted. Also in 2016, more than 20,000 children "aged out" of foster care without permanent families. Research has shown that those who leave care without being linked to a "forever family" have a higher likelihood than the general youth population to experience homelessness, unemployment, and incarceration as adults.

Is there room in your heart and family for a child in need? There are many ways to get involved, some that do not even require foster care. One recommendation: volunteer with the National CASA (Court Appointed Special Advocates) Association for Children. You can find out more information here: www.casaforchildren.org.

Or consider small ways to connect to children in need—after-school tutoring at your public library. Volunteering at a community center. Buy Christmas gifts for a family in need through an Adopt-a-Family program with a local church. Support a family who does provide foster care with respites—babysitting or meals. There are many ways to get involved to care for children in need. And every little bit makes a difference.

Sources: US Department of Health and Human Services, Administration for Children and Families, Administration on Children, Youth and Families, Children's Bureau, "AFCARS Report No. 24," https://www.acf.hhs.gov/sites/default/files /cb/afcarsreport24.pdf (accessed May 16, 2018); and US Department of Health and Human Services, Administration for Children and Families, Administration on Children, Youth and Families, Children's Bureau, "AFCARS Report No. 20," https:// www.acf.hhs.gov/sites/default/files/cb/afcarsreport20.pdf (accessed May 16, 2018).

Suzanne Woods Fisher is an award-winning, bestselling author of more than thirty books, including *Mending Fences*, as well as the Nantucket Legacy, Amish Beginnings, The Bishop's Family, and The Inn at Eagle Hill series, among other novels. She is also the author of several nonfiction books about the Amish, including *Amish Peace* and *Amish Proverbs*. She lives in California. Learn more at www.suzanne woodsfisher.com and follow Suzanne on Facebook @Suzanne WoodsFisherAuthor and Twitter @suzannewfisher.

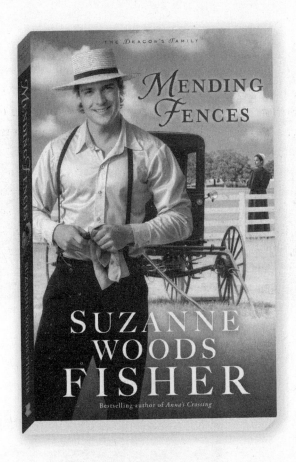

IMMERSE YOURSELF IN THESE HEARTWARMING—AND SURPRISING—TALES OF *young love*, *forgiveness*, AND *healing*.

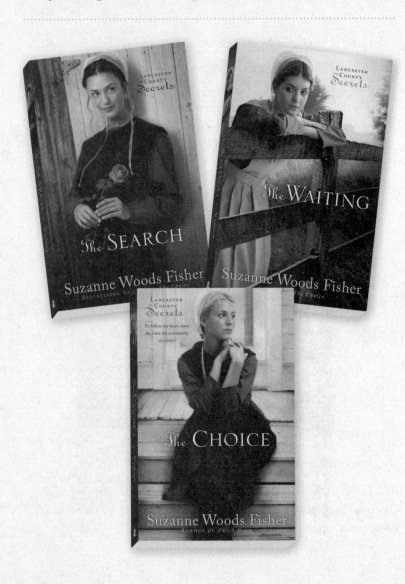

"Fans of Suzanne Woods Fisher will love this story of three sisters coming together on a rugged Maine island to refurbish a camp. *On a Summer Tide* is an enduring tale of love and restoration."

—DENISE HUNTER, bestselling author of *On Magnolia Lane*

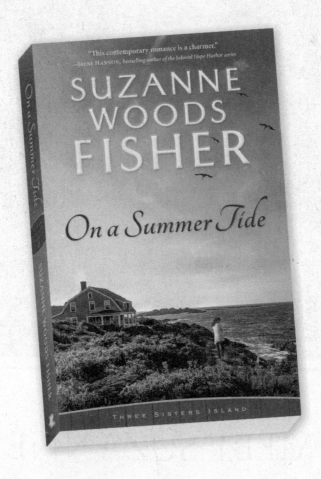

MEET SUZANNE

www.SuzanneWoodsFisher.com